The Concise Bible

The Concise Bible

A condensation by
Frances Kanes Hazlitt

LibertyPress

Indianapolis

Liberty Press is a publishing imprint of Liberty Fund, Inc., a foundation established to encourage study of the ideal of a society of free and responsible individuals.

The cuneiform inscription that serves as the design motif of our endpapers is the earliest known written appearance of the word "freedom" (*ama-gi*), or liberty. It is taken from a clay document written about 2300 B.C. in the Sumerian city-state of Lagash.

Library of Congress Catalog Card No.: 76-26330
ISBN 0-913966-17-7

Contents

PREFACE 7

THE OLD TESTAMENT

BOOK
1. Genesis 15
2. Exodus 32
3. Leviticus 42
4. Numbers 46
5. Deuteronomy 50
6. Joshua 53
7. Judges 57
8. Ruth 61
9. I Samuel 62
10. II Samuel 67
11. I Kings 72
12. II Kings 80
13. I Chronicles 89
14. II Chronicles 90
15. Ezra 91
16. Nehemiah 93
17. Esther 95
18. Job 98
19. Psalms 107
20. Proverbs 113
21. Ecclesiastes 119
22. The Song of Solomon 123
23. Isaiah 126
24. Jeremiah 133
25. Lamentations 136
26. Ezekiel 137
27. Daniel 141
28. Hosea 144
29. Joel 146
30. Amos 147
31. Obadiah 148
32. Jonah 149
33. Micah 150
34. Nahum 151
35. Habakkuk 152

36. Zephaniah 153
37. Haggai 153
38. Zechariah 154
39. Malachi 155

THE NEW TESTAMENT

40. St. Matthew 159
41. St. Mark 184
42. St. Luke 186
43. St. John 193
44. The Acts of the Apostles 198
45. Romans 210
46. I Corinthians 214
47. II Corinthians 216
48. Galatians 217
49. Ephesians 218
50. Philippians 219
51. Colossians 220
52. I Thessalonians 220
53. II Thessalonians 221
54. I Timothy 221
55. II Timothy 222
56. Titus 223
57. Philemon 224
58. Hebrews 224
59. James 225
60. I Peter 227
61. II Peter 228
62. I John 228
63. II John 229
64. III John 229
65. Jude 230
66. Revelation 230

APPENDIX 237

BIBLIOGRAPHY 249

INDEX 253

Preface

Throughout Western civilization the Bible has been regarded for centuries, and is still regarded, as the most
important book in the world. "How many ages and generations," wrote Walt Whitman, "have brooded and wept and
agonized over this book! What untellable joys and ecstasies,
what support to martyrs at the stake, from it! To what
myriads has it been the shore and rock of safety—the refuge
from driving tempest and wreck! Translated in all languages,
how it has united this diverse world! Of its thousands there
is not a verse, not a word, but is thick-studded with human
emotion."

The Bible has not only been for millions a source from
which they sought daily guidance, consolation, courage and
faith, but, particularly in the King James Version, the highest model of English prose. Macaulay declared that the King
James Bible is "a book which, if everything else in our language should perish, would alone suffice to show the whole
extent of its beauty and power."

Yet in our own generation the Bible has fallen into com-
parative neglect. As Ernest Sutherland Bates has put it:

"Few things could be culturally more deplorable than that today the average college graduate, who fancies himself educated, should never have read the Book of Job, should be unfamiliar with Isaiah, and should hardly be able to identify those mighty men of valor, Joshua the son of Nun, Gideon, and Jephthah . . . and should not only thus be abysmally ignorant but should feel no incentive to be otherwise."

One of the chief reasons for this neglect is the formidable length of the Bible. It consists of sixty-six separate books, thirty-nine in the Old Testament, and twenty-seven in the New. It runs to a total of some 900,000 words, the equivalent of at least ten average length books, and twelve times as long as the present volume. Few modern men, outside the ranks of the ministry, have the pertinacity of John Quincy Adams, who wrote in his diary: "I have made it a practice for several years to read the Bible through in the course of every year." How many modern men, not in the clergy, can truly say that they have read the Bible through even once?

One other fact accounts for this contemporary neglect. To most present-day readers, whether for good or ill, the Bible is very uneven in its interest and appeal. Some passages, because of the sheer fascination of their stories or the nobility and eloquence of their prose, are read over and over, or even learned by heart; while the greater part of the Bible remains practically unread and unknown. And, indeed, the sixty-six books of the Bible are extremely diverse in content. This is indicated in its very name. The word "Bible" is derived through the Medieval Latin, *ta Biblia,* from a Greek word which simply means "the books." This greatest of all books is a heterogeneous collection of writings spread over a thousand years, made up of legends, stories, histories, chronicles, biographies, genealogies, prophecies, poems, proverbs, prayers, gospels, and epistles. To emphasize its diversity Sir

Arthur Quiller-Couch, in his essay, "On Reading the Bible," has asked us to imagine as a modern equivalent a volume including the great books of our literature all bound together in some such order as "Paradise Lost," Darwin's "Descent of Man," "The Anglo-Saxon Chronicle," "The Annual Register," "Domesday Book," Palgrave's "Golden Treasury," Bacon's "Essays," Fitzgerald's "Omar Khayyám," Newman's "Apologia," Donne's "Sermons," etc.

The present abridgement and condensation is intended for those who have been intimidated by the sheer length of the Bible and the difficulty of many parts of it, but who sense that they have missed great literary and religious treasures, who would like to be introduced to it in shorter form, and yet would like to feel that they are reading the story and the message of the Bible as far as possible in its own words.

This little book synopsizes each of the sixty-six books of the King James Bible. Wherever possible, I have kept this synopsis in the words of the King James Version itself. My own synopsis appears in italics. Wherever passages, sentences, or even phrases are directly quoted, they are set in roman type.

I have tried to include in this condensation nearly every familiar quotation from the Bible and a good many less known. The reader will find here the full text, in the language of the King James Version, of the story of Creation, the Ten Commandments, the most famous Psalms and Proverbs, and the Sermon on the Mount. He will find nearly every quotation in the narrative context that explains it. And as all these direct quotations or excerpts are set in roman type, he will be able to know clearly when he is reading the original words of the King James Bible and when he is reading (in italics) merely the words of my condensation.

In recent years there have been several abridgements of the Bible of varying length and merit. These of course serve a useful purpose. But they do not take the place of a condensation of the present type. They consist essentially of excerpts from a few selected books or chapters of books. In most cases chapter and verse are not indicated. In practically all cases the reader is given no hint of what he is missing from the selected chapters or books or which books are missing altogether.

The Concise Bible is, to my knowledge, the only condensation or abridgement of this short length that gives chapter and verse for every quotation and includes condensations of all sixty-six books of the King James Bible. It is intended to serve as an introduction to the Bible for the general reader. It is designed to be read independently, simply for itself, so that the reader may learn the outlines of all the great stories, find all the most famous quotations, and know the precise chapter and verse in which they occur. But it is also the author's hope that this little book will awaken many of its readers to a new interest in the entire Bible, will encourage them to turn to it for the great stories in all their vivid details, and to read at least some of its sixty-six books in full, after they have been given a taste of what they have missed.

To increase the value of *The Concise Bible* both as a guide and as a work of reference, I have included in an appendix additional familiar quotations that could not conveniently be fitted into the condensed narrative. I have also provided a selective Index to guide the reader to principal chapters and events, and appended a short bibliography with some comments on the various available translations of the Bible and a few leading commentaries. As *The Concise Bible* is a condensation, and not a commentary, I have re-

frained from any attempt at comment or even interpretation
except as this might be unavoidable in any condensation.

Since the King James Version, which first appeared in
1611, new translations of the Bible have made their appearance—among the most famous the Revised Version of
1881, the American Standard Version of 1901, the Revised
Standard Version of 1952, and the New English Bible
(New Testament only) of 1961. All of these, as well as
several translations made by individual scholars, have their
special merits. Several of them are more accurate in some
respects than the King James Version, and certainly more
modern in phraseology and sometimes more intelligible. But
none of them can compare with the King James in nobility
and grandeur. H. L. Mencken, not distinguished for religious
fervor, called the King James Version "probably the most
beautiful piece of writing in all the literature of the world,"
and in this respect "stupendously superior to all the other
texts." Even, therefore, though a passage in some other
translation, such as the Revised Standard Version, occasion-
ally seemed to me clearer or otherwise superior, I decided
in the interests of familiarity and consistency to take all my
direct quotations from the King James Version.

The Old Testament

GENESIS

THE CREATION

In the beginning God created the heaven and the earth.

And the earth was without form, and void; and darkness was upon the face of the deep. And the spirit of God moved upon the face of the waters. And God said, Let there be light: and there was light. And God saw the light, that it was good: and God divided the light from the darkness. And God called the light Day, and the darkness he called Night. And the evening and the morning were the first day.

And God said, Let there be a firmament in the midst of the waters, and let it divide the waters from the waters. And God made the firmament, and divided the waters which were under the firmament from the waters which were above the firmament: and it was so. And God called the firmament Heaven. And the evening and the morning were the second day.

And God said, Let the waters under the heaven be gathered together unto one place, and let the dry land appear: and it was so. And God called the dry land Earth; and the gathering together of the waters called he Seas: and God saw that it was good. And God said, Let the earth bring forth grass, the herb yielding seed, and the fruit tree yielding fruit after his kind, whose seed is in itself, upon the earth: and it was so. And the earth brought forth grass, and herb yielding seed after his kind, and the tree yielding fruit, whose seed was in itself, after his kind: and God saw that it was good. And the evening and the morning were the third day.

And God said, Let there be lights in the firmament of the heaven to divide the day from the night; and let them be for signs, and for seasons, and for days, and years: And let them be for lights in the firmament of the heaven to give light upon the earth: and it was so. And God made two great lights; the greater light to rule the day, and the lesser light to rule the night: he made the stars also. And God set them in the firmament of the heaven to give light upon the earth, and to rule over the day and over the night, and to divide the light from the darkness: and God saw that it was good. And the evening and the morning were the fourth day.

And God said, Let the waters bring forth abundantly the moving creature that hath life, and fowl that may fly above the earth in the open firmament of heaven. And God created great whales, and every living creature that moveth, which the waters brought forth abundantly, after their kind: and God saw that it was good. And God blessed them, saying, Be fruitful, and multiply, and fill the waters in the seas, and let fowl multiply in the earth. And the evening and the morning were the fifth day.

And God said, Let the earth bring forth the living creature after his kind, cattle, and creeping things, and beast of the earth after his kind: and it was so. And God made the beast of the earth after his kind, and cattle after their kind, and every thing that creepeth upon the earth after his kind: and God saw that it was good.

And God said, Let us make man in our image, after our likeness; and let them have dominion over the fish of the sea, and over the fowl of the air, and over the cattle, and over all the earth, and over every creeping thing that creepeth upon the earth. So God created man in his own image, in the image of God created he him; male and female created he them. And God blessed them, and God said unto them, Be fruitful, and multiply, and replenish the earth, and subdue it: and have dominion over the fish of the sea, and over the fowl of the air, and over every living thing that moveth upon the earth. And God said, Behold, I have given you every herb bearing seed, which is upon the face of all the earth, and every tree, in the which is the fruit of a tree yielding seed; to you it shall be for meat. And to every beast of the earth, and to every fowl of the air, and to every thing that creepeth upon the earth, wherein there is life, I have given every green herb for meat: and it was so. And God saw every thing that he had made, and, behold, it was very good. And the evening and the morning were the sixth day.

Thus the heavens and the earth were finished, and all the host of them. And on the seventh day God ended his work which he had made; and he rested on the seventh day from all his work which he had made. And God blessed the seventh day, and sanctified it: because that in it he had rested from all his work which God created and made.[1:1-31, 2:1-3]

THE GARDEN OF EDEN

And the Lord God planted a garden eastward in Eden.[2:8]
Here He causes to grow every tree that is pleasant to the sight and good for food; the tree of life also in the midst of the garden, and the tree of knowledge of good and evil.[2:9] *And here He puts the man He has formed saying,* Of every

tree of the garden thou mayest freely eat: But of the tree of
the knowledge of good and evil, thou shalt not eat of it: for
in the day that thou eatest thereof thou shalt surely die.[2:16-17]

Then God says, It is not good that the man should be
alone.[2:18]

And the Lord God caused a deep sleep to fall upon Adam,
and he slept: and he took one of his ribs, and closed up the
flesh instead thereof. And the rib, which the Lord God had
taken from man, made he a woman, and brought her unto
the man. And Adam said, This is now bone of my bones,
and flesh of my flesh; she shall be called Woman, because
she was taken out of man.

Therefore shall a man leave his father and his mother,
and shall cleave unto his wife: and they shall be one
flesh.[2:21-24]

And they were both naked, the man and his wife, and
were not ashamed.[2:25]

But as the woman is walking in the Garden of Eden, a
serpent appears.

Now the serpent was more subtil than any beast of the
field which the Lord God had made.[3:1]

He tempts the woman to taste of the fruit of the forbidden
tree. She gives some also to her husband to eat.

And the eyes of them both were opened, and they knew
that they were naked; and they sewed fig leaves together,
and made themselves aprons.

And they heard the voice of the Lord God walking in the
garden in the cool of the day.[3:7-8]

God says to Adam, Hast thou eaten of the tree? *Adam*
replies, The woman whom thou gavest to be with me, she
gave me of the tree, and I did eat. *To the woman, God says,*
What is this that thou hast done? *She answers,* The serpent
beguiled me, and I did eat.[3:11-13]

The Lord then says to the serpent, Because thou hast

done this, thou art cursed above . . . every beast of the field;
upon thy belly shalt thou go, and dust shalt thou eat all
the days of thy life.[3:14]

Upon the woman God lays a burden of sorrow and pain:
In sorrow thou shalt bring forth children.[3:16]

*For Adam's sin, God curses the very ground which must
give them food:* In the sweat of thy face shalt thou eat bread,
till thou return unto the ground: for out of it wast thou
taken: for dust thou art, and unto dust shalt thou return.[3:19]

So God drives them out of the Garden of Eden.

And Adam called his wife's name Eve;* because she was
the mother of all living.[3:20]

THE GENERATIONS OF ADAM

*Two sons are born to Adam and Eve: Cain and Abel.
Cain becomes a tiller of the soil. Abel becomes a shepherd.
From the fruit of their labors, both make an offering to the
Lord. But Cain sees that his brother's offering is regarded
above his own, and he is full of wrath. One day he kills
Abel. When the Lord asks where Abel is, Cain replies,* I
know not; Am I my brother's keeper?[4:9]

The Lord says, What hast thou done? the voice of thy
brother's blood crieth unto me from the ground.[4:10] *He
banishes Cain, upon whom He also lays a curse: the ground
shall not yield to him, and he shall be a fugitive and a vaga-
bond upon the earth. Cain cries,* My punishment is greater
than I can bear. . . . From thy face shall I be hid . . . and
every one that findeth me shall slay me. *The Lord says,*
Whosoever slayeth Cain, vengeance shall be taken on him
sevenfold.

And the Lord set a mark upon Cain, lest any finding him
should kill him.

---

* I.e., "living," or "life."

And Cain went out from the presence of the Lord, and dwelt in the land of Nod, on the east of Eden.[4:13-16]

His wife gives birth to a son; and Cain builds a city and calls it after his son, Enoch.

God sends another son to Adam and Eve, in place of the murdered Abel. This son, Seth, has many descendants.

Then began men to call upon the name of the Lord.[4:26]

In the sixth generation after Seth is born Enoch:

An Enoch walked with God: and he was not; for God took him.[5:24]

Enoch's son is Methuselah, whose years number nine hundred and sixty-nine. And Methuselah's grandson is Noah, who begets three sons: Shem, Ham, and Japheth.

THE FLOOD

As men multiply over the land, great wickedness arises among them.

And it repented the Lord that he had made man on the earth. . . . And the Lord said, I will destroy man whom I have created from the face of the earth.[6:6-7]

But Noah is a just man; he finds grace in the eyes of the Lord.

The Lord tells Noah to build an ark of gopher wood made tight inside and out with pitch, giving him exact dimensions. He says to Noah: Thou shalt come into the ark, thou, and thy sons, and thy wife, and thy son's wives with thee. And of every living thing of all flesh, two of every sort shalt thou bring into the ark.[6:18-19]

And take thou unto thee of all food that is eaten . . . and it shall be food for thee, and for them.[6:21]

Then the windows of heaven are opened. Floods of water pour down upon the earth. It rains for forty days and forty nights. As the waters increase, the ark is lifted up above the earth.

*The waters rise to a height of more than fifteen cubits.** *The mountains are inundated. Every living thing on earth is destroyed.*

Noah only remained alive, and they that were with him in the ark. And the waters prevailed upon the earth an hundred and fifty days.[7:23-24]

Then a wind arises. The rain ceases. One day the ark comes to rest atop Mount Ararat. After forty days more, Noah opens the window of the ark and sends forth a dove, to learn if the waters have abated.

But the dove found no rest for the sole of her foot.[8:9]

In seven days he again releases the dove. This time she returns, bearing an olive leaf in her mouth: the waters are abating. In seven days more, Noah again sends forth the dove. The bird does not return.

And Noah removed the covering of the ark, and looked, and, behold, the face of the ground was dry.[8:13]

More than a year has gone by since they entered the ark.

God speaks to Noah, telling him to go forth from the ark with all those that are with him.

He returns to dry land, and builds an altar and makes offerings to the Lord.

And the Lord said in his heart, I will not again curse the ground any more for man's sake; for the imagination of man's heart is evil from his youth. . . . While the earth remaineth, seedtime and harvest, and cold and heat, and summer and winter, and day and night shall not cease.[8:21-22]

God blesses Noah and his sons. He sets a rainbow in the sky for a token: never again, though storms threaten, shall the waters rise to a flood, to destroy His creatures.

And all the days of Noah were nine hundred and fifty years: and he died.[9:29]

---

* An ancient measure of length, about 18-22 inches.

THE TOWER OF BABEL

The sons of Noah are Shem, Ham, and Japheth. Their families multiply and spread and begin to repopulate the earth.

And by these were the nations divided in the earth after the flood.[10:32]

But Ham commits a sinful act of disrespect toward his father, which so angers Noah that he withholds his blessings from him and puts a curse upon Ham's son, Canaan.

From Canaan, in the generations that follow, are descended the Jebusites, the Amorites, the Hivites, and all the other tribes that inhabit the region called the land of Canaan.

Until now all the people of the earth speak one language. They spread from the east as far as the great plain of Shinar. Then they say to each other, Let us build us a city, and a tower, whose top may reach unto heaven.[11:4] *They pile bricks and mortar to a great height.*

But the Lord looks with disfavor upon their arrogance. He confounds their language; they cannot understand one another. They leave off building the tower, and in confusion scatter far and wide over the earth.

ABRAHAM AND SARAH

Terah, who is descended from Noah's son Shem, leaves his ancestral home in Ur of the Chaldees to journey toward the land of Canaan. He takes with him his son Abram, Abram's wife Sarai, and Terah's orphaned grandson, Lot. They come to a place called Haran, where they make their home. Terah dies in Haran.

The Lord speaks to Abram, saying, Get thee out of thy country . . . unto a land that I will show thee: And I will make of thee a great nation.[12:1-2]

Abram, with Sarai and Lot, journeys into the land of Canaan, to Sichem. Here he builds an altar; and the Lord appears to him and says, Unto thy seed will I give this land.[12:7]

They journey to the south. But because there is a famine in the land they go to sojourn in Egypt.

Now Sarai is a beautiful woman. Fearing the Egyptians, she and Abram agree to say that she is his sister. But the Pharaoh, hearing of Sarai's beauty, sends for her and takes her into his house. Abram receives many gifts of cattle and of servants.

Punishment comes from the Lord. Great plagues spread over the land. Then the Pharaoh learns the truth about Sarai and Abram and, in fear of the Lord's vengeance, sends them, with all their goods, out of the land.

They make their way back to the land of Canaan, to a place where Abram had built an altar; and here he calls on the name of the Lord.

Both Abram and Lot own herds of cattle and flocks of sheep; and strife arises between their herdsmen. Abram says to Lot, Let there be no strife, I pray thee, between me and thee . . . for we be brethren.[13:8] *He gives Lot choice of all the land in this region for his herd. Lot chooses the fertile plain of Jordan. So they separate, Abram remaining in the land of Canaan, Lot dwelling in the cities of the plain, pitching his tents toward Sodom.*

But the men of Sodom were wicked and sinners before the Lord exceedingly.[13:13]

Abram pitches his tents on the plain of Mamre, in Hebron.

At this time the kings of Sodom and Gomorrah are defeated in battle by a fierce warrior king named Chedorlaomer, who takes many captives and much goods. Among the captives is Lot. Abram arms himself and his servants and goes in pursuit. He kills Chedorlaomer, and returns with all the captives and goods. The king of Sodom offers to reward him; but Abram refuses: for he has sworn to the Lord that he will take nothing from Sodom.

Abram's wife, Sarai, to her great grief, is barren. She gives her handmaiden, Hagar, an Egyptian, to Abram to be his wife, to bear him a son. But when she is with child, Hagar despises her childless mistress. Sarai deals harshly with her, and the girl goes weeping into the wilderness. The angel of the Lord appears to her, telling her that she shall bear a son, whose name shall be Ishmael:* his hand will be against every man, and every man's hand against him.[16:12]

In Abram's ninety-ninth year, the Lord appears to him and says, Thou shalt be a father of many nations. Neither shall thy name any more be called Abram, but thy name shall be Abraham**....[17:4-5]

This is my covenant, which ye shall keep, between me and you and thy seed after thee; Every man child among you shall be circumcised.[17:10]

And the uncircumcised man child whose flesh of his foreskin is not circumcised, that soul shall be cut off from his people; he hath broken my covenant.

As for Sarai thy wife, thou shalt not call her name Sarai, but Sarah*** shall her name be. And I will bless her, and give thee a son also of her.[17:14-16]

The wickedness of the people of Sodom and Gomorrah is grievous to the Lord. He sends two angels to destroy them. These two strangers are roughly treated by the men of Sodom; but Lot, though not knowing who they are, befriends them and takes them into his house. They say to

---

* God hears.
** Father of a multitude.
*** Princess.

him, Escape for thy life; look not behind thee . . . lest thou be consumed.[19:17]

Then the Lord rained upon Sodom and upon Gomorrah brimstone and fire . . . and he overthrew those cities, and all the plain, and all the inhabitants of the cities, and that which grew upon the ground.[19:24-25]

Lot escapes to the mountain, taking his wife and their two daughters.

But his wife looked back from behind him, and she became a pillar of salt.[19:26]

The Lord's promise to Abraham is fulfilled: Sarah now bears him a son, whom they call Isaac.

As the child grows, Sarah distrusts Hagar, the Egyptian, who has mocked her, and Hagar's son, Ishmael. She begs Abraham to cast them out. He receives comfort from the Lord, who says, also of the son of the bondwoman will I make a nation, because he is thy seed.[21:13] *Hagar and her son are sent away.*

They wander in the desert. The jug of water they have been given is soon spent. Hagar weeps, for she sees that the boy will die. But the Lord speaks to her. He opens her eyes, and she sees a well of water nearby.

And God was with the lad; and he grew. . . . And he dwelt in the wilderness of Paran: and his mother took him a wife out of the land of Egypt.[21:20-21]

THE LORD TEMPTS ABRAHAM

God is with Abraham in all that he does. Now He commands him to offer up his son Isaac for a sacrifice. Abraham takes Isaac to the mountain of Moriah; and when the lad says, but where is the lamb for a burnt offering? *Abraham replies,* My son, God will provide himself a lamb.[22:7-8] *He takes his knife and stretches out his hand to slay Isaac.*

The voice of the Lord calls to him: Lay not thine hand

upon the lad . . . for now I know that thou fearest God, seeing thou hast not withheld thy son, thine only son, from
me.²²:¹²

*At once, Abraham sees a ram caught by his horns in a
nearby thicket. He takes the ram and offers it up for a sacrifice in place of his son.*

THE DEATH OF ABRAHAM

*Sarah dies here in Hebron. Weeping, Abraham mourns
her. He buys from the Canaanites a field in which there is a
cave, known as the cave of Machpelah. Here he buries his
wife.*

And Abraham was old, and well stricken in age: and the
Lord had blessed Abraham in all things.²⁴:¹

*He sends his old and faithful servant to look for a wife
for Isaac,* saying, Thou shalt not take a wife unto my son
of the daughters of the Canaanites, among whom I dwell:
But thou shalt go into my country and to my kin-
dred. . . .²⁴:³⁻⁴ *The servant journeys east, toward Mesopo-
tamia, to the city of Haran. He stands by the well where
the women come to draw water, and prays to the Lord for
a sign. There appears a fair maiden with her pitcher upon
her shoulder, who gives him water to drink from her pitcher.
She is Rebekah, the daughter of Abraham's nephew, Bethuel. She accompanies Abraham's servant to Hebron, to the
home of his master.*

*Isaac is waiting for them in a field at eventide. He takes
Rebekah and leads her into the tent of his mother, Sarah.*

And she became his wife; and he loved her.²⁴:⁶⁷

Then Abraham gave up the ghost, and died in a good
old age, an old man, and full of years; and was gathered
to his people. And his sons Isaac and Ishmael buried him in
the cave of Machpelah.²⁵:⁸⁻⁹

ISAAC AND REBEKAH

Rebekah gives birth to twins.

And the first came out red, all over like a hairy garment; and they called his name Esau. And after that came his brother out, and his hand took hold on Esau's heel; and his name was called Jacob. . . . And the boys grew: and Esau was a cunning hunter, a man of the field; and Jacob was a plain man, dwelling in tents. And Isaac loved Esau, because he did eat of his venison: but Rebekah loved Jacob.[25:25-28]

One day Esau, being very hungry, asks Jacob for some of his pottage. Jacob replies, Sell me this day thy birthright.[25:31] *Being hungry almost to starvation, Esau does so.*

Thus Esau despised his birthright.[25:34]

Isaac is now old and his eyes are dim. To receive the eldest son's blessing, Rebekah tells Jacob to go to his father in place of his older brother. Behold, *says Jacob,* my brother is a hairy man, and I am a smooth man.[27:11] *But Rebekah puts the skins of young kids upon his hands and neck and sends him to his father.*

Laying his hands upon Jacob, Isaac says, The voice is Jacob's voice, but the hands are the hands of Esau. . . .[27:22] *But he gives Jacob his blessing.*

Then Esau comes for the blessing which is rightfully his; and Isaac says, Thy brother came with subtilty and hath taken away thy blessing.[27:35] *Esau hears this with a great and bitter cry. He hates Jacob, and swears to kill him.*

JACOB AND RACHEL

To protect him from Esau, Rebekah sends Jacob to her father, Bethuel, in Haran.

On the way, Jacob rests and falls asleep.

And he dreamed, and behold a ladder set up on the earth, and the top of it reached to heaven: and behold the angels of God ascending and descending on it. And, behold, the Lord stood above it, and said, I am the Lord God of Abraham thy father, and the God of Isaac: the land whereon thou liest, to thee will I give it, and to thy seed.[28:12-13]

Jacob awakes, and says, Surely the Lord is in this place; and I knew it not.[28:16]

When he comes to Haran, Jacob sees a maiden leading a flock of sheep. She is Rachel, the daughter of his mother's brother, Laban. Jacob stays for a month in Laban's house, and looks after Laban's flock. Then Laban says, Tell me, what shall thy wages be?[29:15] *Jacob replies,* I will serve thee seven years for Rachel.[29:18]

And Jacob served seven years for Rachel; and they seemed unto him but a few days, for the love he had to her.[29:20]

When the seven years are fulfilled, Laban tricks Jacob: he gives him his other daughter, Leah, and prevails upon Jacob to pledge seven more years of service in return for receiving Rachel also for his wife.

And he went in also unto Rachel, and he loved also Rachel more than Leah.[29:30]

Leah bears him many sons; but Rachel is barren. Jacob is forty years old when at last the Lord sends Rachel a son, whom they call Joseph.

Laban is warned by the Lord against doing further harm to his kinsman. Therefore out of fear he makes his peace with Jacob. They build a heap of stones as a witness; and they call it Mizpah:* for Laban says, The Lord watch between me and thee, when we are absent one from another.[31:49]

Jacob takes his family and his goods and returns to Hebron. But on the way an angel comes and wrestles with

---

* Watchtower.

him all one night, but cannot prevail against him; he meets
his brother, Esau, whom he fears, but who runs to meet him
and embraces him; God appears to him at Luz, in the land
of Canaan; He says, Thy name shall not be called any more
Jacob, but Israel shall be thy name. . . .[35:10]

And Jacob called the name of the place where God spake
with him, Beth-el.[35:15]

A little further on, near Bethlehem, Rachel gives birth to
another son, Benjamin. Then she dies. Jacob sets a pillar
upon her grave: That is the pillar of Rachel's grave unto
this day.[35:20]

In Hebron, Jacob is at last united with Isaac, his father.

And the days of Isaac were a hundred and fourscore
years. And Isaac gave up the ghost, and died, and was
gathered unto his people . . . and his sons Esau and Jacob
buried him.[35:28-29]

JOSEPH AND HIS BRETHREN

Jacob, who is now called Israel, lives on in the land of
Canaan.

Now Israel loved Joseph more than all his children, because he was the son of his old age; and he made him a coat
of many colors.[37:3]

His brothers hate Joseph. One day when they are pas-
turing their father's flocks they seize him, strip him of his
fine coat, and throw him into a pit. They plan to kill him.
But just then some Ishmaelite traders pass by, to whom the
brothers sell Joseph for twenty pieces of silver. Then they
dip his torn coat in goat's blood and bring it to their father,
who is told that Joseph has been devoured by a wild beast.
Israel rends his garments and weeps, refusing to be com-
forted.

Meanwhile Joseph is taken to Egypt, where the Ish-
maelites sell him to an officer of the Pharaoh, Potiphar.

The Lord is with Joseph: Potiphar makes him overseer of his house and places him in charge of all his goods.

Joseph is very handsome; now he is also prosperous. Soon his master's wife casts her eyes upon him.

And she caught him by his garment, saying, Lie with me: and he left his garment in her hand, and fled. . . .[39:12] *The angry woman, by false accusations, causes him to be thrown into prison.*

Two years pass. One day Joseph is summoned to appear before the Pharaoh, who has been told that this Hebrew has the power to interpret dreams.

The Pharaoh had dreamed of seven fat cows and seven gaunt cows; and of seven good ears of corn and seven thin ears. The lean cows have eaten up the fat cows; and the thin ears of corn have devoured the good ears.

Joseph says to the Pharaoh, Behold, there come seven years of great plenty through all the land of Egypt: And there shall arise after them seven years of famine.[41:29-30] Let the Pharaoh look out for a man discreet and wise, and set him over the land of Egypt. . . . And let him appoint officers over the land, and take up the fifth part of the land of Egypt in the seven plenteous years. And let them gather all the food of those good years . . . for store to the land against the seven years of famine.[41:33-36]

The Pharaoh replies, Forasmuch as God hath showed thee all this, there is none so discreet and wise as thou art: Thou shalt be over my house, and according unto thy word shall all my people be ruled: only in the throne will I be greater than thou.[41:39-40]

He gives Joseph a priest's daughter, Asenath, for his wife; and they prosper greatly in the seven plenteous years. Two sons are born to them: Manasseh and Ephraim.

Then the famine sets in. Joseph opens the storehouse,

*and sells corn to the Egyptians. He sells also to those of
other lands who come to buy: and among these, sent here
by their father, are ten of Joseph's brothers.*

And Joseph knew his brethren, but they knew not him.[42:8]

*He is deeply moved by the sight of them; but he speaks
to them roughly:* Ye are spies, to see the nakedness of the
land ye are come.[42:9] *He contrives to have them accused of
stealing. To prove themselves innocent, they must go to
their home and bring back their youngest brother, Benjamin.
Meanwhile one of them must remain here in prison as surety.*

*Terrified, the brothers return to Hebron. Israel weeps
bitterly upon hearing their story. But he tells them to take
Benjamin and return to Egypt:* If mischief befall him by the
way . . . then shall ye bring down my gray hairs with sorrow
to the grave.[42:38]

*When Joseph sees his brothers standing before him, and
Benjamin with them, he can scarcely hide his tears. Still he
sets them one more trial. Benjamin is accused of theft. To
save him, one of the brothers, Judah, takes the blame upon
himself.*

Joseph can restrain himself no longer. He says, I am
Joseph, your brother, whom ye sold into Egypt.[45:4]

The brothers cannot speak. But Joseph says, Be not
grieved, nor angry with yourselves . . . for God did send me
before you to preserve life.[45:5] Ye shall tell my father of all
my glory in Egypt, and of all that ye have seen; and ye shall
haste and bring down my father hither.[45:13]

*Returned home, they tell all this to their father. Israel
says,* It is enough: Joseph my son is yet alive: I will go and
see him before I die.[45:28]

*Joseph's rule under the Pharaoh is discreet and wise, and
the people of Egypt are saved from starvation.*

Israel and his family live and prosper in the land of

Egypt. One day Israel sends for Joseph and says, Behold, I die; but God shall be with you, and bring you again unto the land of your fathers.[48:21]

Then he gathers his twelve sons together and speaks to each in turn, prophesying the future: Reuben, thou art my firstborn. . . . Unstable as water, thou shalt not excel. . . .[49:3] Judah is a lion's whelp . . . who shall rouse him up?[49:9] Joseph is a fruitful bough. . . .[49:22]

All these are the twelve tribes of Israel. . . .[49:28]

Then Israel says to his sons, I am to be gathered unto my people: bury me with my fathers in the cave that is in the field of Machpelah.[49:29-30]

Joseph sees his children grow up, into the third generation. When he is dying, he says to his people, God will surely visit you, and bring you out of this land unto the land which he sware to Abraham, to Isaac and to Jacob. . . . And ye shall carry up my bones from hence.[50:24-25]

EXODUS

THE BIRTH OF MOSES

Those who have come into Egypt from the land of Canaan are Israel, his sons, the sons' wives, and all their households: seventy souls in all. As years go by they multiply and spread over the land.

A king arises who distrusts these strangers in Egypt and turns his people against them. Taskmasters are set over them. They are forced into cruel bondage. Their lives are made bitter with hard labor. Their newborn babies, if they are boys, are taken from them and cast into the river, by order of the Pharaoh.

Therefore a woman of the house of Levi hides away her newborn son.

And when she could no longer hide him, she took for him an ark of bulrushes, and daubed it with slime and with pitch, and put the child therein; and she laid it in the flags by the river's brink. And his sister stood afar off, to wit what would be done to him.

And the daughter of Pharaoh came down to wash herself at the river. . . . And when she saw the ark among the flags, she sent her maid to fetch it. And when she had opened it, she saw the child: and, behold, the babe wept. And she had compassion on him, and said, This is one of the Hebrews' children. Then said his sister to Pharaoh's daughter, Shall I go and call to thee a nurse of the Hebrew women, that she may nurse the child for thee? And Pharaoh's daughter said to her, Go. And the maid went and called the child's mother.

And Pharaoh's daughter said unto her, Take this child away, and nurse it for me, and I will give thee thy wages. And the woman took the child, and nursed it. And the child grew, and she brought him unto Pharaoh's daughter, and he became her son. And she called his name Moses:* and she said, Because I drew him out of the water.[2:3-10]

When he grows to manhood and goes out among his own people, Moses sees their burdens. He sees an Egyptian beating a Hebrew; he kills the Egyptian.

But afterwards one of his own brethren, whom Moses reproaches for striking a fellow Hebrew, says to him, Who made thee a prince and a judge over us? Intendest thou to kill me, as thou killedst the Egyptian?[2:14]

Moses is forced to flee for his life. He escapes into the land of Midian.

The priest of Midian, Reuel, takes him into his house and gives him his daughter, Zipporah, for his wife. She

---

* To draw out.

*bears him a son whom he calls Gershom:** for, he says, I have been a stranger in a strange land.²⁝²²

One day Moses leads the flock of his father-in-law into the desert. He comes to mount Horeb:

And the Angel of the Lord appeared unto him in a flame of fire out of a bush: and he looked, and, behold, the bush burned with fire, and the bush was not consumed.³⁝²

The voice of God called to Moses out of the bush: Draw not nigh hither: put off thy shoes from off thy feet; for the place whereon thou standest is holy ground.

I am the God of thy father, the God of Abraham, the God of Isaac, and the God of Jacob.

And Moses hid his face; for he was afraid to look upon God.

And the Lord said, I have surely seen the affliction of my people which are in Egypt. . . . I am come down to deliver them out of the hand of the Egyptians, and to bring them up out of that land unto a good land and a large, unto a land flowing with milk and honey. . . .³⁝⁵⁻⁸

Come now therefore, and I will send thee unto Pharaoh, that thou mayest bring forth my people the children of Israel out of Egypt.³⁝¹⁰

But Moses says, When I come unto the children of Israel, and shall say unto them, The God of your fathers hath sent me unto you; and they shall say to me, What is his name? what shall I say unto them? *The Lord replies,* I AM THAT I AM: . . . Say unto the children of Israel, I AM hath sent me unto you.³⁝¹³⁻¹⁴

He commands Moses to go to the Pharaoh and beseech him to let the Hebrew people go only three days' journey into the wilderness, to worship and to sacrifice to their God. Moses pleads, O my Lord, I am not eloquent . . . but I am

---

* A stranger there.

slow of speech, and of a slow tongue. *The Lord says,* Who hath made man's mouth?[4:10-11] Is not Aaron the Levite thy brother? I know that he can speak well. . . . Thou shalt speak unto him, and put words in his mouth: and I will be with thy mouth, and with his mouth, and will teach you what ye shall do.[4:14-15]

And thou shalt take this rod in thine hand, wherewith thou shalt do signs.[4:17]

And Moses took his wife, and his sons, and set them upon an ass, and he returned to the land of Egypt: and Moses took the rod of God in his hand.[4:20]

Moses and Aaron go to the Pharaoh. But in answer to their request he says, I know not the Lord, neither will I let Israel go.[5:2] *Instead he lays a heavier burden of labor upon the Hebrews. They are beaten, and called idle.*

The Lord says to Moses and Aaron, I will harden Pharaoh's heart, and multiply my signs and my wonders in the land of Egypt.[7:3]

And the Egyptians shall know that I am the Lord.[7:5]

Take thy rod, and cast it before Pharaoh, and it shall become a serpent.[7:9]

They obey. But Pharaoh summons his wise men and sorcerers; and they also cause their rods to become serpents.

But Aaron's rod swallowed up their rods.[7:12]

With the rod of the Lord, Moses turns the water of the river into blood. There is no water to drink. Still the Pharaoh refuses to let the children of Israel go.

Then the Lord smites Egypt with a scourge of frogs, a scourge of flies, a murrain upon cattle, a plague of boils.

Goshen, where the Israelites live, has neither plague nor pestilence: but elsewhere in Egypt there are terrible storms; armies of locusts cover the earth; there is a darkness over the land—even darkness which may be felt.[10:21]

Still the heart of the Pharaoh remains hardened.

Moses goes to him and says, Thus saith the Lord . . . all the firstborn in the land of Egypt shall die, from the first-born of Pharaoh . . . even unto the firstborn of the maid-servant that is behind the mill; and all the firstborn of beasts.[11:4-5] *But this too is without avail.*

The Lord tells Moses and Aaron what now must be done:
On the tenth day of Abib,* each household is to take for itself a lamb. On the fourteenth day the lambs shall be slaughtered and with the blood a mark shall be made on each house of the children of Israel. That night the flesh is to be roasted and eaten, with unleavened bread and with bitter herbs. It must be eaten in haste: it is the Lord's passover.[12:11]

For I will pass through the land of Egypt this night, and will smite all the firstborn in the land of Egypt. . . .

And when I see the blood, I will pass over you. . . .

And this day shall be unto you for a memorial; and ye shall keep it a feast to the Lord throughout your genera-tions. . . . Seven days shall ye eat unleavened bread. . . . Whosoever eateth leavened bread from the first day until the seventh day, that soul shall be cut off from Israel.[12:12-15]

At midnight on the fourteenth day the plague strikes.

And there was a great cry in Egypt: for there was not a house where there was not one dead.[12:30]

Summoned by night, Moses and Aaron are told by the Pharaoh, Get you forth from among my people, both ye and the children of Israel. . . . Also take your flocks and your herds . . . and be gone. . . .[12:31-32]

And it came to pass at the end of four hundred and thirty years . . . that all the hosts of the Lord went out from the land of Egypt.[12:41]

---

* April.

PHARAOH PURSUES ISRAEL

And the Lord went before them by day in a pillar of a cloud, to lead them the way; and by night in a pillar of fire, to give them light. [13:21]

The Pharaoh pursues them with all his army. The Israelites are greatly afraid. But Moses holds the rod of the Lord over the sea. The waters divide. The children of Israel walk through the sea on dry ground, with a wall of water on their right and on their left.

Then the waters return; and the Egyptians, pursuing them into the sea, are all drowned.

Thus the Lord saved Israel that day out of the hand of the Egyptians. [14:30]

Moses and his people sing and dance, and a great song of praise goes up to the Lord:

I will sing unto the Lord, for he hath triumphed gloriously: the horse and his rider hath he thrown into the sea. The Lord is my strength and song, and he is become my salvation: he is my God, and I will prepare him a habitation. . . .

The Lord is a man of war. . . . [15:1-3]

THE PILGRIMAGE TO SINAI

They journey through the wilderness. They suffer thirst and hunger: but the Lord teaches Moses to sweeten waters that are bitter; to smite a rock with his rod and draw water. Their hunger becomes so great that the people murmur against Moses, saying, Would to God we had died by the hand of the Lord in the land of Egypt, when we sat by the fleshpots, and when we did eat bread to the full. [16:3]

The Lord rains down bread upon them from the heavens. It is manna:

And the children of Israel did eat manna forty years, until they came . . . unto the borders of the land of Canaan.[16:35]

They are set upon by the Amalekites (a tribe of the Edomites, descendants of Esau), but these fierce tribesmen are driven off.

In the third month of their wanderings, they come to the desert of Sinai, where they encamp before the mount.

THE TEN COMMANDMENTS

It is the morning of the third day of their encampment. There are thunder and lightning, and a thick cloud settles upon the mountain. They hear the sound of a trumpet, long and loud. The whole mountain quakes: the people tremble in fear.

The Lord descends in fire upon the top of mount Sinai.

And the Lord called Moses up to the top of the mount; and Moses went up.[19:20]

And God spake all these words, saying,

I am the Lord thy God, which have brought thee out of the land of Egypt, out of the house of bondage.

Thou shalt have no other gods before me.

Thou shalt not make unto thee any graven image, or any likeness of any thing that is in heaven above, or that is in the earth beneath, or that is in the water under the earth: Thou shalt not bow down thyself to them, nor serve them: for I the Lord thy God am a jealous God, visiting the iniquity of the fathers upon the children unto the third and fourth generation of them that hate me; and showing mercy unto thousands of them that love me, and keep my commandments.

Thou shalt not take the name of the Lord thy God in vain; for the Lord will not hold him guiltless that taketh his name in vain.

Remember the sabbath day, to keep it holy. Six days shalt thou labor, and do all thy work: But the seventh day is the sabbath of the Lord thy God: in it thou shalt not do any work, thou, nor thy son, nor thy daughter, thy manservant, nor thy maidservant, nor thy cattle, nor thy stranger that is within thy gates: For in six days the Lord made heaven and earth, the sea, and all that in them is, and rested the seventh day: wherefore the Lord blessed the sabbath day, and hallowed it.

Honor thy father and thy mother: that thy days may be long upon the land which the Lord thy God giveth thee.

Thou shalt not kill.

Thou shalt not commit adultery.

Thou shalt not steal.

Thou shalt not bear false witness against thy neighbor.

Thou shalt not covet thy neighbor's house, thou shalt not covet thy neighbor's wife, nor his manservant, nor his maidservant, nor his ox, nor his ass, nor any thing that is thy neighbor's.[20:1-17]

THE JUDGMENTS

The Lord says to Moses, These are the judgments which thou shalt set before them.[21:1] *The people are instructed in every detail of their lives: in their relations with each other, and their relations with God; in the laws of justice, and in the rules for cleanliness; in the foods to be eaten, and those that are forbidden; in the manner in which they are to build their houses; in the laws governing the making of sacrifices and offerings, the atonement for sins, the observance of feast days, the reaping of the harvest.*

There are over a hundred judgments. These are among them:

Thou shalt neither vex a stranger, nor oppress him: for ye were strangers in the land of Egypt.[22:21]

Ye shall not afflict any widow, or fatherless child. If thou afflict them in any wise, and they cry at all unto me, I will surely hear their cry; and my wrath shall wax hot. . . .[22:22-24]

If thou lend money to any of my people that is poor by thee, thou shalt not be to him as a usurer.[22:25]

Thou shalt not raise a false report: put not thine hand with the wicked to be an unrighteous witness.[23:1]

Thou shalt not suffer a witch to live.[22:18]

He that smiteth a man, so that he die, shall be surely put to death.[21:12]

Eye for eye, tooth for tooth, hand for hand, foot for foot. Burning for burning, wound for wound, stripe for stripe.[21:24-25]

The Lord says to Moses, And let them make me a sanctuary; that I may dwell among them.[25:8] *He gives Moses minute particulars for the building of His sanctuary.*

Aaron and his sons, and their descendants forever, are to be His priests.

And he gave unto Moses, when he had made an end of communing with him upon mount Sinai, two tables of testimony, tables of stone, written with the finger of God.[31:18]

THE GOLDEN CALF

Moses is on the mount forty days and forty nights. The people lose hope. They say to Aaron, Up, make us gods, which shall go before us.[32:1] *They break off their golden earrings; and Aaron makes a calf of gold.*

The Lord tells Moses the people have corrupted themselves. Behold, it is a stiffnecked people.[32:9] *He will destroy them.*

When Moses descends from the mount, and sees the golden calf and the people dancing around it, his anger is so great that he dashes to pieces the two tables of testimony, and destroys the golden calf.

Yet he feels sympathy and compassion for his people: he returns to the mountain and says to the Lord, Oh, this people have sinned a great sin. . . . Yet now, if thou wilt forgive their sin—; and if not, blot me, I pray thee, out of thy book which thou hast written.[32:31-32]

The Lord replies, Whoever hath sinned against me, him will I blot out of my book. Therefore now go, lead the people unto the place of which I have spoken unto thee. . . .[32:33-34]

And the Lord spake unto Moses face to face, as a man speaketh unto his friend.[33:11] And he was there with the Lord forty days and forty nights; he did neither eat bread, nor drink water. And he wrote upon the tables the words of the covenant, the ten commandments.[34:28]

Moses returns, and gathers the congregation together and says, These are the words which the Lord hath commanded, that ye should do them.[35:1]

They build a tabernacle to the Lord, each man and each woman willingly bringing to it an offering of goods or of labor.

A canopy of fine embroidered linen is made, spread over a framework overlaid with gold: it is the holy place, the tent of the congregation. Within, behind a curtain of blue and purple and scarlet, is the Ark of the Lord, overlaid with pure gold and encircled by a golden crown. This is the Holy of Holies. Before it stands the sacrificial altar; within are the two tables of testimony.

Above the Ark, betwixt two golden cherubim with outstretched wings, stands the mercy seat—the throne of God.

And Moses did look upon all the work, and, behold, they had done it as the Lord had commanded . . . and Moses blessed them.[39:43]

Then a cloud covered the tent of the congregation, and the glory of the Lord filled the tabernacle.[40:34]

And when the cloud was taken up from over the taber-

nacle, the children of Israel went onward in all their journeys: But if the cloud were not taken up, then they
journeyed not. . . . For the cloud of the Lord was upon the
tabernacle by day, and fire was on it by night . . . throughout all their journeys.⁴⁰:³⁶⁻³⁸

LEVITICUS

*The Book of Leviticus is a manual for the priests of Israel.
The more than four hundred laws set forth in its pages gov-
ern the rituals of sacrifice, the consecration of priests, the
rites of purification and atonement, the dietary laws. They
also contain the Holiness Code.*

These are a few of the Laws of Leviticus:

THE LAW OF THE OFFERINGS

And the Lord called unto Moses, and spake unto him out
of the tabernacle of the congregation, saying, Speak unto
the children of Israel, and say unto them, If any man of you
bring an offering unto the Lord, ye shall bring your offering
of the cattle, even of the herd, and of the flock. . . . Let him
offer a male without blemish: he shall offer it of his own
voluntary will at the door of the tabernacle of the congregation before the Lord.

And he shall put his hand upon the head of the burnt
offering; and it shall be accepted for him to make atonement
for him. And he shall kill the bullock before the Lord: and
the priests, Aaron's sons, shall bring the blood, and sprinkle
the blood round about upon the altar. . . .¹:¹⁻⁵

And the priest shall burn all on the altar, to be a burnt
sacrifice, an offering made by fire, of a sweet savor unto the
Lord.¹:⁹

THE CONSECRATION OF PRIESTS

And Moses brought Aaron and his sons, and washed
them with water.⁸:⁶

And Moses said unto Aaron, Go unto the altar, and offer thy sin offering, and thy burnt offering, and make an atonement for thyself, and for the people . . . as the Lord commanded.[9:7]

And Aaron . . . came down from offering of the sin offering, and the burnt offering, and peace offerings. And Moses and Aaron went into the tabernacle of the congregation, and came out, and blessed the people: and the glory of the Lord appeared unto all the people.[9:22-23]

And the Lord spake unto Aaron, saying, Do not drink wine nor strong drink, thou, nor thy sons with thee, when ye go into the tabernacle of the congregation, lest ye die: it shall be a statute for ever throughout your generations.[10:8-9]

THE DIETARY LAWS

Whatever parteth the hoof, and is cloven-footed, and cheweth the cud, among the beasts, that shall ye eat.[11:3]

The swine . . . he is unclean to you.[11:7]

The camel, the coney, and the hare are forbidden: Of their flesh shall ye not eat, and their carcass shall ye not touch; they are unclean to you.[11:8]

Of creatures that live in the waters, those having fins and scales may be eaten; all others are forbidden.

The eagle and the osprey, the vulture and the kite, the raven, the owl, the nighthawk, the cuckoo, the cormorant, the stork, are among the fowl that are not to be eaten.

The weasel, the mouse, the tortoise and the ferret, the chameleon, the lizard, the snail and the mole are pronounced unclean.

This is the law. . . . To make a difference between the unclean and the clean, and between the beast that may be eaten and the beast that may not be eaten.[11:46-47]

THE LAWS OF CLEANLINESS

If a woman have conceived seed, and borne a man child, then she shall be unclean seven days. . . . And in the eighth day the flesh of his foreskin shall be circumcised. And she shall then continue in the blood of her purifying three and thirty days; she shall touch no hallowed thing, nor come into the sanctuary until the days of her purifying be fulfilled.[12:2-4]

When a man shall have in the skin of his flesh a rising, a scab, or bright spot, and it be . . . the plague of leprosy; then he shall be brought unto Aaron the priest, or unto one of his sons. . . .[13:2]

The priests are told how to recognize the signs of leprosy.

The leper in whom the plague is, his clothes shall be rent, and his head bare, and he shall put a covering upon his upper lip, and shall cry, Unclean, unclean.

He shall dwell alone; without the camp shall his habitation be.[13:45-46]

THE DAY OF ATONEMENT

And this shall be a statute for ever unto you: that in the seventh month, on the tenth day of the month, ye shall afflict your souls, and do no work at all. . . .

For on that day shall the priest make an atonement for you, to cleanse you, that ye may be clean from all your sins before the Lord.[16:29-30]

THE MORAL LAWS

After the doings of the land of Egypt, wherein ye dwelt, shall ye not do.[18:3]

None of you shall approach to any that is near of kin to him, to uncover their nakedness.[18:6]

Also thou shalt not approach unto a woman to uncover her nakedness, as long as she is put apart for her uncleanness. Moreover, thou shalt not lie carnally with thy neighbor's wife, to defile thyself with her.[18:19-20]

Thou shalt not lie with mankind, as with womankind: it is abomination. Neither shalt thou lie with any beast to defile thyself therewith: neither shall any woman stand before a beast to lie down thereto: it is confusion.[18:22-23]

THE HOLINESS CODE

Ye shall be holy: for I the Lord your God am holy.

Ye shall fear every man his mother, and his father, and keep my sabbaths: I am the Lord your God.[19:2-3]

Ye shall not steal, neither deal falsely, neither lie one to another.

And ye shall not swear by my name falsely, neither shalt thou profane the name of thy God: I am the Lord.

Thou shalt not defraud thy neighbor, neither rob him: the wages of him that is hired shall not abide with thee all night until the morning.

Thou shalt not curse the deaf, nor put a stumblingblock before the blind, but shalt fear thy God.

Ye shall do no unrighteousness in judgment: thou shalt not respect the person of the poor, nor honor the person of the mighty: but in righteousness shalt thou judge thy neighbor.

Thou shalt not go up and down as a talebearer among thy people: neither shalt thou stand against the blood of thy neighbor.

Thou shalt not hate thy brother in thine heart: thou shalt in any wise rebuke thy neighbor, and not suffer sin upon him.

Thou shalt not avenge, nor bear any grudge against the children of thy people, but thou shalt love thy neighbor as thyself: I am the Lord.[19:11-18]

Do not prostitute thy daughter, to cause her to be a whore, lest the land fall to whoredom, and the land become full of wickedness.[19:29]

And if a stranger sojourn with thee in your land, ye shall

not vex him. But the stranger . . . shall be unto you as one born among you. . . .

Ye shall do no unrighteousness in judgment, in meteyard, in weight, or in measure. Just balances, just weights . . . shall ye have.

Observe all my statutes, and all my judgments, and do them: I am the Lord.[19:33-37]

NUMBERS

The Lord speaks to Moses, saying, On this wise ye shall bless the children of Israel, saying unto them,

The Lord bless thee, and keep thee:

The Lord make his face shine upon thee, and be gracious unto thee:

The Lord lift up his countenance upon thee, and give thee peace.[6:23-26]

It is the second year of their deliverance. They are still encamped in the wilderness of Sinai. Here they keep the Passover.

The Lord commands Moses to make a count of the men of all the tribes of the congregation except those of the tribe of Levi, whom He has sanctified and set aside to serve in the tabernacle. When the count is made, Israel numbers more than six hundred thousand men as her fighting force.

THE DEPARTURE FROM SINAI

On the twentieth day of the second month, the cloud of the Lord lifts from over the tabernacle. The children of Israel resume their march, the Ark of the Lord borne forward in their midst.

Still their only food is manna. The people weep and complain, saying, Give us flesh, that we may eat.[11:13] *At last*

Moses says to the Lord, I am not able to bear all this people alone, because it is too heavy for me.[11:14] *The Lord tells him to choose seventy men from among the elders, men who are wise and trustworthy, to help bear his burden.*

Two of these men, Eldad and Medad, feeling the Spirit of the Lord within them, take it upon themselves to prophesy within the camp. Then Joshua the son of Nun, loyal and valiant, goes to Moses and says, My lord Moses, forbid them. *But Moses replies,* Enviest thou for my sake? Would God that all the Lord's people were prophets, and that the Lord would put his spirit upon them.[11:28-29]

They draw near to the Promised Land. Moses sends messengers ahead—among them Joshua the son of Nun, and Caleb, the son of Jephunneh—to bring back a report. It is indeed a land of plenty, flowing with milk and honey: but, say the messengers, the people are strong, the cities are walled, and giants live there. The Israelites weep and wail. They refuse to go on.

But Joshua the son of Nun, and Caleb the son of Jephunneh, speak to them, saying it is a good land: Neither fear ye the people of the land . . . the Lord is with us. . . .[14:9] *For saying this, they are almost stoned.*

The Lord says to Moses, How long will this people provoke me? . . .[14:11]

He tells Moses to turn and proceed by way of the Red Sea. As for those who have murmured and complained, they shall never see the Promised Land: they shall fall in this wilderness; and their children shall wander in the wilderness for forty years.

They journey on. Still the people complain against Moses and Aaron. They rebel, and are punished by the Lord. The earth opens and swallows the leaders of the rebellion. A plague wipes out thousands of the disobedient.

In the desert of Zin they suffer a thirst so terrible that even Moses and Aaron lose heart. Then the Lord tells Moses to take his rod and draw water from a nearby rock. But Moses angrily turns on the people: Hear now, ye rebels; must we fetch you water out of this rock?²⁰:¹⁰

Nevertheless he strikes the rock, and water flows from it. The Lord say to Moses and Aaron, Because ye believed me not, to sanctify me in the eyes of the children of Israel, therefore ye shall not bring this congregation into the land which I have given them.²⁰:¹²

They come to the land of Edom, but are refused passage through the country: they must journey a long way around its borders.

At mount Hor, on the border of Edom, the Lord says to Moses, Aaron shall be gathered unto his people. . . .

Take Aaron and Eleazar his son, and bring them up unto mount Hor: And strip Aaron of his garments, and put them on Eleazar. . . . ²⁰:²⁴⁻²⁶

And Aaron died there in the top of the mount: and Moses and Eleazar came down from the mount.²⁰:²⁸

THE STORY OF BALAAM AND THE ASS

It is the fortieth year of the journey through the wilderness. The children of Israel have won many great battles and taken many cities. They have become mighty.

When they approach the land of Moab, Balak, the king of Moab, sends a message to a renowned prophet named Balaam: Curse me this people . . . for I wot that he whom thou blessest is blessed, and he whom thou cursest is cursed.²²:⁶

As Balaam is riding toward Moab on the back of an ass, an angel of the Lord stands in his way. The ass refuses to move. Three times Balaam beats her with his staff, until she falls to the ground. Then the Lord opens the mouth of the ass: she says to her master, What have I done unto thee, that thou hast smitten me these three times?²²:²⁸

Then Balaam's eyes are opened and he sees the angel. He falls on his face, saying, I have sinned. . . . I will get me back again.²²:³⁴ *The angel tells him to proceed to Moab:* But only the word that I shall speak unto thee, that thou shalt speak. . . .²²:³⁵

In Moab, Balaam stands with the king on a hill overlooking the forces of the Israelites. Three time he prepares to curse them. But each time he blesses them instead.

At last he says to the king, How shall I curse, whom God hath not cursed? or how shall I defy, whom the Lord hath not defied?²³:⁸

Who can count the dust of Jacob. . . . Let me die the death of the righteous, and let my last end be like his!²³:¹⁰

How goodly are thy tents, O Jacob, and thy tabernacles, O Israel!²⁴:⁵

Balak says angrily, I called thee to curse mine enemies, and, behold, thou hast altogether blessed them these three times.²⁴:¹⁰ *Balaam replies,* I cannot go beyond the commandment of the Lord, to do either good or bad of mine own mind. . . .²⁴:¹³

There shall come a Star out of Jacob, and a Sceptre shall rise out of Israel, and shall smite the corners of Moab. . . . And Edom shall be a possession . . . and Israel shall do valiantly.²⁴:¹⁷⁻¹⁸

THE SECOND CENSUS

A second count is made; the children of Israel now number more than six hundred thousand men of fighting age. The Lord says to Moses, Unto these the land shall be divided for an inheritance. . . .²⁶:⁵³

But of those who were counted at Sinai, there is not a man left—save Caleb the son of Jephunneh, and Joshua the son of Nun.

DEUTERONOMY

Thou hast seen how that the Lord thy God bare thee, as a man doth bear his son, in all the way that ye went, until ye came into this place.[1:31]

The book of Deuteronomy takes its name from the Greek "deuteronomion": the law repeated. It consists of Moses' parting counsels to his people on the eve of their entry into the land which the Lord has given them.

They have wandered for forty years in the wilderness. They have fought their way through savage lands. Now they are within sight of the Promised Land.

The Lord has told Moses that he will not enter into this land. Moses calls the people together and says, The Lord was angry with me for your sakes, and sware that I should not go over the Jordan. . . .

But ye shall go over, and possess that good land.

Take heed unto yourselves, lest ye forget the covenant of the Lord your God, which he made with you. . . .[4:21-23]

He reminds them of past tribulations from which God in His goodness and mercy delivered them; he exhorts them to obey the Law, and warns them of terrible punishments for trespasses; he repeats, in substance, the Ten Command-ments[5:6-21] for the generation which has grown up in the wilderness; and he gives the people scores of commandments for their life in the new land.

When they come into this land, and have conquered its people, they must drive out and utterly destroy them: for the Lord has said, Not for thy righteousness, or for the uprightness of thine heart, dost thou go to possess their land: but for the wickedness of these nations the Lord thy God doth drive them out from before thee. . . .[9:5]

In the land of plenty which is to be theirs, they are to remember, Moses says, how the Lord fed them manna in the wilderness: That he might make thee know that man doth not live by bread only, but by every word that proceedeth out of the mouth of the Lord, doth man live.[8:3]

They shall not harden their hearts to the needy: For the poor shall never cease out of the land: therefore I command thee, saying, Thou shalt open thine hand wide unto thy brother, to thy poor, and to thy needy, in thy land.[15:11]

Judgments are to be rendered with justice: Thou shalt not respect persons, neither take a gift: for a gift doth blind the eye of the wise, and pervert the words of the righteous.[16:19]

And in all things they are to obey the statutes and the judgments of the Lord: in gleaning the fields; in dividing the land (Cursed be he that removeth his neighbor's land-mark[27:17]); *in marriage and in divorce; in waging war and in the taking of prisoners, in dealing with crime; in the punishment of adulterers, of usurers, of those guilty of murder; in matters of tithing; and in the giving of charity to strangers, to the fatherless, and to widows.*

If they obey the commandments, they will be blessed above all people: And thou shalt rejoice in every good thing which the Lord thy God hath given unto thee, and unto thine house, thou, and the Levite, and the stranger that is among you.[26:11]

But if they forsake the commandments and the statutes of the Lord, His curse will fall upon them: Cursed shalt thou be in the city, and cursed shalt thou be in the field.[28:16] The Lord shall send upon thee cursing, vexation, and rebuke, in all that thou settest thine hand unto for to do, until thou be destroyed. . . .[28:20] And thou shalt become an astonishment, a proverb, and a byword, among all nations whither the Lord shall lead thee.[28:37]

THE RENEWAL OF THE COVENANT

The Lord commands Moses to reestablish the covenant made between Him and the children of Israel at Sinai.

Moses speaks to the people: Ye stand this day all of you before the Lord your God; your captains of your tribes, your elders, and your officers, with all the men of Israel, your little ones, your wives, and the stranger that is in thy camp, from the hewer of thy wood unto the drawer of thy water: That thou shouldest enter into covenant with the Lord thy God, and into his oath, which the Lord thy God maketh with thee this day: That he may establish thee today for a people unto himself, and that he may be unto thee a God, as he hath said unto thee, and as he hath sworn unto thy fathers. . . . [29:10-13]

The secret things belong unto the Lord our God: but those things which are revealed belong unto us and to our children for ever, that we may do all the words of this law.[29:29]

And Moses says to the people, I have set before you life and death, blessing and cursing: therefore choose life, that both thou and thy seed may live.[30:19]

THE DEATH OF MOSES

The Lord says to Moses, Behold, thy days approach that thou must die. . . . [31:14]

He reveals a future for Israel full of evils and troubles: Therefore write ye this song for you, and teach it the children of Israel: put it in their mouths, that this song may be a witness for me against the children of Israel.[31:19]

It is a song of prophecy. The people will forsake God still, say the words of the song, and He will punish them with terrible misfortunes. But in the end they will repent; and God will show them His mercy:

Moses writes down the song and teaches it to the people. It begins:

> Give ear, O ye heavens, and I will speak; and hear, O earth, the words of my mouth.
> My doctrine shall drop as the rain, my speech shall distill as the dew, as the small rain upon the tender herb, and as the showers upon the grass:
> Because I will publish the name of the Lord: ascribe ye greatness unto our God. He is the Rock, his work is perfect. . . .[32:1-4]

Moses goes up from the plains of Moab to the top of mount Pisgah, and looks down upon the promised land.

The Lord says to him, I have caused thee to see it with thine eyes, but thou shalt not go over thither.[34:4]

Moses dies in the land of Moab. He is buried in a valley: but no man knoweth of his sepulchre unto this day.

And Moses was a hundred and twenty years old when he died: his eye was not dim, nor his natural force abated.[34:6-7]

And Joshua the son of Nun was full of the spirit of wisdom; for Moses had laid his hands upon him: and the children of Israel hearkened unto him. . . .

And there arose not a prophet since in Israel like unto Moses, whom the Lord knew face to face. [34:9-10]

JOSHUA

After the death of Moses the Lord speaks to Joshua, who has been closer to Moses than any other man, and commands him to cross the Jordan: Thou, and all this people. . . .

Every place that the sole of your foot shall tread upon, that have I given unto you, as I said unto Moses.[1:2-3]

As I was with Moses, so I will be with thee: I will not fail thee, nor forsake thee.[1:5]

Be strong and of good courage; be not afraid, neither be thou dismayed: for the Lord thy God is with thee whithersoever thou goest.[1:9]

Joshua sends two men across the river into Jericho, to spy out the land. They lodge in the house of a harlot named Rahab, who hides them when the king's men come to seize them. She then says to the two men, I know that the Lord hath given you the land.[2:9] *They learn from her that all Jericho is in terror of the Israelites, for whom the Lord fights.*

When it is safe to do so, Rahab lets the two men down by a cord from a window. In return for her kindness, they swear that the lives of all under her roof will be spared when Jericho falls. When we come into the land, *they tell her,* thou shalt bind this line of scarlet thread in the window which thou didst let us down by. . . .[2:18]

Joshua, when he hears the two men's report, gives the command for the people to move forward, across the Jordan.

Before them go the priests, bearing the Ark of the Covenant. As the feet of the priests touch the water, the river dries up: And the priests stood firm on dry ground in the midst of Jordan, and all the Israelites passed over on dry ground. . . .[3:17]

About forty thousand prepared for war passed over before the Lord unto battle, to the plains of Jericho. On that day the Lord magnified Joshua in the sight of all Israel; and they feared him, as they feared Moses, all the days of his life.[4:13-14]

THE WALLS OF JERICHO

Their first encampment in the Promised Land is at Gilgal, in the plains of Jericho. Here they keep the Passover. The

*next day, the manna ceases. From this time they eat the pro-
duce of the land of Canaan.*

The Lord says to Joshua, I have given into thine hand
Jericho, and the king thereof, and the mighty men of
valor.[6:2] *And He gives Joshua explicit directions for the
capture of the city.*

*Each day, for six days, the army marches once around the
city. In its midst goes the Ark of the Covenant, led by seven
priests bearing seven trumpets. On the seventh day the city
is encompassed seven times. Then the priests blow a blast on
their trumpets:* And it came to pass, when the people heard
the sound of the trumpet, and the people shouted with a
great shout, that the wall fell down flat, so that the people
went up into the city . . . and they took the city.[6:20]

*Every living thing in the city is destroyed—men, women,
children, and cattle. But* Joshua saved Rahab the harlot
alive, and her father's household, and all that she had . . .
because she hid the messengers which Joshua sent to spy
out Jericho.[6:25]

So the Lord was with Joshua; and his fame was noised
throughout all the country.[6:27]

THE CONQUEST OF CANAAN

*Five kings of the Amorites, fearing Joshua, now gather to
make war on Israel. The Lord says to Joshua,* Fear them
not: for I have delivered them into thine hand. . . .[10:8]

And the Lord discomfited them before Israel, and slew
them with a great slaughter at Gibeon. . . .[10:10]

Then spake Joshua to the Lord . . . and he said in the
sight of Israel, Sun, stand thou still upon Gibeon; and thou,
Moon, in the valley of Ajalon.

And the sun stood still, and the moon stayed, until the
people had avenged themselves upon their enemies. . . .

And there was no day like that before it or after it, that

the Lord hearkened unto the voice of a man: for the Lord fought for Israel.[10:12-14]

So Joshua took all that land, the hills, and all the south country, and all the land of Goshen, and the valley, and the plain, and the mountain of Israel, and the valley of the same.[11:16]

But there is still much land to be taken: and Joshua is now growing old. The Lord tells him to divide by lot among the tribes of Israel all the countries in the land of Canaan, so each tribe may go and claim its inheritance.

When the land has been allotted, Joshua chooses for his own inheritance the city of Timnath-serah, in the region of mount Ephraim. He builds up this city and lives in it.

THE DEATH OF JOSHUA

And the Lord gave unto Israel all the land which he sware to give unto their fathers. . . .[21:43]

There failed not aught of any good thing which the Lord had spoken unto the house of Israel; all came to pass.[21:45]

Israel is now at peace. Joshua calls together the people and says, Therefore fear the Lord, and serve him in sincerity and in truth: and put away the gods which your fathers served on the other side of the flood, and in Egypt. . . .[24:14]

And the people say, The Lord our God will we serve, and his voice will we obey.[24:24]

They solemnly renew the covenant with God: as witness to which they set up a great stone near the tabernacle of the Lord.

So Joshua let the people depart, every man unto his inheritance.

And it came to pass after these things, that Joshua the son of Nun, the servant of the Lord, died, being a hundred and ten years old.[24:28-29]

JUDGES

A new generation arises in Israel which does not remember Joshua.

In those days there was no king in Israel, but every man did that which was right in his own eyes.[17:6]

The commandments are broken; sacrifices are made to strange gods on forbidden altars; the conquered people of the land are not driven out, as the Lord has commanded, saying They shall be as thorns in your sides,[2:3] *but instead they live side by side with the Israelites and pay tribute to them.*

And the anger of the Lord was hot against Israel, and he delivered them into the hands of spoilers . . . and he sold them into the hands of their enemies. . . .[2:14]

The Book of Judges is the history of Israel in the Promised Land, as the people fall from grace and are punished by the Lord; as they repent; and as the Judges whom the Lord raises up from among them deliver them each time from oppression.

DEBORAH AND BARAK

For twenty years the children of Isreal live in cruel servitude to Jabin, king of Canaan—for they have done evil in the sight of the Lord. Their Judge is Deborah, a prophetess, and to her they turn at last for help. She calls upon Barak, a man of valor; and together they raise ten thousand fighting men whom they lead to mount Tabor.

In the valley below them is Sisera, invincible commander of king Jabin's forces, with nine hundred iron chariots and a great a'my.

Deborah says to Barak, Up; for this is the day in which the Lord hath delivered Sisera into thine hand.[4:14] *The*

Israelites sweep down from mount Tabor. The enemy is routed.

Sisera flees for refuge to the tent of Heber the Kenite, whom he believes to be friendly. Heber's wife, Jael, draws him into the tent. She gives him milk to drink. She covers him with a mantle.

Then Jael Heber's wife took a nail of the tent, and took a hammer in her hand, and went softly unto him, and smote the nail into his temples, and fastened it into the ground: for he was fast asleep and weary. So he died.[4:21]

Israel is victorious. King Jabin is killed and his kingdom subdued.

Then Deborah and Barak sing a song of exultation, and of praise to the Lord:

I will sing praise to the Lord God of Israel.[5:3]

The inhabitants of the villages ceased, they ceased in Israel, until that I Deborah arose, that I arose a mother in Israel.[5:7]

Then . . . the Lord made me have dominion over the mighty.[5:13]

They fought from heaven; the stars in their courses fought against Sisera.[5:20]

Blessed above women shall Jael the wife of Heber the Kenite be. . . .[5:24]

At her feet he bowed, he fell, he lay down. . . . where he bowed, there he fell down dead.

The mother of Sisera looked out at a window. . . . Why tarry the wheels of his chariots? . . . Have they not divided the prey; to every man a damsel or two? . . .[5:27-30]

So let all thine enemies perish, O Lord. . . .[5:31]

THE MIGHTY MEN OF VALOR

And the land had rest forty years.[5:31]

And the children of Israel did evil in the sight of the Lord. . . .[6:1]

In the two hundred years following the death of Joshua, these are among the men whom the Lord raises up to be Judges and leaders of Israel:

GIDEON, who overthrows an altar to the god Baal; and who with three hundred picked men attacks a great horde of the enemy—the Midianites. By making a sudden great noise the three hundred, dispersed about the enemy camp, shouting The sword of the Lord, and of Gideon,[7:20] *throw the Midianites into such confusion that they are utterly routed.*

JEPHTHAH, the son of a harlot, who is driven out of his father's house in Gilead. But when the city is attacked by Ammonites, Jephthah is sent for. He makes a vow to the Lord: If thou shalt without fail deliver the children of Ammon into mine hands then it shall be, that whatsoever cometh forth of the doors of my house to meet me, when I return in peace from the children of Ammon, shall surely be the Lord's, and I will offer it up for a burnt offering.[11:30-31] *He returns home victorious. It is his young daughter, his only child, who dances forth to meet him.*

Jephthah cries, Alas my daughter! thou hast brought me very low.[11:35] *But the girl knows what must be done: Jephthah's vow to the Lord is fulfilled.*

SAMSON, of the tribe of Dan, who with his own two hands begins Israel's deliverance when through their disobedience they have fallen into the power of the Philistines. Samson is a Nazarite, dedicated at birth to the Lord: no wine or strong drink must ever pass his lips, no razor must ever touch his hair. The Spirit of the Lord is upon him; the strength of many men is in his hands.

He marries a daughter of the Philistines. But a great enmity arises between him and his wife's people, in consequence of which they kill both the woman and her father. Samson goes to avenge them.

And he smote them hip and thigh with a great slaughter. . . .[15:8]

He is captured, but easily breaks his bonds. Taking the first weapon at hand, the jawbone of an ass, he strikes out: And Samson said, With the jawbone of an ass . . . have I slain a thousand men.[15:16]

Samson is Judge over Israel for twenty years.

He falls in love with Delilah, whom the Philistines bribe to be their tool. She presses him to tell her wherein lies his strength. At last Samson says, If I be shaven, then my strength will go from me. . . .[16:17]

While he is asleep, Delilah has his head shaved. Then she says, The Philistines be upon thee, Samson. *He awakens:* And he wist not that the Lord was departed from him. [16:20] *The Philistines take him, put out his eyes, and bring him into the city of Gaza.*

Blind and in fetters, standing between two pillars of the house in which the Philistines have gathered to make sport of him, Samson calls upon the Lord: Strengthen me, I pray thee, only this once, O God, that I may be at once avenged of the Philistines for my two eyes.[16:28] *Taking hold of the two pillars, he bows himself with all his might. The house falls, killing all that are in it.*

So the dead which he slew at his death were more than they which he slew in his life.[16:30]

THE DAUGHTERS OF SHILOH

In Gibeah, inhabited by the tribe of Benjamin, an atrocity is committed upon an innocent wayfarer. All Israel gathers against the Benjamites. The cities of Gibeah are destroyed, its inhabitants are slain: all but six hundred men who flee into the wilderness.

The children of Israel repent, now that one tribe has been cut off from them. They send messengers of peace to the remaining Benjamites. There are no women left in Gibeah, however; and wives must be found for these men.

Now each year there is a feast of the Lord at Shiloh, near Bethel, when the maidens come out to dance. The Benjamites are told to go and hide in the nearby vineyards: If the daughters of Shiloh come out to dance . . . then come ye out of the vineyards, and catch you every man his wife. . . .[21:21]

And the children of Benjamin did so, and took them wives . . . of them that danced, whom they caught: and they went and returned unto their inheritance, and repaired the cities, and dwelt in them[21:23]

RUTH

During a terrible famine, a man of Bethlehem named Elimelech goes to live in the land of Moab, taking with him his wife, Naomi, and their two sons. The sons marry among the Moabites; but both Elimelech and his sons die in Moab. Naomi sorrowfully prepares to return to Bethlehem, telling her daughters-in-law to go home to their own parents.

But one of the young women, whose name is Ruth, says Entreat me not to leave thee, or to return from following after thee: for whither thou goest, I will go; and where thou lodgest, I will lodge: thy people shall be my people, and thy God my God; Where thou diest, will I die, and there will I be buried: the Lord do so to me, and more also, if aught but death part thee and me.[1:16-17]

When the two women come to Bethlehem, Ruth goes out into the fields and says to the men, I pray you, let me glean and gather after the reapers among the sheaves. . . .[2:7]

It happens that the field in which she gleans belongs to Boaz, a rich relative of Ruth's dead father-in-law, Elimelech. Boaz notices Ruth; he sees to it that she is well and generously treated. Ruth bows before him, saying, Why have I found grace in thine eyes . . . seeing I am a stranger?[2:10] *He tells her that he knows of her goodness to her mother-in-law: how she left her own people to come here with Naomi to live among strangers. He gives her six measures of barley, saying,* Go not empty unto thy mother-in-law.[3:17]

On her return home, Ruth learns from Naomi that this powerful man is their near kinsman.

As Naomi's next of kin, Boaz has the right to buy, if he will, the land that belonged to her husband. He redeems this right. And with the purchase of the land he also claims the right to marry the young widow.

So Boaz took Ruth, and she was his wife . . . and she bare a son.[4:13]

And Naomi took the child, and laid it in her bosom, and became nurse unto it.[4:16] *To Naomi it is as if she had a son in place of the two who lie dead in Moab.*

From Ruth and Boaz is directly descended king David: for their son, named Obed, becomes the father of Jesse and the grandfather of David—who will one day be king of Judah and of all Israel.

I SAMUEL

Samuel's mother, Hannah, before his birth makes a vow: O Lord of hosts, if thou wilt . . . give unto thine handmaid a man child, then I will give him unto the Lord all the days of his life. . . .[1:11] *Accordingly after she has weaned the child Hannah places him in the care of Eli, the High Priest at Shiloh.*

Eli's two sons, priests of the temple at Shiloh, are evil men. They greedily seize the congregation's offerings to the Lord; they corrupt the women who assembled at the tabernacle; they desecrate the tabernacle and lead the people into sin.

But the child Samuel ministers before the Lord, girded with a linen ephod.[2:18]

One night Samuel hears the voice of the Lord calling him. He answers, Speak, Lord; for thy servant heareth.[3:9] *The Lord says,* I will do a thing in Israel, at which both the ears of every one that heareth it shall tingle.[3:11]

Eli and his sons are to be terribly punished: because his sons made themselves vile, and he restrained them not.[3:13]

Thus the Lord reveals himself to Samuel: and all Israel knows that he is established to be a prophet of the Lord.

Punishment falls upon the Israelites: They are defeated with great slaughter in a battle against the Philistines. The Ark of the Covenant is captured by the enemy; and the tidings kill their High Priest, Eli:

He fell from off the seat backward by the side of the gate, and his neck brake. . . .[4:18]

Eli's daughter-in-law, dying in childbirth, says, The glory is departed from Israel: for the ark of God is taken.[4:22]

But the Ark brings plagues and disasters to its captors, and they return it. Israel repents its sins. The tribes gather at Mizpeh to fast and pray. Then, in the midst of this, the Philistines fall upon them.

Samuel cries to the Lord to save Israel; and the Lord hears him:

The Lord thundered with a great thunder on that day upon the Philistines . . . and they were smitten before Israel.[7:10]

And Samuel judged Israel all the days of his life.[7:15]

ISRAEL DEMANDS A KING

When Samuel is growing old, the elders come to him and petition him to give them a king: to judge us like all the nations.[8:5] *It displeases the Lord; but He names Saul, of the tribe of Benjamin, to reign over Israel.*

And all the people shouted and said, God save the king.[10:24]

Saul reigns for two years: A choice young man, and a goodly.[9:2] *Under his leadership and that of his brave son, Jonathan, the Israelites win victories over many of their enemies.*

The Lord commands Saul to go and smite the wicked Amalekites, Israel's enemy of old. Saul is utterly to destroy them and all their goods. But Saul rashly disobeys: He takes Agag, king of the Amalekites, alive; and he permits his people to carry off the best of the cattle and the sheep.

The Lord says to Samuel, It repenteth me that I have set up Saul to be king. . . .[15:11]

Reproached by Samuel for his disobedience, Saul says, The people spared the best of the sheep and of the oxen, to sacrifice unto the Lord. . . .[15:15]

Samuel replies, To obey is better than sacrifice, and to hearken than the fat of rams. For rebellion is as the sin of witchcraft, and stubbornness is as iniquity and idolatry. Because thou hast rejected the word of the Lord, he hath also rejected thee from being king.[15:22-23]

Samuel sends for King Agag:

And Agag came unto him delicately. And Agag said, Surely the bitterness of death is past. And Samuel said, As thy sword hath made women childless, so shall thy mother be childless among women.

And Samuel hewed Agag in pieces before the Lord in Gilgal.[15:32-33]

Then the Lord says to Samuel, I will send thee to Jesse the Bethlehemite: for I have provided me a king among his sons.[16:1]

Jesse's oldest son, Eliab, is pleasing to Samuel: but the Lord says, Look not on his countenance, or on the height of his stature; because I have refused him: for the Lord

seeth not as man seeth; for man looketh on the outward
appearance, but the Lord looketh on the heart.[16:7] *Jesse's
youngest son, David, then comes in from tending the sheep:*

Now he was ruddy, and withal of a beautiful countenance,
and goodly to look to. And the Lord said, Arise, anoint him:
for this is he.[16:12]

DAVID AND GOLIATH

*The army of king Saul and that of the Philistines face
each other across a valley in Judah. There comes out a huge
Philistine, wearing mail and a brass helmet. This giant,
Goliath, challenges the Israelites to send out a man against
him:* If he be able to fight with me, and to kill me, then will
we be your servants. . . .[17:9]

The boy David goes to king Saul and says, Let no man's
heart fail because of him; thy servant will go and fight with
this Philistine.[17:32] *Taking his staff in his hand, he chooses
five smooth stones out of the brook.*

The giant, in a rage, shouts at David, Am I a dog, that
thou comest to me with staves?[17:43] *David takes one of the
stones and slings it at him. It sinks into Goliath's forehead,
and kills him.*

So David prevailed over the Philistine with a sling and
with a stone. . . . And when the Philistines saw their
champion was dead, they fled.[17:50-51]

*Saul returns home in triumph, to hear the women of Israel
singing,* Saul hath slain his thousands, and David his ten
thousands.[18:7] *He tells his son Jonathan that David must be
killed. The young man goes at once to warn David: because*
he loved him as his own soul.[18:3]

*David flees into the wilderness, with some four hundred
of his followers. They are pursued by Saul, with an army of
three thousand.*

Hiding among the rocks of the wilderness, David comes

twice upon Saul when the king is alone and helpless; but twice David spares him: the king is the Lord's anointed; he must not be harmed.

Samuel dies, and all Israel mourns the great prophet.

David meanwhile wanders through the wilderness. He takes two wives: one is Ahinoam, of Jezreel; the other is Abigail, a woman of good understanding, and of a beautiful countenance.[25:3]

When David first sees Abigal she is the wife of a rich man named Nabal whom David has in the past befriended, but who refuses him food when David sends asking for it. Abigail however secretly takes food to David and his men; and with tact and wisdom she placates his wrath against her husband. Nabal dies; and Abigail follows David into the wilderness and becomes his wife.

THE WITCH OF ENDOR

To escape from Saul, David goes to live in Gath, the land of the Philistines. He allows Achish, the king of Gath, to look upon him as an enemy of the Israelites. Achish gives him the city of Ziklag for his home.

A great army of the Philistines is gathering against Israel. In fear, Saul goes to see a woman at Endor who is said to have a familiar spirit. He tells her to bring up Samuel. The woman cries out, An old man cometh up; and he is covered with a mantle.[28:14] Saul falls on his face before the dread figure of Samuel, who says, Why hast thou disquieted me, to bring me up?[28:15]

Saul answers, God is departed from me, and answereth me no more. . . .[28:15]

Samuel says, Because thou obeyedst not the voice of the Lord . . . the Lord will also deliver Israel with thee into the hand of the Philistines: and tomorrow shalt thou and thy son be with me. . . .[28:18-19]

Next day, the Philistines march against Israel. David and his men have no choice but to march with the army of king Achish. But the king suspects them. He orders them back to Ziklag.

They find Ziklag burned down, the women and much spoil carried off by the Amalekites. David pursues the raiders and overtakes and destroys them. He restores to Ziklag all the stolen goods and the women—among whom are his own two wives.

The Israelites are hopelessly defeated by the Philistines at mount Gilboa. Jonathan is killed. Saul is wounded: he falls upon his sword rather than be taken by the Philistines.

The nearby cities of the Israelites are abandoned; and the Philistines come in and occupy them.

II SAMUEL

And David lamented with this lamentation over Saul and over Jonathan his son:

The beauty of Israel is slain upon thy high places: how are the mighty fallen! Tell it not in Gath, publish it not in the streets of Askelon; lest the daughters of the Philistines rejoice, lest the daughters of the uncircumcised triumph.

Ye mountains of Gilboa, let there be no dew, neither let there be rain, upon you, nor fields of offerings: for there the shield of the mighty is vilely cast away. . . . [1:17-21]

Saul and Jonathan were lovely and pleasant in their lives, and in their death they were not divided: they were swifter than eagles, they were stronger than lions.

Ye daughters of Israel weep over Saul, who clothed you in scarlet, with other delights; who put on ornaments of gold upon your apparel.[1:23-24]

I am distressed for thee, my brother Jonathan. . . . Thy love to me was wonderful, passing the love of women.

How are the mighty fallen, and the weapons of war
perished![1:26-27]

*The Lord directs David to go to Hebron, and there the
men of Judah anoint him king; while to the north, Abner,
Saul's commander, makes Saul's son Ishbosheth king of all
Israel. There is a long war between the two houses: the
Israelites led by Abner, the men of Judah led by David's
commander, Joab.*

DAVID SUCCEEDS SAUL

*Abner makes himself strong over the Israelites; and Ish-
bosheth therefore picks a quarrel with him. In anger, Abner
goes to David in Hebron and offers to make a league between
Israel and Judah. David bids him go in peace.*

But as Abner is leaving, Joab treacherously kills him.

*When David hears this he proclaims his own innocence,
curses Joab and all his house, and says to his people,* Know
ye not that there is a prince and a great man fallen this day
in Israel?[3:38]

*Ishbosheth, who shows himself to be a feeble king, is
murdered.*

The elders of Israel now go to Hebron and say to David,
Behold, we are thy bone and thy flesh.[5:1] *David makes a
league with them; and they anoint him king. He rules for
thirty-three years over the united kingdoms of Israel and
Judah.*

And David went on, and grew great, and the Lord God
of hosts was with him.[5:10]

*In his reign the Jebusite fortress of Zion is captured;
Jerusalem is taken, and becomes the center and the capital
of the united kingdom; the Philistines are defeated in a great
battle in the valley of Rephaim, west of Jerusalem. And,
with great rejoicing, the Ark of the Lord is brought up to
Zion:*

And David and all the house of Israel played before the Lord on all manner of instruments. . . .[6:5] And David danced before the Lord with all his might. . . .[6:14]

He plans a tabernacle for the Lord: but Nathan the prophet comes and tells him that not David but his son will build God's house.

The Lord delivers all the surrounding hostile nations into David's hands. The Philistines are subdued; Moab is conquered; Syria, the powerful northern nation, is defeated; the Ammonites and the Edomites become vassals of Israel.

David is a good and generous king, who remembers those who were kind to him in his exile. He sends for Jonathan's son, the lame Mephibosheth, takes him into his household, and restores to him all the land that was Saul's.

DAVID AND BATH-SHEBA

But while Joab and the army are in the field, engaged in fighting the Ammonites, David is idly walking on the roof of his house one day, when he sees a woman washing herself: And the woman was very beautiful to look upon.[11:2] *He learns that she is Bath-sheba, the wife of Uriah, a soldier with Joab's army. David sends for Uriah, and gives him a message to take back to Joab:* Set ye Uriah in the forefront of the hottest battle.[11:15] *Uriah is killed.*

When the period of mourning is over, David sends for Bath-sheba; and she becomes his wife. She bears him a son.

But the thing that David had done displeased the Lord.[11:27]

The Lord sends the prophet Nathan to David with a parable:

There were two men in one city; the one rich, and the other poor. The rich man had exceeding many flocks and herds. But the poor man had nothing, save one little ewe lamb, which he had bought and nourished up. . . .

And there came a traveler unto the rich man, and he

spared to take of his own flock . . . to dress for the wayfaring man . . . but took the poor man's lamb, and dressed it for the man that was come to him.[12:1-4]

—   *David's anger is kindled against this rich man. He says,* the man that hath done this thing shall surely die. *Nathan says,* Thou art the man.[12:5-7]

—   *David says,* I have sinned against the Lord.[12:13]

—   *The son of David and Bath-sheba is stricken and is very sick. It is the Lord's punishment. David lies upon the earth,*

—   *and fasts and prays. But the child dies. Then David arises, and washes, and worships the Lord. He says,* Now he is dead, wherefore should I fast? Can I bring him back again? I shall go to him, but he shall not return to me.[12:23]

In time Bath-sheba bears him another son, whom they call Solomon: And the Lord loved him.[12:24]

THE REVOLT OF ABSALOM

A son of David's named Amnon falls in love with his half-sister, Tamar. He forces himself upon the girl, and afterwards puts her out of his house. Tamar's brother, Absalom, kills Amnon, then flees to the kingdom of Geshur, in Syria.

David grieves for his son Absalom. After punishing him for three years, he gives him permission to return. Instead Absalom goes to Hebron, from where he forms a conspiracy to make himself king. Raising an army, he prepares to march on Jerusalem.

To save the city from destruction, David leaves, with all his household and his people. He sends an army against Absalom, but he says to his officers, Deal gently for my sake with the young man, even with Absalom.[18:5]

Absalom's forces are defeated with great slaughter.

When the news is brought to David, he says, Is the young man Absalom safe?[18:32] *He is told that Absalom is dead.*

And the king was much moved, and went up to the

chamber over the gate, and wept: and as he went, thus he
said: O my son Absalom! my son, my son Absalom! Would
God I had died for thee, O Absalom, my son, my son![18:33]

DAVID'S SONG OF THANKSGIVING

And David spake unto the Lord the words of this song,
in the day that the Lord had delivered him out of the hand
of all his enemies. . . .

The Lord is my rock, and my fortress, and my deliverer;

The God of my rock; in him will I trust: he is my shield,
and the horn of my salvation, my high tower, and my refuge,
my saviour. . . . [22:1-3]

*David orders Israel to be numbered: there are in Israel
eight hundred thousand valiant men, and in Judah five hundred thousand.*

*But when the count has been made, David knows that in
making it he has acted sinfully. The prophet Gad comes
to him and, in the name of the Lord, offers him as punishment a choice of evils. David says,* Let us fall now into the
hand of the Lord; for his mercies are great: and let me not
fall into the hand of man.[24:14]

*A pestilence falls upon the people, and many thousands
die. David says to the Lord,* Lo, I have sinned, and I have
done wickedly: but these sheep, what have they done? let
thine hand, I pray thee, be against me, and against my
father's house.[24:17]

*The prophet Gad tells him to build an altar to the Lord.
David buys a threshing-floor on which to build the altar: it
is willingly offered by the owner, but David says,* Nay; but I
will surely buy it of thee at a price: neither will I offer burnt
offerings unto the Lord my God of that which doth cost me
nothing.[24:24] *The altar is built; burnt offerings and peace
offerings are made; the Lord is entreated, and the plague
is stayed from Israel.*

I KINGS

David reigns for forty years: seven in Hebron, thirty-three in Jerusalem.

Adonijah, his eldest son after the death of Absalom, now conspires with Joab, commander of the army, and Abiathar the priest, to make himself king. David, warned of the plot by Bath-sheba, anoints Solomon, his son by Bath-sheba, to be king.

Now the days of David drew nigh that he should die. . . .[2:1]

He charges Solomon to walk in the ways of the Lord and keep His commandments; to show kindness to those who have been loyal to the throne, and to punish those who have plotted against it.

David dies; Solomon sits upon the throne of his father; Joab and Adonijah are put to death; the priest Abiathar is banished.

Solomon makes an alliance with the Pharaoh, whose daughter he marries and brings up from Egypt into Zion, the city of David.

And Solomon loved the Lord, walking in the statutes of David his father: only he sacrificed and burnt incense in high places.[3:3]

One night the Lord appears to him in a dream and says, Ask what I shall give thee. *Solomon replies,* O Lord my God . . . I am but a little child: I know not how to go out or come in.[3:5-7]

Give therefore thy servant an understanding heart to judge thy people, that I may discern between good and bad: for who is able to judge this thy so great a people?[3:9]

The Lord says, Behold I have done according to thy

word: lo, I have given thee a wise and an understanding heart; so that there was none like thee before thee, neither after thee shall any arise like unto thee.

And I have also given thee that which thou hast not asked, both riches and honor: so that there shall not be any among the kings like unto thee all thy days.[3:12-13]

THE WISDOM OF SOLOMON

There are two women, harlots, both living in the same house, each of whom gives birth to a male child. One of the infants dies; whereupon its mother, while the other woman sleeps, takes the living child and claims it for her own.

The women come before king Solomon for judgment. Calling for a sword, he says, Divide the living child in two, and give half to the one, and half to the other. *One of the women consents. The other says,* O my Lord, give her the living child, and in no wise slay it. *The king turns to this second woman, saying,* Give her the living child . . . she is the mother thereof.[3:25-27]

All Israel hears of this judgment: And they feared the king: for they saw that the wisdom of God was in him to do judgment.[3:28]

The land grows great and prosperous under Solomon.
Judah and Israel were many, as the sand which is by the sea in multitude, eating and drinking, and making merry.[4:20]

And Solomon's wisdom excelled the wisdom of all the children of the east country, and all the wisdom of Egypt. . . .

And he spake three thousand proverbs: and his songs were a thousand and five.[4:30-32]

People come from all lands to hear king Solomon's wisdom.

In the fourth year of his reign, in the four hundred and eightieth year of Israel's deliverance, Solomon begins the building of a Temple, raising a levy of thirty thousand men from all Israel to hew timber and to bring stones. The dimensions of the Temple are very great (6:2-6). Its walls are cedar, the furnishings richly carved. Stones are brought to the site already hewn: so that there was neither hammer nor axe nor any tool of iron heard in the house, while it was in building.[6:7]

When the Temple is finished, with its pillars and its altar and its cherubim overlaid with gold, and its vessels of purest gold, Solomon builds the king's house, with a porch for a throne of judgment.

In all, twenty years go by before the Temple and the king's house are completed.

Then the priests bring the Ark of the Lord into the Temple. A great cloud fills the place: the glory of God is in the house of the Lord.

SOLOMON AND THE QUEEN OF SHEBA

When the Queen of Sheba hears of Solomon's fame, she comes to Jerusalem, with a great train, to prove him with hard questions.

She communed with him of all that was in her heart. And Solomon told her all her questions: there was not any thing hid from the king, which he told her not.[10:1-3]

And when the queen of Sheba had seen all Solomon's wisdom . . . there was no more spirit in her. And she said to the king . . . behold, the half was not told me: thy wisdom and prosperity exceedeth the fame which I heard.[10:4-7]

She presents the king with many rich gifts.

And king Solomon gave unto the queen of Sheba all her desire, whatsoever she asked, besides that which Solomon gave her of his royal bounty. So she turned and went to her own country, she and her servants.[10:13]

The king has seven hundred wives, princesses, and three hundred concubines:
King Solomon loved many strange women, together with the daughter of Pharaoh, women of the Moabites, Ammonites, Edomites, Zidonians, and Hittites. . . . Solomon clave unto these in love.[11:1-2]
They turn away his heart from the Lord; and he builds altars to their strange gods.
The Lord tells Solomon that He will rend the kingdom away from him. For David's sake, however, He will not do so in Solomon's reign, but in that of his son: Howbeit . . . I will give one tribe to thy son for David my servant's sake, and for Jerusalem's sake which I have chosen.[11:13]
The Lord stirs up adversaries against the king. Among these is Jeroboam, a valorous and able young man whom the king, noting his industry, has placed in charge of all the men of the house of Joseph. But Jeroboam is told by a prophet that he will be king over Israel; therefore, Solomon seeks to have him killed. Jeroboam escapes into Egypt, where he remains while the king lives.
Solomon reigns for forty years. Upon his death he is succeeded by his son, Rehoboam.

The people now recall Jeroboam from Egypt.
Solomon's son, Rehoboam, goes to Shechem, at mount Ephraim, to be made king. Here the people, led by Jeroboam, make a request of him: Thy father made our yoke grievous: now therefore make thou the grievous service of thy father, and his heavy yoke which he put upon us, lighter, and we will serve thee.[12:4]

*Rehoboam chooses to listen to rash young counselors.
They tell him to say this to the people:* My little finger shall
be thicker than my father's loins. And now whereas my
father did lade you with a heavy yoke, I will add to your
yoke: my father hath chastised you with whips, but I will
chastise you with scorpions.[12:10-11]

Their request being thus roughly refused, the people cry,
To your tents, O Israel: now see to thine own house,
David.[12:16] *They rebel. Rehoboam flees to Jerusalem. Once
more Israel is torn asunder: Jeroboam is made king of Israel,
while Rehoboam reigns in Jerusalem, where only the tribe
of Judah remains faithful to him.*

And there was war between Rehoboam and Jeroboam all
their days.[14:30]

*But both kingdoms worship images of gold. They break
the Lord's commandments. They practice sodomy and all
the abominations of the people whom the Lord cast out
before them.*

*In the fifth year of Rehoboam's reign, Jerusalem is at-
tacked by the Egyptians, who raid the Temple and the house
of the king and carry off the treasures of king Solomon.*

*King Jeroboam is warned by the prophet Ahijah that the
Lord will smite Israel and destroy the house of Jeroboam:
but he continues in his sins, as do the kings who come after
him: Nadab, Jeroboam's son, an evil king, is slain by one
Baasha, who destroys all those of the house of Jeroboam
and makes himself king. His son Elah, who succeeds him, is
conspired against by one of his officers, Zimri. Finding the
king drunk in the house of his steward, Zimri kills him, and
then destroys all the house of Baasha.*

*Zimri reigns only seven days: because of his treason to the
throne the people rise against him. He kills himself. The commander of the army, Omri, is chosen to be king. In his reign,*

*Omri buys a hill for two talents of silver and builds a city
which he calls Samaria. From here he rules Israel, but he
also does evil in the eyes of the Lord.*

*The sixth king of Israel after Jeroboam is Ahab, son of
Omri: He takes Jezebel, daughter of the king of Tyre, for his
wife, and builds a temple to the god Baal.*

THE PROPHET ELIJAH

*A holy man of Gilead called Elijah the Tishbite warns
king Ahab that the land will suffer a great drought. Then
Elijah is commanded by the Lord to go and hide:*
He went and dwelt by the brook Cherith, that is before
Jordan. And the ravens brought him bread and flesh in the
morning, and bread and flesh in the evening; and he drank
of the brook.[17:5-6]

*The drought comes. The brook dries up. Elijah is directed
by the Lord to go to Zarephath in Zidon. The Lord says,* I
have commanded a widow woman there to sustain thee.[17:9]

*The widow is gathering sticks at the gates of Zarephath
when Elijah comes, asking for water and a morsel of bread.
She says,* I have . . . but a handful of meal in a barrel, and
a little oil in a cruse: and . . . I am gathering two sticks,
that I may go in and dress it for me and my son, that we
may eat it, and die. *Elijah says,* Fear not; go and do as thou
hast said. . . . *She obeys.*

And she, and he, and her house, did eat many days. And
the barrel of meal wasted not, neither did the cruse of oil
fail. . . .[17:12-16]

*The widow's son falling sick to death, Elijah pleads with
the Lord for the child's life: and the Lord hears him. The
boy revives. The mother says to Elijah,* Now by this I know
that thou art a man of God. . . .[17:24]

*In the third year of the drought, the Lord sends Elijah to
the king. When Ahab sees him he says,* Art thou he that

troubleth Israel? *The prophet replies,* I have not troubled Israel; but thou, and thy father's house, in that ye have forsaken the commandments of the Lord. . . .[18:17-18]

He tells Ahab to gather at mount Carmel all the people of Israel, all the prophets of Baal, and all the prophets of the groves who eat at the table of Jezebel, king Ahab's wife. Standing before the multitude, Elijah says, How long halt ye between two opinions? If the Lord be God, follow him: but if Baal, then follow him.[18:21] *He says to the prophets of Baal,* Call ye on the name of your gods, and I will call on the name of the Lord: and the God that answereth by fire, let him be God.[18:24]

The prophets call in vain, from morning until noon, upon Baal. Elijah mocks them: Either he is talking, or he is pursuing, or he is in a journey, or peradventure he sleepeth, and must be awaked.[18:27]

Then it is Elijah's turn: Hear me O Lord, hear me, that this people may know that thou art the Lord God. . . .[18:37]

The fire of the Lord comes and consumes the burnt sacrifice. The people fall on their faces, crying, The Lord, he is the God.[18:39]

Elijah speaks to the king: Get thee up, eat and drink; for there is a sound of abundance of rain.[18:41]

Jezebel swears to have Elijah killed, to avenge her prophets. He flees into the wilderness:
And came and sat down under a juniper tree: and he requested for himself that he might die; and said, It is enough; now, O Lord, take away my life. . . .[19:4]

The word of the Lord comes to him: Go forth, and stand upon the mount. . . .

And, behold, the Lord passed by, and a great and strong wind rent the mountains . . . but the Lord was not in the wind: and after the wind an earthquake; but the Lord was

not in the earthquake: and after the earthquake a fire; but
the Lord was not in the fire; and after the fire a still small
voice.[19:11-12]

*The Lord commands Elijah to go to Damascus, there to
anoint Hazael to be king of Syria:* And Jehu . . . shalt thou
anoint to be king over Israel: and Elisha . . . shalt thou
anoint to be prophet in thy room. And it shall come to pass,
that him that escapeth the sword of Hazael shall Jehu slay:
and him that escapeth from the sword of Jehu shall Elisha
slay. . . .

Yet I have left me seven thousand in Israel, all the knees
which have not bowed unto Baal, and every mouth which
hath not kissed him.[19:16-18]

THE DEATH OF AHAB

*There is a vineyard in Jezreel, hard by the palace of the
king, which king Ahab covets; but its owner, Naboth, refuses to part with it. Jezebel taunts the king: she plots
against Naboth, so that he is accused of blasphemy and
stoned to death. Ahab then takes possession of the vineyard.*

*The Lord sends Elijah the Tishbite to the king. When
Ahab sees him he says,* Hast thou found me, O mine enemy?
Elijah says, I will bring evil upon thee, and will take away
thy posterity. . . .[21:20-21]

*In Jerusalem, Solomon's son, Rehoboam, dies, and is
succeeded by his son Abijam.*

And he walked in all the sins of his father, which he had
done before him. . . .[15:3]

*Asa, Abijam's son, rules after him. He destroys the idols
out of the land. He drives out the sodomites, builds cities,
and, by making a league with Ben-hadad, king of Syria,
saves Judah from the hands of king Baasha of Israel. After
Asa's death his son, Jehoshaphat, also rules righteously.*

Jehoshaphat makes peace with king Ahab of Israel. He and Ahab agree to march against Ramoth in Gilead, to take the city away from the king of Syria. Their victory is assured them by all the prophets of Israel save one, Micaiah, of whom Ahab says, I hate him; for he doth not prophesy good concerning me, but evil.²²:⁸ *Micaiah, prophesying, says,* I saw all Israel scattered upon the hills, as sheep that have not a shepherd.²²:¹⁷ *Ahab says to Jehoshaphat,* Did I not tell thee that he would prophesy no good concerning me, but evil?²²:¹⁸ Put this fellow in the prison, and feed him with bread of affliction and with water of affliction, until I come in peace. *Micaiah replies,* If thou return at all in peace, the Lord hath not spoken by me.²²:²⁷⁻²⁸

The two kings go up to Ramoth-gilead. The battle goes against them.

And a certain man drew a bow at a venture, and smote the king of Israel between the joints of the harness.²²:³⁴

Ahab dies. Jehoshaphat flees. And at sunset word goes out among the Israelites and the Judeans: Every man to his city, and every man to his own country.²²:³⁶

Jehoshaphat returns to Jerusalem, where he reigns yet for many years over Judah.

Ahab is buried in Samaria. Israel is now ruled by Ahaziah, the son of Ahab and Jezebel. Like his father and mother, Ahaziah worships Baal, and does great evil in the eyes of the Lord.

II KINGS

One day king Ahaziah is injured in a fall from his upper window; and he sends to Baalzebub, the god of Ekron, to inquire if he will recover.

The Lord sends Elijah the Tishbite to the king with this message:

Forasmuch as thou hast sent messengers to inquire of Baalzebub the god of Ekron, is it not because there is no God in Israel to inquire of his word? Therefore thou shalt not come down off that bed on which thou art gone up, but shalt surely die.[1:16]

Ahaziah dies. As he has no son to succeed him, his brother Jehoram reigns in his place.

THE ASCENSION OF ELIJAH

Elijah knows that his days are nearing an end. As he is walking with his disciple, Elisha, by the river Jordan, Elijah says to him, Ask what I shall do for thee. *Elisha answers,* I pray thee, let a double portion of thy spirit be upon me.[2:9]

And it came to pass, as they still went on, and talked, that, behold, there appeared a chariot of fire, and horses of fire, and parted them asunder; and Elijah went up by a whirlwind into heaven.

Elisha cries out, My father, my father, the chariot of Israel, and the horsemen thereof![2:11-12] *Elijah vanishes from sight. But the other prophets, when they see Elisha, exclaim,* The spirit of Elijah doth rest on Elisha.[2:15] *And they bow down before him.*

Moab, which has been vassal to Israel, now rebels. Three kings unite and take the field against the king of Moab: Jehoram of Israel, Jehoshaphat of Judah, and the king of Edom. But there is no water for their armies: they face defeat.

The prophet Elisha is summoned; but he says to the king of Israel, What have I to do with thee? get thee to the prophets of thy father. . . .[3:13] *But for the sake of Jehoshaphat he tells them what to do: Ditches are dug, through which water pours in through the land. The Moabites attack and are defeated.*

Elisha is now a great prophet in Israel, working many wonders among the people. A pot of oil, all that a poor widow has in her house, is increased until she has an abundance. A dead boy, whose mother has befriended Elisha, is restored to life. During a famine, Elisha tells a company of prophets to gather wild herbs for a pottage. They say, There is death in the pot;[4:40] *whereupon Elisha renders the pottage harmless. He feeds a hundred people with a few loaves and a little corn, and he cures Naaman, the great Syrian general, of his leprosy.*

Elisha foretells the end of a siege of Samaria by the Syrians. The beleaguered city instead suffers a terrible famine; and the king swears to have Elisha put to death. The prophet says, Thus saith the Lord, tomorrow about this time shall a measure of fine flour be sold for a shekel and two measures of barley for a shekel in the gate of Samaria.[7:1] *The Lord causes the Syrians to hear a great noise of chariots: they flee in the night, leaving their tents filled with provisions. So, as Elisha has said, that day a measure of fine flour is sold for a shekel in Samaria.*

Elisha then goes to Damascus to anoint Hazael king of Syria, as Elijah was instructed by the Lord (I Kgs., 19:15). Elisha tells Hazael he shall be king in place of his master, Ben-hadad. Thereupon Hazael kills Ben-hadad, and makes himself king of Syria.

Jehoram, the son of king Jehoshaphat of Judah, reigns after his father. His wife is a daughter of Ahab of Israel. In Jehoram's reign Edom, and also Libnah, revolt from Judah.

After Jehoram comes Ahaziah, his son, the grandson of Ahab and Jezebel and cousin to king Jehoram of Israel. The two kings, Ahaziah and Jehoram, join in a war against Hazael of Syria, in Ramoth-gilead. Jehoram, wounded in battle, goes to Jezreel to be healed; and Ahaziah goes there to see him.

Elisha the prophet sends a disciple to Ramoth-gilead to anoint a young officer named Jehu, whom the Lord has appointed through His prophet Elijah (I Kgs., 19:16) to be king of Israel. The disciple says to Jehu, Thus saith the Lord God of Israel . . . thou shalt smite the house of Ahab thy master, that I may avenge the blood of my servants. . . . For the whole house of Ahab shall perish. . . .

And the dogs shall eat Jezebel in the portion of Jezreel, and there shall be none to bury her.[9:6-10]

With his comrades, Jehu rides in a chariot to Jezreel. They are met by a messenger who asks, Is it peace? *Jehu replies,* What hast thou to do with peace? Turn thee behind me.[9:17-18]

This is told to the king by his messenger, who says, The driving is like the driving of Jehu the son of Nimshi; for he driveth furiously.[9:20]

The two kings, Jehoram and Ahaziah, go out in their chariots against Jehu. They meet in Naboth's vineyard. Is it peace, Jehu? *calls Jehoram. Jehu answers,* What peace, so long as the whoredom of thy mother Jezebel and her witchcrafts are so many?[9:22] *He draws his bow and kills Jehoram. Ahaziah turns to escape; he too is killed.*

Jezebel heard of it; and she painted her face, and tired her head, and looked out at a window. And as Jehu entered in at the gate, she said, Had Zimri peace, who slew his master?

And he lifted up his face to the window, and said, Who is on my side? Who? And there looked out to him two or three eunuchs. And he said, Throw her down. So they threw her down. . . . And he trod her under foot.

He says, Go, see now this cursed woman, and bury her: for she is a king's daughter.

And they went to bury her: but they found no more of her than the skull, and the feet, and the palms of her hands.[9:30-35]

THE END OF THE HOUSE OF AHAB

Jehu puts to death all the remaining men of the house of Ahab in Jezreel and in Samaria. The priests and the prophets of Baal, all in Israel who worship Baal, the image and the temple of the god—all are destroyed.

But Jehu breaks the laws that the Lord has laid down for Israel.

In those days the Lord began to cut Israel short: and Hazael [*king of Syria*] smote them in all the coasts of Israel.[10:31-32]

Jehu rules Israel for twenty-eight years. After him, from father to son, the kings of Israel are Jehoahaz, Jehoash, Jeroboam the Second. All these trespass against the Law: the golden calves of Jeroboam still remain in Israel. But the Lord is gracious. He will not yet destroy his people because of his covenant with Abraham, Isaac, and Jacob.

Zachariah, son of Jeroboam the Second, succeeds his father on the throne, but only for six months: he is killed by a conspirator, Shallum, who makes himself king. Shallum himself, having reigned for one month, is killed by Menahem. Having seized the throne, Menahem gives the king of Assyria, Pul, a thousand talents of silver—which he exacts from the people in taxes—in order to turn aside an attack upon Israel and to strengthen his own power.

Menahem's son, Pekahiah, rules for two years, after which he is killed by one of his officers, Pekah, in whose reign Tiglath-pileser, king of Assyria, captures many of Israel's possessions and carries away captive large numbers of the people. Then there is a conspiracy against Pekah, who is killed. Hoshea is the new king; and he is the last king of Israel.

Hoshea pays tribute to the king of Assyria, who is now Shalmaneser, and is virtually his servant.

For so it was, that the children of Israel had sinned against the Lord their God . . . and walked in the statutes of the heathen. . . . And the children of Israel did secretly those things that were not right against the Lord their God. . . .[17:7-9]

Shalmaneser comes up and takes Samaria. Israel is carried away into slavery in Assyria.

And the king of Assyria brought men from Babylon, and from Cuthah, and from Ava, and from Hamath, and from Sepharvaim, and placed them in the cities of Samaria instead of the children of Israel: and they possessed Samaria, and dwelt in the cities thereof.[17:24]

THE LAST DAYS OF JERUSALEM

When Ahaziah, king of Judah, is killed at Jezreel, his mother, Athaliah, seizes the throne. This evil woman reigns for six years, when there is an uprising against her, led by the priest Jehoiada. Athaliah is killed. The temple of Baal is destroyed. The rightful king, Ahaziah's young son Jehoash, is set upon the throne.

The priest Jehoiada makes a new covenant with the Lord, that they will be His people; and a covenant also between the king and the people.

Jehoash reigns for forty years in Jerusalem. He buys off the king of Syria with all the hallowed things and the gold in the Temple and in the king's house, thus saving Jerusalem from attack. But Jehoash is conspired against and is killed. His slayers are put to death by Amaziah, Jehoash's son, who succeeds him, and who is a righteous king.

One day Amaziah sends a challenge to the king of Israel, Jehoash: Come, let us look one another in the face.[14:8] *The meeting is at Beth-shemesh in Judah. Amaziah is defeated. The king of Israel goes to Jerusalem, breaks down the wall, takes treasure and hostages, and returns to Samaria.*

Amaziah is deposed and killed. His sixteen-year-old son, Azariah (also called Uzziah), is made king. He reigns for fifty-two years with righteousness, as did his father before him. Yet the people worship and sacrifice on the high places everywhere. The Lord smites Azariah: he is a leper until he dies, dwelling apart, while his son, Jotham, rules Judah.

After Azariah, and then Jotham, Jotham's son Ahaz begins to reign:

But he walked in the way of the kings of Israel, yea, and made his son to pass through the fire, according to the abominations of the heathen. . . .[16:3]

His son is Hezekiah, a righteous king. He removes the images and the groves, he keeps the commandments, and trusts in the Lord.

And the Lord was with him; and he prospered whithersoever he went forth: and he rebelled against the king of Assyria, and served him not.[18:7]

In the fourteenth year of the reign of Hezekiah, Sennacherib, king of Assyria, comes up against Judah. Although Hezekiah humbles himself, and sends him gifts of gold and treasure, Sennacherib attacks and captures the fortified cities of Judah. Then his messengers, along with a great army, come up to Jerusalem itself and call upon the people to surrender.

Hezekiah prays: Lord, bow down thine ear, and hear: open, Lord, thine eyes and see: and hear the words of Sennacherib, which hath sent him to reproach the living God.[19:16]

In the night, the angel of the Lord comes and smites the camp of the Assyrians. A hundred and eighty-five thousand are dead by morning. Sennacherib returns to Nineveh. As he is worshipping in the temple of his god, Nisroch, his own sons leap upon him with swords and kill him.

And Hezekiah slept with his fathers: and Manasseh his son reigned in his stead.²⁰:²¹

Manesseh does great evil in the land; and he seduces the people into evil ways. Manesseh shed innocent blood very much, till he had filled Jerusalem from one end to another.²¹:¹⁶ *His son, Amon, rules after him: he likewise forsakes God.*

Then comes Josiah, the son of Amon, who observes the Law and obeys the commandments.

He orders the Temple of the Lord to be repaired. As the work is being done, there is found, hidden within the Temple, the book of the Law.

When the king hears the words of the book, he rends his clothes, crying, Great is the wrath of the Lord that is kindled against us, because our fathers have not hearkened unto the words of this book. . . .²²:¹³

Gathering together the people and the priests and the prophets, he reads to them all the words of the book.

And the king stood by a pillar, and made a covenant before the Lord, to walk after the Lord, and to keep his commandments and his testimonies and his statutes with all their heart and all their soul, to perform the words of this covenant that were written in this book. And all the people stood to the covenant.²³:³

And the king commanded all the people, saying, Keep the passover unto the Lord your God, as it is written in the book of this covenant.

Surely there was not holden such a passover from the days of the judges that judged Israel. . . .²³:²¹⁻²²

Notwithstanding, the Lord turned not from the fierceness of his great wrath . . . against Judah. . . . And the Lord said, I will remove Judah also out of my sight, as I have removed Israel. . . .²³:²⁶⁻²⁷

But He says to Josiah, Because thine heart was tender . . . thou shalt be gathered into thy grave in peace; and thine eyes shall not see all the evil which I will bring upon this place.[22:19-20]

The king of Egypt having advanced, against the king of Assyria, as far as the Euphrates, Josiah goes up to oppose him. The Pharaoh kills him at Megiddo, in the plain of Jezreel.

Judah is now a servant of Egypt. The new king, Josiah's son Jehoahaz, is carried off to Egypt, where he dies. His brother, Jehoiakim, is taken by the Pharaoh and set on the throne: and he taxes the people to give silver and gold to the Pharaoh.

Then Nebuchadnezzar, king of Babylon, comes and invades Jerusalem. Jehoiakim is his vassal for three years; then he rebels. But bands of the Chaldeans, bands of the Syrians, bands of the Moabites and of the Ammonites attack the city, destroying wherever they are able.

Jehoiakim dies. His son Jehoiachin succeeds him; and in the eighth year of his reign Nebuchadnezzar, who meanwhile has defeated Egypt and has taken land from the river of Egypt unto the river Euphrates all that pertained to the king of Egypt,[24:7] *lays siege to Jerusalem. Jehoiachin comes out to him and surrenders. He is carried away prisoner to Babylon: and with him go his mother, his wives, his officers, and all the mighty of the land. None remain but* the poorest sort of people of the land.[24:14]

All the men of might, even seven thousand, and craftsmen and smiths a thousand, all that were strong and apt for war, even them the king of Babylon brought captive to Babylon.[24:16]

Nebuchadnezzar puts Zedekiah, an uncle of Jehoiachin's,

*on the throne of Judah. He reigns for eleven years: then he
too rebels against Babylon. Nebuchadnezzar comes up with
a great host. Jerusalem is utterly despoiled. Its walls are
torn down, the Temple is burned, the king's house and all
the great houses of the city are destroyed. The brass pillars
of the Temple, all the vessels of brass, the bowls and pans of
gold and silver, all are carried off to Babylon.*

*Zedekiah flees; but he is taken. His sons are slain before
his eyes. The king himself is bound with fetters of brass, his
eyes are put out, and he is carried to Babylon.*

So Judah was carried away out of their land.[25:21]

*Those people whom Nebuchadnezzar permits to remain,
live only in constant fear. At last they flee for safety to
Egypt.*

I CHRONICLES

*The two Books of Chronicles form a supplement to II
Samuel and Kings, repeating in substance the history of
events from the death of king Saul to the Babylonian captivity. In Chronicles, however, there are both additions to
and omissions from the story; it is told more briefly and in
less detail than in the Books of Samuel and Kings.*

*The first nine chapters of the First Book of Chronicles
consist of a catalogue of the official genealogies of the children of Israel, beginning with Creation.*

*After the genealogies, I Chronicles describes again
Israel's defeat by the Philistines at mount Gilboa, the death
of Saul, the anointing of David as king over all Israel, the
capture of Zion and of Jerusalem, the bringing in of the
Ark into Zion, the wars of David.*

*Peculiar to I Chronicles is a detailed account of David's
instructions and preparations for the building of the Temple
and his directions for its rituals. It is upon the completion*

of these preparations that he utters his great prayer of thanksgiving, quoted here in part:

Blessed be thou, Lord God of Israel our father, for ever and ever. . . .

Both riches and honor come of thee, and thou reignest over all. . . .

Now therefore, our God, we thank thee, and praise thy glorious name.

But who am I, and what is my people, that we should be able to offer so willingly after this sort? for all things come of thee, and of thine own have we given thee. For we are strangers before thee, and sojourners, as were all our fathers: our days on the earth are as a shadow, and there is none abiding.[29:10-15]

O Lord God of Abraham, Isaac, and of Israel, our fathers, keep this for ever in the imagination of the thoughts of the heart of thy people, and prepare their heart unto thee.[29:18]

II CHRONICLES

And Solomon the son of David was strengthened in his kingdom, and the Lord his God was with him, and magnified him exceedingly.[1:1]

The Second Book of Chronicles covers a period of more than four hundred years. With some additions and omissions, it closely parallels the narrative in Kings—from the opening of the reign of king Solomon (I Kings, 2:12), through the ever increasing apostasy of Judah and Israel interrupted only by brief periods of reform, to the final destruction of Jerusalem and the deportation of its people to be captives in Babylon (II Kings, 25:11).

EZRA

Fifty years have gone by since the fall of Jerusalem. The Persians have captured Babylon which, as the Book of Ezra opens, is governed by king Cyrus of Persia.

In the first year of his reign, Cyrus issues a proclamation: The Jews of the captivity are to return, if they wish, to their own land; they are to take with them the holy vessels which Nebuchadnezzar carried away from the Temple; they are to be helped by their neighbors with money and with goods; and with the king's permission they are to rebuild the Temple in Jerusalem.

Then rose up the chief of the fathers of Judah and Benjamin, and the priests, and the Levites, with all them whose spirit God had raised, to go up to build the house of the Lord which is in Jerusalem.[1:5]

An official register is compiled of all who choose to go with Zerubbabel, their leader. They are upward of forty-two thousand souls.

In the seventh month of their return to Judah, each man having gone to his own city, they gather together in Jerusalem. Here they build an altar to the Lord, offer burnt offerings, and keep the feast of tabernacles according to the Law.

In the second year of their return, led by Zerubbabel and by Jeshua, a priest, amid tears and rejoicing they finish laying the foundation of the Temple.

But they meet with opposition from the people who have been living here in this land since the time of the exile. These people hire counselors against the Jews. Letters are sent to the king accusing them of sedition.

In spite of these intrigues, in spite of delays and obstacles, the work goes forward. Some twenty years after the founda-

tion is laid, in the sixth year of the reign of king Darius of Persia, the Temple is finished.

And the children of Israel, the priests, and the Levites, and the rest of the children of the captivity, kept the dedication of this house of God with joy.[6:16]

THE ARRIVAL OF EZRA IN JERUSALEM

It is sixty years later, when king Artaxerxes rules Persia, that the priest Ezra, a ready scribe in the law of Moses,[7:6] *who is in the service of Artaxerxes and in his favor, obtains the king's permission to go up from Babylon to Jerusalem:*

For Ezra had prepared his heart to seek the law of the Lord, and to do it, and to teach in Israel statutes and judgments.[7:10]

He carries a letter of authority from the king; and with him go some of the children of Israel and some of the priests and Levites.

Arrived in the Holy City, Ezra is astonished and grief-stricken: for he learns that the children of Israel, disobeying the Law, are taking wives from among the people of the land.

And when I heard this thing . . . I fell upon my knees, and spread out my hands unto the Lord my God, and said, O my God, I am ashamed and blush to lift up my face to thee, my God: for our iniquities are increased over our head, and our trespass is grown up unto the heavens.[9:3-6]

Ezra weeps and the people weep with him. He says, Ye have transgressed. . . . Now therefore make confession unto the Lord God of your fathers, and do his pleasure: and separate yourselves from the people of the land, and from the strange wives.

Then all the congregation answers with a loud voice, As thou hast said, so must we do.[10:10-12]

NEHEMIAH

Fourteen years after Ezra's departure from Babylon, word comes that the Jewish remnant in Jerusalem is living in great affliction and that the city itself lies waste, its walls and gates in ruins.

Nehemiah, cupbearer to king Artaxerxes, prevails upon the king to send him to rebuild Jerusalem. He is given letters of safe passage, an order unto the keeper of the king's forest for timber, and an escort of soldiers and horsemen for his journey.

Nehemiah tells his own story: So I came to Jerusalem. . . . And I went out by night . . . and viewed the walls of Jerusalem, which were broken down, and the gates thereof were consumed with fire.[2:11-13]

He appeals to the officials and to the priests, the nobles, and the people: Ye see the distress that we are in, how Jerusalem lieth waste, and the gates thereof are burned with fire: come, and let us build up the wall of Jerusalem, that we be no more a reproach.

Then I told them of the hand of my God which was good upon me; as also the king's words. . . . And they said, Let us rise up and build.[2:17-18]

They are laughed to scorn by their adversaries: Sanballat the Horonite, Tobiah the Ammonite, Geshem the Arabian. Nehemiah says, The God of heaven, he will prosper us.[2:20] *Work is allotted to men and to families. The people have a mind to work. The wall begins to rise.*

Sanballat and the others plan to surprise and kill the builders of the wall. Nehemiah reassures them: Be not ye afraid of them: Remember the Lord, which is great and terrible, and fight for your brethren, your sons, and your daughters, your wives and your houses.[4:14]

Half the people work while the other half stand guard, armed with spears and shields and bows.

They which builded on the wall . . . every one with one of his hands wrought in the work, and with the other hand held a weapon.[4:17]

The wall is finished in fifty-two days.

And Ezra the priest brought the law before the congregation. . . . And he read therein. . . .[8:2-3]

Now . . . the children of Israel were assembled with fasting, and with sackclothes, and earth upon them. . . . And they stood up in their place, and read in the book of the law of the Lord their God one fourth part of the day; and another fourth part they confessed, and worshipped the Lord their God.[9:1-3]

After a period of years Nehemiah, who has returned to the Persian court, again obtains the permission of the king to go to Jerusalem.

He finds that the High Priest, Eliashib, has made an alliance with Tobiah the Ammonite and that this old enemy of the Jews is living within the very courts of the Temple. Tithes have neither been collected nor distributed. The Sabbath is profaned. The men of the congregation are once more taking wives from among the heathen: the High Priest's son has married the daughter of Sanballat the Horonite.

Nehemiah is grief-stricken as he contends with these evils.

Tobiah is cast forth from his chamber with all his household goods. The people bring in the tithes and they are distributed according to law. Nehemiah exacts an oath of the congregation not to marry among the heathen. He drives out Sanballat's son-in-law.

Thus cleansed I them from all strangers. . . .

Remember me, O my God, for good.[13:30-31]

ESTHER

During the reign of king Ahasuerus of Persia, a search is made for the most beautiful young girls in the kingdom, one of whom will become queen: for the haughty queen Vashti has been deposed.

In Shushan, the capital, live a Jew of the captivity named Mordecai and his orphaned cousin, Esther, a girl of rare beauty whom Mordecai has raised as his own child. She is chosen among the others to be brought to the king's palace; but Mordecai counsels her to say nothing of her nationality.

So Esther was taken unto king Ahasuerus into his house royal. . . . And the king loved Esther above all the women, and she obtained grace and favor in his sight more than all the virgins; so that he set the royal crown upon her head, and made her queen instead of Vashti.[2:16-17]

Meanwhile Mordecai, sitting in the king's gate, overhears a plot to kill Ahasuerus. He tells Esther, who goes at once to the king and, in Mordecai's name, warns him of his danger. The story is found to be true. The conspirators are seized and hanged.

The king's grand vizier, Haman, is a man of such power that all men bow down before him: all but Mordecai, who refuses to bow. Haman is full of wrath. But he disdains to punish this one Jew; instead he will destroy all the Jews in the kingdom.

Having cast Pur (that is, lots) to find the auspicious day on which to act, Haman petitions the king for his consent to destroy the Jews out of the land. In return he promises to pay ten thousand talents of silver into the king's treasury. The king gives him his signet ring, saying, The silver is given to thee, the people also, to do with them as it seemeth good to thee.[3:11]

Haman's decree, sealed with the king's ring, goes out to the governors of all the provinces: To destroy, to kill, and to cause to perish, all Jews, both young and old, little children and women . . . and to take the spoil of them for a prey.[3:13]

There is great mourning and anguish among the Jews.

Esther sends to Mordecai, who tells her she must go and plead with the king for her people.

To enter unbidden the inner court of the palace, unless the king, by holding out his golden sceptre, gives permission, means death.

But Esther sends word to Mordecai, Go, gather together all the Jews . . . and fast ye for me. . . . I also and my maidens will fast. . . .[4:16]

Dressed in her royal robes, she goes and stands in the inner court of the palace. Here, from his throne, the king can see her. Raising the golden sceptre that is in his hand, he holds it out toward her.

As Esther draws near, the king says, What wilt thou, queen Esther? And what is thy request? It shall be even given thee to the half of the kingdom. *She replies,* Let the king and Haman come this day unto the banquet that I have prepared for him.[5:3-4]

Afterwards Haman boasts to his wife and his friends of Esther's request, which the king has granted. Yet all this availeth me nothing, *he complains,* so long as I see Mordecai the Jew sitting at the king's gate.[5:13] Let a gallows be made of fifty cubits high, *they advise him,* and tomorrow speak thou unto the king that Mordecai may be hanged thereon: then go thou in merrily with the king unto the banquet.[5:14]

The king, reading meanwhile in the book of records, learns it was Mordecai who saved his life from the conspirators. He sends for Haman and says, What shall be done

unto the man whom the king delighteth to honor?[6:6] *This
man whom the king would honor, proudly replies Haman,
should first be arrayed in royal apparel; he should be
mounted on the king's own horse; he should then be led
through the streets by one of the king's most noble princes
who will proclaim,* Thus shall it be done to the man whom
the king delighteth to honor.

The king says to Haman, Make haste, and take the apparel and the horse, as thou hast said, and do even so to
Mordecai, the Jew. . . .[6:9-10]

ESTHER DELIVERS HER PEOPLE

*At Esther's banquet, which is attended by the king and
Haman, the king asks,* What is thy petition, queen Esther?[7:2]
She begs him to save her life and the lives of her people:
For we are sold, I and my people, to be destroyed, to be
slain, and to perish.[7:4]

Who dares to do this, the king asks; and Esther says,
The adversary and enemy is this wicked Haman.[7:6]

*Then the king learns of the gallows built in Haman's
house to receive Mordecai.*

Hang Haman thereon, orders the king.

*So they hang Haman on the gallows he had prepared for
Mordecai.*

*The decree which Haman issued against the Jews cannot
however be changed: it was made in the king's name and
sealed with his ring.*

*Esther falls weeping at the king's feet. Though he cannot
change the decree, he can issue a new one: The Jews are
now permitted to defend themselves, even to the death,
against the enemies who would destroy them.*

*The danger is past. The days of their deliverance the
Jews name Purim, after Haman's casting of Pur, or lots, to
find the auspicious time for their destruction; and these days*

they set aside for feasting and gladness. And the Jews had light, and gladness, and joy, and honor.[8:17]

For Mordecai the Jew was next unto king Ahasuerus and great among the Jews . . . and speaking peace to all his seed.[10:2-3]

JOB

The problem of suffering in relation to sin is dealt with in this poetic drama: the story of a pious man's struggle to retain his faith in God when beset by terrible and undeserved misfortune. The chief participants in the drama are God, Job, and Satan. The problem dealt with is, Why do the godly suffer?

There was a man in the land of Uz, whose name was Job; and that man was perfect and upright, and one that feared God, and eschewed evil.

And there were born unto him seven sons and three daughters.

His substance also was seven thousand sheep, and three thousand camels, and five hundred yoke of oxen, and five hundred she asses, and a very great household; so that this man was the greatest of all the men of the east.[1:1-3]

There is a council in heaven, when the Lord gives Satan leave to test the faith and integrity of Job:

Now there was a day when the sons of God came to present themselves before the Lord, and Satan came also among them. And the Lord said unto Satan, whence comest thou? Then Satan answered the Lord, and said, From going to and fro in the earth, and from walking up and down in it. And the Lord said unto Satan, Hast thou considered my servant Job that there is none like him in the earth, a perfect and an upright man, one that feareth God, and escheweth evil?

Then Satan answered the Lord, and said, Doth Job fear God for nought? Hast not thou made a hedge about him, and about his house, and about all that he hath on every side? . . . But put forth thine hand now, and touch all that he hath, and he will curse thee to thy face. And the Lord said unto Satan, Behold, all that he hath is in thy power; only upon himself put not forth thine hand.[1:6-12]

THE TRIALS OF JOB

Suddenly great blows fall upon Job. The Sabeans steal his cattle and kill his men. Lightning destroys his sheep. The Chaldeans carry off his camels. A wind blows down the house in which his sons and daughters are feasting and kills them all.

Job's consolation in this dark hour is his faith in God.

Then Job arose, and rent his mantle, and shaved his head, and fell down upon the ground, and worshipped. And said, Naked came I out of my mother's womb, and naked shall I return thither: The Lord gave, and the Lord hath taken away; blessed be the name of the Lord.[1:20-21]

The Lord says to Satan, Hast thou considered my servant Job . . . still he holdeth fast his integrity, although thou movedst me against him, to destroy him without cause.[2:3]

Satan replies, Skin for skin, yea, all that a man hath will he give for his life. But put forth thine hand now, and touch his bone and his flesh, and he will curse thee to thy face. *The Lord says,* He is in thine hand; but save his life.[2:4-6]

Job is smitten by boils that cover him from head to foot. Still he turns aside from his wife's bitter rejection of God:

He took him a potsherd to scrape himself withal; and he sat down among the ashes. Then said his wife unto him, Dost thou still retain thine integrity? Curse God, and die. But he said unto her . . . What? shall we receive good at the hand of God, and shall we not receive evil?[2:8-10]

JOB'S COMFORTERS

Job's three close friends come to mourn with him and to comfort him: Eliphaz the Temanite, Bildad the Shuhite, and Zophar the Naamathite. Job, sitting on an ash heap outside his village, is so ravaged that his friends weep at sight of him.

Now at last he gives voice to his anguish and despair.

And Job spake, and said, Let the day perish wherein I was born, and the night in which it was said, There is a man child conceived.[3:2-3]

Why died I not from the womb? why did I not give up the ghost when I came out of the belly?[3:11]

For now should I have lain still and been quiet, I should have slept. . . .[3:13]

Wherefore is light given to him that is in misery, and life unto the bitter in soul; which long for death, but it cometh not. . . .[3:20-21]

Then each of his three friends speaks in turn. Each urges repentance; for Job's sufferings must be the harvest of his own sins.

Eliphaz speaks first: Behold, thou hast instructed many, and thou hast strengthened the weak hands. . . .

But now it is come upon thee, and thou faintest; it toucheth thee, and thou art troubled.[4:3-5]

Remember, I pray thee, who ever perished, being innocent? or where were the righteous cut off? . . . They that plow iniquity, and sow wickedness, reap the same. [4:7-8]

Although affliction cometh not forth of the dust, neither doth trouble spring out of the ground; yet man is born unto trouble, as the sparks fly upward.

I would seek unto God, and unto God would I commit my cause. [5:6-8]

He taketh the wise in their own craftiness.[5:13]

Behold, happy is the man whom God correcteth: there-

fore despise not thou the chastening of the Almighty. For he
maketh sore, and bindeth up: he woundeth, and his hands
make whole. [5:17-18]

Thou shalt come to thy grave in a full age, like as a shock
of corn cometh in in his season.[5:26]

*Job's answer is a reproach to Eliphaz for his injustice, and
a plea for compassion:*

To him that is afflicted pity should be showed from his
friend. . . . My brethren have dealt deceitfully as a brook,
and as the stream of brooks they pass away.[6:14-15]

They were confounded because they had hoped; they
came thither, and were ashamed. For now ye are nothing;
ye see my casting down, and are afraid. Did I say, bring
unto me? or, Give a reward for me of your substance? or,
Deliver me from the enemy's hand?[6:20-23]

How forcible are right words! But what doth your arguing
reprove? Do ye imagine to reprove words, and the speeches
of one that is desperate, which are as wind? Yea, ye over-
whelm the fatherless, and ye dig a pit for your friend.[6:25-27]

My flesh is clothed with worms and clods of dust; my skin
is broken, and become loathsome. My days are swifter than
a weaver's shuttle, and are spent without hope. O remember
that my life is wind: mine eye shall no more see good.[7:5-7]

Therefore I will not refrain my mouth; I will speak in the
anguish of my spirit; I will complain in the bitterness of my
soul.[7:11]

How long wilt thou not depart from me, nor let me alone
till I swallow down my spittle? I have sinned; what shall I
do unto thee, O thou preserver of men? Why hast thou set
me as a mark against thee, so that I am a burden to myself?
And why dost thou not pardon my transgression, and take
away mine iniquity?[7:19-21]

*Bildad speaks. He reproves Job for questioning divine
justice; and he accuses him of hypocrisy:*

How long wilt thou speak these things? And how long shall the words of thy mouth be like a strong wind? Doth God pervert justice?[8:2-3]

If thou wouldest seek unto God betimes, and make thy supplication to the Almighty; if thou wert pure and upright; surely now he would awake for thee, and make the habitation of thy righteousness prosperous.[8:5-6]

Can the rush grow up without mire? can the flag grow without water? . . . So are the paths of all that forget God; and the hypocrite's hope shall perish . . . whose trust shall be a spider's web.[8:11-14]

But Job demands to know how man, ignorant and helpless, can prove himself innocent to God—a God of infinite wisdom and terrible might:

But how should man be just with God? If he will contend with him, he cannot answer him one of a thousand. He is wise in heart, and mighty in strength: who hath hardened himself against him, and hath prospered?[9:2-4]

Behold, he taketh away, who can hinder him? Who will say unto him, What doest thou?[9:12]

For he is not a man, as I am, that I should answer him, and we should come together in judgment. Neither is there any daysman [*i.e., umpire*] betwixt us, that might lay his hand upon us both. Let him take his rod away from me, and let not his fear terrify me: Then would I speak, and not fear him; but it is not so with me.[9:32-35]

If I be wicked, woe unto me; and if I be righteous, yet will I not lift up my head. I am full of confusion. . . . Thou huntest me as a fierce lion: and again thou showest thyself marvelous upon me.[10:15-16]

Are not my days few? Cease then, and let me alone, that I may take comfort a little, before I go whence I shall not return, even to the land of darkness and the shadow of death. A land of darkness, as darkness itself . . . where the light is as darkness.[10:20-22]

Zophar, his third friend, also reproaches Job. If God were to speak, Zophar says, Job would realize that his sufferings are light compared to his iniquities:

Thou hast said, My doctrine is pure, and I am clean in thine eyes. But oh that God would speak, and open his lips against thee; and that he would show thee the secrets of wisdom, that they are double to that which is! Know therefore that God exacteth of thee less than thine iniquity deserveth. Canst thou by searching find out God? Canst thou find out the Almighty unto perfection? It is as high as heaven; what canst thou do? deeper than hell; what canst thou know?[11:4-8]

If iniquity be in thine hand, put it far away, and let not wickedness dwell in thy tabernacles.[11:14]

Job bitterly replies. He resents the easy platitudes of his three visitors: What ye know, the same do I know also: I am not inferior unto you.[13:2] *He sarcastically rejects their insincere arguments. He affirms his innocence. God has stripped him of everything, has destroyed him in His wrath; yet he has abiding trust in Him—for God knows Job's integrity and will vindicate him:*

No doubt but ye are the people, and wisdom shall die with you. But I have understanding as well as you. . . . Yea, who knoweth not such things as these?[12:2-3]

Hold your peace, let me alone, that I may speak, and let come on me what will. . . . Though he slay me, yet will I trust in him: but I will maintain mine own ways before him.[13:13-15]

Behold, I cry out of wrong, but I am not heard: I cry aloud, but there is no judgment.[19:7]

He hath destroyed me on every side, and I am gone: and mine hope hath he removed like a tree.[19:10]

He hath put my brethren far from me, and mine acquaintance are verily estranged from me. My kinsfolk have failed, and my familiar friends have forgotten me.[19:13-14]

My breath is strange to my wife. . . .[19:17]

My bone cleaveth to my skin and to my flesh, and I am escaped with the skin of my teeth.[19:20]

Have pity upon me, have pity upon me, O ye my friends; for the hand of God hath touched me. Why do ye persecute me as God, and are not satisfied with my flesh? Oh that my words were now written! Oh that they were printed in a book![19:21-23]

For I know that my Redeemer liveth, and that he shall stand at the latter day upon the earth: And though after my skin worms destroy this body, yet in my flesh shall I see God.[19:25-26]

Job asks for fair judgment. He challenges the Lord to answer him:

What portion of God is there from above? and what inheritance of the Almighty from on high? Is not destruction to the wicked? and a strange punishment to the workers of iniquity? Doth not he see my ways, and count all my steps? If I have walked with vanity, or if my foot hath hasted to deceit; let me be weighed in an even balance, that God may know mine integrity.[31:2-6]

Oh that one would hear me! behold, my desire is, that the Almighty would answer me, and that mine adversary had written a book.* Surely I would take it upon my shoulder, and bind it as a crown to me.[31:35-36]

The words of Job are ended.[31:40]

Then the Lord answered Job out of the whirlwind, and said, Who is this that darkeneth counsel by words without knowledge? Gird up now thy loins like a man; for I will demand of thee, and answer thou me.

Where wast thou when I laid the foundations of the earth? declare, if thou hast understanding. . . .

---

* The RSV translation is: *Oh, that I had the indictment written by my adversary!*

Whereupon are the foundations thereof fastened? or who laid the corner stone thereof; when the morning stars sang together, and all the sons of God shouted for joy? Or who shut up the sea with doors, when it brake forth, as if it had issued out of the womb? When I made the cloud the garment thereof, and thick darkness a swaddling band for it. . . .

And said, Hitherto shalt thou come, but no further: and here shall thy proud waves be stayed?

Hast thou commanded the morning since thy days; and caused the dayspring to know his place? . . . [38:1-12]

Hath the rain a father? or who hath begotten the drops of dew?[38:28]

Canst thou bind the sweet influences of Pleiades, or loose the bands of Orion? Canst thou bring forth Mazzaroth in his season? or canst thou guide Arcturus with his sons?[38:31-32]

Hast thou given the horse strength? hast thou clothed his neck with thunder? . . . the glory of his nostrils is terrible. He paweth in the valley, and rejoiceth in his strength: he goeth on to meet the armed men.[39:19-21]

He swalloweth the ground with fierceness and rage: neither believeth he that it is the sound of the trumpet. He saith among the trumpets, Ha, ha! and he smelleth the battle afar off, the thunder of the captains, and the shouting.[39:24-25]

Behold now behemoth, which I made with thee. . . .[40:15]

His bones are as strong pieces of brass; his bones are like bars of iron. He is the chief of the ways of God: he that made him can make his sword to approach unto him.[40:18-19]

Canst thou draw out leviathan with a hook? . . . Canst thou put a hook into his nose? . . . Will he make many supplications unto thee? will he speak soft words unto thee?[41:1-3]

Wilt thou play with him as with a bird? or wilt thou bind him for thy maidens?[41:5]

Shall he that contendeth with the Almighty instruct him? he that reproveth God, let him answer it.[40:2]

Wilt thou also disannul my judgment? wilt thou condemn me, that thou mayest be righteous?

Hast thou an arm like God? or canst thou thunder with a voice like him? Deck thyself now with majesty and excellency; and array thyself with glory and beauty. Cast abroad the rage of thy wrath: and behold every one that is proud, and abase him. Look on every one that is proud, and bring him low; and tread down the wicked in their place. . . .

Then will I also confess unto thee that thine own right hand can save thee. [40:8-14]

JOB REPENTS AND IS BLESSED BY THE LORD

Then Job answered the Lord, and said, I know that thou canst do every thing, and that no thought can be withholden from thee. . . .

Therefore have I uttered that I understood not; things too wonderful for me, which I knew not. . . .

I have heard of thee by the hearing of the ear; but now mine eye seeth thee: Wherefore I abhor myself, and repent in dust and ashes. [42:1-6]

The Lord then speaks to Eliphaz: My wrath is kindled against thee, and against thy two friends: for ye have not spoken of me the thing that is right, as my servant Job hath. . . .

My servant Job shall pray for you: for him will I accept: lest I deal with you after your folly, in that ye have not spoken of me the thing which is right, like my servant Job. [42:7-8]

And the Lord turned the captivity of Job, when he prayed for his friends: also the Lord gave Job twice as much as he had before. [42:10]

So the Lord blessed the latter end of Job more than his beginning. [42:12]

After this lived Job a hundred and forty years, and saw his sons, and his sons' sons, even four generations.

So Job died, being old and full of days.[42:16-17]

PSALMS

Blessed is the man that walketh not in the counsel of the ungodly, nor standeth in the way of sinners, nor sitteth in the seat of the scornful. But his delight is in the law of the Lord; and in his law doth he meditate day and night.

And he shall be like a tree planted by the rivers of water, that bringeth forth his fruit in his season; his leaf also shall not wither; and whatsoever he doeth shall prosper.

The ungodly are not so: but are like the chaff which the wind driveth away.

Therefore the ungodly shall not stand in the judgment, nor sinners in the congregation of the righteous.

For the Lord knoweth the way of the righteous: but the way of the ungodly shall perish.[1:1-6]

This is the First Psalm. There are a hundred and fifty songs, hymns, chants, and prayers which together form the Book of Psalms. Many of them are attributed to David, the sweet psalmist of Israel (II Samuel, 23:1). The Ninetieth Psalm gives Moses as its author. Others are of unknown authorship.

The Book of Psalms is in five sections, each ending in a doxology:

1. Psalms 1-41; 2. Psalms 42-72; 3. Psalms 73-89; 4. Psalms 90-106; 5. Psalms 107-150.

The Eighth and the Twenty-third Psalms are given below in their entirety followed by a selection of great passages from the others.

O Lord our Lord, how excellent is thy name in all the earth! who hast set thy glory above the heavens.

Out of the mouth of babes and sucklings hast thou ordained strength because of thine enemies, that thou mightest still the enemy and the avenger.

When I consider thy heavens, the work of thy fingers, the moon and the stars, which thou hast ordained;

What is man, that thou art mindful of him? and the son of man, that thou visitest him?

For thou hast made him a little lower than the angels, and hast crowned him with glory and honor.

Thou madest him to have dominion over the work of thy hands; thou hast put all things under his feet: All sheep and oxen, yea, and the beasts of the field; the fowl of the air, and the fish of the sea, and whatsoever passeth through the paths of the seas.

O Lord our Lord, how excellent is thy name in all the earth! [8:1-9]

The Lord is my shepherd; I shall not want.

He maketh me to lie down in green pastures: he leadeth me beside the still waters.

He restoreth my soul: he leadeth me in the paths of righteousness for his name's sake.

Yea, though I walk through the valley of the shadow of death, I will fear no evil: for thou art with me; thy rod and thy staff they comfort me.

Thou preparest a table before me in the presence of mine enemies; thou anointest my head with oil; my cup runneth over.

Surely goodness and mercy shall follow me all the days of my life: and I will dwell in the house of the Lord for ever. [23:1-6]

I will both lay me down in peace, and sleep: for thou, Lord, only makest me dwell in safety. [4:8]

The fool hath said in his heart, There is no God. [14:1]

The lines are fallen unto me in pleasant places; yea, I have a goodly heritage.[16:6]

Keep me as the apple of the eye, hide me under the shadow of thy wing, from the wicked that oppress me, from my deadly enemies, who compass me about.[17:8-9]

The sorrows of death compassed me, and the floods of ungodly men made me afraid.[18:4]

He bowed the heavens also, and came down: and darkness was under his feet. And he rode upon a cherub, and did fly: yea, he did fly upon the wings of the wind.[18:9-10]

The heavens declare the glory of God; and the firmament showeth his handiwork.

Day unto day uttereth speech, and night unto night showeth knowledge. There is no speech nor language, where their voice is not heard.[19:1-3]

His going forth is from the end of the heaven, and his circuit unto the ends of it: and there is nothing hid from the heat thereof.[19:6]

The fear of the Lord is clean, enduring forever: the judgments of the Lord are true and righteous altogether. More to be desired are they than gold, yea, than much fine gold: sweeter also than honey and the honeycomb.[19:9-10]

Let the words of my mouth, and the meditation of my heart, be acceptable in thy sight, O Lord, my strength, and my redeemer.[19:14]

My God, my God, why hast thou forsaken me?[22:1]

My times are in thy hand.[31:15]

From the place of his habitation he looketh upon all the inhabitants of the earth. He fashioneth their hearts alike; he considereth all their works. [33:14-15]

The meek shall inherit the earth; and shall delight themselves in the abundance of peace.[37:11]

I have been young, and now am old; yet have I not seen the righteous forsaken, nor his seed begging bread.[37:25]

I have seen the wicked in great power, and spreading himself like a green bay tree.[37:35]

Mark the perfect man, and behold the upright: for the end of that man is peace.[37:37]

Surely every man walketh in a vain show: surely they are disquieted in vain: he heapeth up riches, and knoweth not who shall gather them.[39:6]

Blessed is he that considereth the poor: the Lord will deliver him in time of trouble.[41:1]

As the hart panteth after the water brooks, so panteth my soul after thee, O God.[42:1]

God is our refuge and strength, a very present help in trouble. Therefore will not we fear, though the earth be removed, and though the mountains be carried into the midst of the sea.[46:1-2]

Be still, and know that I am God.[46:10]

Beautiful for situation, the joy of the whole earth, is mount Zion, on the sides of the north, the city of the great King.[48:2]

Wash me, and I shall be whiter than snow.[51:7]

Create in me a clean heart, O God; and renew a right spirit within me.[51:10]

Oh that I had wings like a dove! for then would I fly away, and be at rest.[55:6]

For it was not an enemy that reproached me. . . . But it was thou, a man mine equal, my guide, and mine acquaintance. We took sweet counsel together, and walked unto the house of God in company.[55:12-14]

The wicked are estranged from the womb. . . . They are like the deaf adder that stoppeth her ear; which will not hearken to the voice of charmers, charming never so wisely.[58:3-5]

Give us help from trouble: for vain is the help of man.[60:11]

Lead me to the rock that is higher than I.[61:2]

Surely men of low degree are vanity, and men of high degree are a lie: to be laid in the balance, they are altogether lighter than vanity.[62:9]

Also unto thee, O Lord, belongeth mercy: for thou renderest to every man according to his work.[62:12]

Thou crownest the year with thy goodness.[65:11]

God is the judge: he putteth down one, and setteth up another.[75:7]

A day in thy courts is better than a thousand. I had rather be a doorkeeper in the house of my God, than to dwell in the tents of wickedness.[84:10]

Mercy and truth are met together; righteousness and peace have kissed each other. [85:10]

A thousand years in thy sight are but as yesterday when it is past, and as a watch in the night.[90:4]

The days of our years are threescore years and ten; and if by reason of strength they be fourscore years, yet is their strength labor and sorrow; for it is soon cut off, and we fly away.[90:10]

So teach us to number our days, that we may apply our hearts unto wisdom.[90:12]

Establish thou the work of our hands upon us; yea, the work of our hands establish thou it.[90:17]

Thou shalt not be afraid for the terror by night . . . nor for the pestilence that walketh in darkness; nor for the destruction that wasteth at noonday.[91:5-6]

There shall no evil befall thee. . . . For he shall give his angels charge over thee, to keep thee in all thy ways.[91:10-11]

The Lord on high is mightier than the noise of many waters.[93:4]

The Lord reigneth; let the earth rejoice.[97:1]

As for man, his days are as grass: as a flower of the field, so he flourisheth. For the wind passeth over it, and it is gone; and the place thereof shall know it no more.[103:15-16]

They that go down to the sea in ships, that do business in great waters; these see the works of the Lord, and his wonders in the deep.[107:23-24]

The fear of the Lord is the beginning of wisdom: a good understanding have all they that do his commandments.[111:10]

From the rising of the sun unto the going down of the same the Lord's name is to be praised.[113:3]

Precious in the sight of the Lord is the death of his saints.[116:15]

The stone which the builders refused is become the head stone of the corner. This is the Lord's doing; it is marvelous in our eyes. This is the day which the Lord hath made; we will rejoice and be glad in it.[118:22-24]

Thy word is a lamp unto my feet, and a light unto my path.[119:105]

They that sow in tears shall reap in joy.[126:5]

Except the Lord build the house, they labor in vain that build it. . . . It is vain for you to rise up early, to sit up late, to eat the bread of sorrows: for so he giveth his beloved sleep.[127:1-2]

Behold, how good and how pleasant it is for brethren to dwell together in unity![133:1]

By the rivers of Babylon, there we sat down, yea, we wept, when we remembered Zion. We hanged our harps upon the willows in the midst thereof. For there they that carried us away captive required of us a song. . . . How shall we sing the Lord's song in a strange land? If I forget thee, O Jerusalem, let my right hand forget her cunning.[137:1-5]

Whither shall I go from thy Spirit? or whither shall I flee from thy presence. . . .

If I take the wings of the morning, and dwell in the uttermost parts of the sea; even there shall thy hand lead me. . . .[139:7-10]

I will praise thee; for I am fearfully and wonderfully made.[139:14]

Praise ye the Lord. Praise God in his sanctuary: praise him in the firmament of his power. Praise him for his mighty acts: praise him according to his excellent greatness.[150:1-2]

Let every thing that hath breath praise the Lord. Praise ye the Lord.[150:6]

PROVERBS

Wisdom is the principal thing; therefore get wisdom: and with all thy getting get understanding.[4:7]

Nearly all the sayings in the Book of Proverbs are attributed in the Bible itself to Solomon. Here are the more famous:

ADVICE TO SONS

My son, if sinners entice thee, consent thou not.[1:10]

Surely in vain the net is spread in the sight of any bird.[1:17]

Wisdom crieth out; she uttereth her voice in the streets.[1:20]

Be not wise in thine own eyes: fear the Lord, and depart from evil.[3:7]

Whom the Lord loveth he correcteth; even as a father the son in whom he delighteth.[3:12]

Happy is the man that findeth wisdom. . . .[3:13] Length of days.is in her right hand; and in her left hand riches and honor. Her ways are ways of pleasantness, and all her paths are peace.[3:16-17]

Withhold not good from them to whom it is due, when it is in the power of thine hand to do it.[3:27]

Keep my commandments, and live.[4:4]

The lips of a strange woman drop as a honeycomb, and

her mouth is smoother than oil: but her end is bitter as wormwood, sharp as a two-edged sword.$^{5:3-4}$

Go to the ant, thou sluggard; consider her ways, and be wise.$^{6:6}$

Yet a little sleep, a little slumber, a little folding of the hands to sleep: So shall thy power come as one that traveleth, and thy want as an armed man.$^{6:10-11}$

These six things doth the Lord hate; yea, seven are an abomination unto him: A proud look, a lying tongue, and hands that shed innocent blood, a heart that deviseth wicked imaginations, feet that be swift in running to mischief, a false witness that speaketh lies, and he that soweth discord among brethren.$^{6:16-19}$

The commandment is a lamp; and the law is light.$^{6:23}$

Can a man take fire to his bosom, and his clothes not be burned?$^{6:27}$

Behold, there met him a woman with the attire of a harlot, and subtil of heart. . . .

So she caught him, and kissed him, and with an impudent face said unto him. . . .

I have perfumed my bed with myrrh, aloes, and cinnamon. Come, let us take our fill of love until the morning: let us solace ourselves with loves. For the goodman is not at home, he is gone a long journey.$^{7:10-19}$

He goeth after her straightway, as an ox goeth to the slaughter, or as a fool to the correction of the stocks.$^{7:22}$

Her house is the way to hell, going down to the chambers of death.$^{7:27}$

IN PRAISE OF WISDOM

Wisdom is better than rubies; and all the things that may be desired are not to be compared to it.$^{8:11}$

I wisdom dwell with prudence. . . .$^{8:12}$ I love them that love me. . . .$^{8:17}$

Wisdom hath builded her house, she hath hewn out her seven pillars.[9:1]

The fear of the Lord is the beginning of wisdom.[9:10]

A foolish woman is clamorous.[9:13] As for him that wanteth understanding, she saith to him, stolen waters are sweet, and bread eaten in secret is pleasant. But he knoweth not that the dead are there; and that her guests are in the depths of hell.[9:16-18]

A wise son maketh a glad father: but a foolish son is the heaviness of his mother.[10:1]

The memory of the just is blessed.[10:7]

Hatred stirreth up strifes: but love covereth all sins.[10:12]

The destruction of the poor is their poverty.[10:15]

THE FOLLY OF WICKEDNESS— THE WISDOM OF RIGHTEOUSNESS

Where no counsel is, the people fall: but in the multitude of counselors there is safety.[11:14]

As a jewel of gold in a swine's snout, so is a fair woman which is without discretion.[11:22]

A virtuous woman is a crown to her husband.[12:4]

A righteous man regardeth the life of his beast: but the tender mercies of the wicked are cruel.[12:10]

Hope deferred maketh the heart sick.[13:12]

He that spareth his rod hateth his son: but he that loveth him chasteneth him betimes.[13:24]

Fools make a mock at sin.[14:9]

The heart knoweth his own bitterness; and a stranger doth not intermeddle with his joy.[14:10]

In all labor there is profit: but the talk of the lips tendeth only to penury.[14:23]

Righteousness exalteth a nation.[14:34]

A soft answer turneth away wrath: but grievous words stir up anger.[15:1]

A merry heart maketh a cheerful countenance.[15:13]

He that is of a merry heart hath a continual feast.[15:15]

Better is a dinner of herbs where love is, than a stalled ox and hatred therewith.[15:17]

A word spoken in due season, how good is it![15:23]

A man's heart deviseth his way: but the Lord directeth his steps.[16:9]

Pride goeth before destruction, and a haughty spirit before a fall.[16:18]

Pleasant words are as a honeycomb, sweet to the soul. . . .[16:24]

The hoary head is a crown of glory. . . .[16:31]

He that is slow to anger is better than the mighty; and he that ruleth his spirit than he that taketh a city.[16:32]

A reproof entereth more into a wise man than a hundred stripes into a fool.[17:10]

He that begetteth a fool doeth it to his sorrow.[17:21]

A merry heart doeth good like a medicine.[17:22]

Even a fool, when he holdeth his peace, is counted wise.[17:28]

Whoso findeth a wife findeth a good thing. . . .[18:22]

There is a friend that sticketh closer than a brother.[18:24]

Wealth maketh many friends; but the poor is separated from his neighbor.[19:4]

He that hath pity upon the poor lendeth unto the Lord.[19:17]

WARNINGS AND INSTRUCTIONS

Wine is a mocker, strong drink is raging.[20:1]

The hearing ear, and the seeing eye, the Lord hath made even both of them.[20:12]

Meddle not with him that flattereth with his lips.[20:19]

To do justice and judgment is more acceptable to the Lord than sacrifice.[21:3]

It is better to dwell in a corner of the housetop, than with a brawling woman in a wide house.[21:9]

Whoso stoppeth his ears at the cry of the poor, he also shall cry himself, but shall not be heard.[21:13]

A good name is rather to be chosen than great riches. . . .[22:1]

Train up a child in the way he should go: and when he is old, he will not depart from it.[22:6]

The borrower is servant to the lender.[22:7]

Seest thou a man diligent in his business? he shall stand before kings.[22:29]

Riches certainly make themselves wings.[23:5]

As he thinketh in his heart, so is he.[23:7]

The drunkard and the glutton shall come to poverty: and drowsiness shall clothe a man with rags.[23:21]

Despise not thy mother when she is old.[23:22]

Who hath woe? who hath sorrow? who hath contentions? who hath babbling? who hath wounds without cause? who hath redness of eyes? They that tarry long at the wine; they that go to seek mixed wine. Look not thou upon the wine when it is red, when it giveth his color in the cup, when it moveth itself aright. At the last it biteth like a serpent, and stingeth like an adder.[23:29-32]

A wise man is strong; yea, a man of knowledge increaseth strength.[24:5]

If thou faint in the day of adversity, thy strength is small.[24:10]

A just man falleth seven times, and riseth up again: but the wicked shall fall into mischief. Rejoice not when thine enemy falleth, and let not thine heart be glad when he stumbleth: lest the Lord see it, and it displease him, and he turn away his wrath from him.[24:16-18]

The heart of kings is unsearchable.[25:3]

A word fitly spoken is like apples of gold in pictures of silver.[25:11]

Hast thou found honey? Eat so much as is sufficient for thee, lest thou be filled therewith, and vomit it.[25:16]

Withdraw thy foot from thy neighbor's house; lest he be weary of thee, and so hate thee.[25:17]

As he that taketh away a garment in cold weather, and as vinegar upon nitre, so is he that singeth songs to a heavy heart.[25:20]

If thine enemy be hungry, give him bread to eat; and if he be thirsty, give him water to drink: For thou shalt heap coals of fire upon his head, and the Lord shall reward thee.[25:21-22]

As cold waters to a thirsty soul, so is good news from a far country.[25:25]

Answer not a fool according to his folly, lest thou also be like unto him.[26:4]

Answer a fool according to his folly, lest he be wise in his own conceit.[26:5]

As a dog returneth to his vomit, so a fool returneth to his folly.[26:11]

Seest thou a man wise in his own conceit? there is more hope of a fool than of him.[26:12]

The slothful man saith, There is a lion in the way; a lion is in the streets.[26:13]

The sluggard is wiser in his own conceit than seven men that can render a reason.[26:16]

Whoso diggeth a pit shall fall therein.[26:27]

Boast not thyself of tomorrow; for thou knowest not what a day may bring forth.[27:1]

Let another man praise thee, and not thine own mouth; a stranger, and not thine own lips.[27:2]

Open rebuke is better than secret love.[27:5]

Faithful are the wounds of a friend; but the kisses of an enemy are deceitful.[27:6]

Better is a neighbor that is near than a brother far off.[27:10]

A continual dropping in a very rainy day and a contentious woman are alike.[27:15]

Iron sharpeneth iron; so a man sharpeneth the countenance of his friend.[27:17]

The wicked flee when no man pursueth; but the righteous are bold as a lion.[28:1]

He that maketh haste to be rich shall not be innocent.[28:20]

He that giveth unto the poor shall not lack.[28:27]

A fool uttereth all his mind: but a wise man keepeth it in all afterwards.[29:11]

The rod and reproof give wisdom: but a child left to himself bringeth his mother to shame.[29:15]

Where there is no vision, the people perish.[29:18]

The horseleach hath two daughters, crying, Give, give.[30:15]

There be three things which are too wonderful for me, yea, four which I know not: The way of an eagle in the air; the way of a serpent upon a rock; the way of a ship in the midst of the sea; and the way of a man with a maid.[30:18-19]

Who can find a virtuous woman? for her price is far above rubies.[31:10] She layeth her hands to the spindle, and her hands hold the distaff.[31:19] In her tongue is the law of kindness.[31:26] She looketh well to the ways of her household, and eateth not the bread of idleness.[31:27] Her children arise up, and call her blessed; her husband also, and he praiseth her. Many daughters have done virtuously, but thou excellest them all.[31:28-29]

ECCLESIASTES
The Preacher

Vanity of vanities; all is vanity.[1:2]

Thus begins the most despairing book in the Bible. The author of Ecclesiastes (Greek for "the Preacher") is not known; but the work is ascribed in the Bible to Solomon:

The words of the Preacher, the son of David, king in Jerusalem.[1:1]

Vanity of vanities, saith the Preacher, vanity of vanities; all is vanity. What profit hath a man of all his labor which he taketh under the sun? One generation passeth away, and another generation cometh: but the earth abideth for ever.[1:2-4]

All the rivers run into the sea; yet the sea is not full; unto the place from whence the rivers come, thither they return again.

All things are full of labor; man cannot utter it: the eye is not satisfied with seeing, nor the ear filled with hearing.

There is no new thing under the sun. Is there any thing whereof it may be said, See, this is new? It hath been already of old time, which was before us.[1:7-10]

I have seen all the works that are done under the sun; and, behold, all is vanity and vexation of spirit.[1:14]

For in much wisdom is much grief: and he that increaseth knowledge increaseth sorrow.[1:18]

And I turned myself to behold wisdom, and madness, and folly. . . . Then I saw that wisdom excelleth folly, as far as light excelleth darkness. The wise man's eyes are in his head; but the fool walketh in darkness: and I myself perceived also that one event happeneth to them all.[2:12-14]

A TIME FOR ALL THINGS

To everything there is a season, and a time to every purpose under the heaven: A time to be born, and a time to die; a time to plant, and a time to pluck up that which is planted; a time to kill, and a time to heal; a time to break down, and a time to build up; a time to weep, and a time to laugh; a time to mourn, and a time to dance . . . ;[3:1-4] a time to keep silence, and a time to speak; a time to love, and a time to hate; a time of war, and a time of peace.[3:7-8]

Be not rash with thy mouth, and let not thine heart be hasty to utter any thing before God: for God is in heaven, and thou upon earth: therefore let thy words be few.[5:2]

Better is it that thou shouldest not vow, than that thou shouldest vow and not pay.[5:5]

SORROW IS BETTER THAN LAUGHTER

It is better to go to the house of mourning than to go to the house of feasting: for that is the end of all men.[7:2]

Sorrow is better than laughter: for by the sadness of the countenance the heart is made better.[7:3]

As the crackling of thorns under a pot, so is the laughter of the fool.[7:6]

Better is the end of a thing than the beginning thereof.[7:8]

Say not thou, What is the cause that the former days were better than these? for thou dost not inquire wisely concerning this.[7:10]

Be not righteous over much; neither make thyself over wise: why shouldest thou destroy thyself? Be not over much wicked, neither be thou foolish: why shouldest thou die before thy time?[7:16-17]

One man among a thousand have I found; but a woman among all those have I not found. Lo, this only have I found, that God hath made man upright; but they have sought out many inventions.[7:28-29]

There is no man that hath power over the spirit to retain the spirit; neither hath he power in the day of death: and there is no discharge in that war.[8:8]

Go thy way, eat thy bread with joy, and drink thy wine with a merry heart; for God now accepteth thy works.[9:7]

Whatsoever thy hand findeth to do, do it with thy might;

for there is no work, nor device, nor knowledge, nor wisdom, in the grave, whither thou goest. . . . The race is not to the swift, nor the battle to the strong, neither yet bread to the wise, nor yet riches to men of understanding, nor yet favor to men of skill: but time and chance happeneth to them all.[9:10-11]

CAST THY BREAD UPON THE WATERS

Cast thy bread upon the waters: for thou shalt find it after many days. . . . If the clouds be full of rain, they empty themselves upon the earth: and if the tree fall toward the south, or toward the north, in the place where the tree falleth, there it shall be.[11:1-3]

He that observeth the wind shall not sow; and he that regardeth the clouds shall not reap. . . . In the morning sow thy seed, and in the evening withhold not thine hand: for thou knowest not whether shall prosper, either this or that. . . .[11:4-6]

Truly the light is sweet, and a pleasant thing it is for the eyes to behold the sun.[11:7] Rejoice, O young man, in thy youth; and let thy heart cheer thee in the days of thy youth, and walk in the ways of thine heart . . . but know thou, that for all these things God will bring thee into judgment.[11:9]

REMEMBER NOW THY CREATOR

Remember now thy Creator in the days of thy youth, while the evil days come not, nor the years draw nigh, when thou shalt say, I have no pleasure in them.[12:1] In the day when the keepers of the house shall tremble, and the strong men shall bow themselves, and the grinders cease because they are few. . . . And the doors shall be shut in the streets, when the sound of the grinding is low, and he shall rise up at the voice of the bird, and all the daughters of music shall be brought low; also when . . . the grasshopper shall be a burden, and desire shall fail: because man goeth to his long home, and the mourners go about the streets:

Or ever the silver cord be loosed, or the golden bowl be broken, or the pitcher be broken at the fountain, or the wheel broken at the cistern.

Then shall the dust return to the earth as it was: and the spirit shall return unto God who gave it.[12:3-7]

Let us hear the conclusion of the whole matter: Fear God, and keep his commandments: for this is the whole duty of man. For God shall bring every work into judgment, with every secret thing, whether it be good, or whether it be evil.[12:13-14]

THE SONG OF SOLOMON

The song of songs, which is Solomon's:

Let him kiss me with the kisses of his mouth: for thy love is better than wine. . . . Thy name is as ointment poured forth, therefore do the virgins love thee.[1:1-3]

The king hath brought me into his chamber: we will be glad and rejoice in thee, we will remember thy love more than wine. . . .

I am black, but comely, O ye daughters of Jerusalem, as the tents of Kedar, as the curtains of Solomon.[1:4-5]

Tell me, O thou whom my soul loveth, where thou feedest, where thou makest thy flock to rest at noon.[1:7]

A bundle of myrrh is my well-beloved unto me; he shall lie all night betwixt my breasts.[1:13]

I am the rose of Sharon, and the lily of the valleys.[2:1]

He brought me to the banqueting house, and his banner over me was love. Stay me with flagons, comfort me with apples: for I am sick of love. His left hand is under my head, and his right hand doth embrace me. I charge you, O ye daughters of Jerusalem . . . that ye stir not up, nor awake my love, till he please.[2:4-7]

RISE UP, MY LOVE

Rise up, my love, my fair one, and come away. For lo, the winter is past, the rain is over and gone; the flowers appear on the earth; the time of the singing birds is come, and the voice of the turtle is heard in our land.[2:10-12]

Take us the foxes, the little foxes, that spoil the vines: for our vines have tender grapes.

My beloved is mine, and I am his: he feedeth among the lilies.

Until the day break, and the shadows flee away, turn, my beloved, and be thou like a roe or a young hart upon the mountains of Bether.[2:15-17]

By night on my bed I sought him whom my soul loveth: I sought him, but I found him not.[3:1]

Behold, thou are fair, my love; behold, thou art fair; thou hast doves' eyes within thy locks: thy hair is as a flock of goats, that appear from mount Gilead. Thy teeth are like a flock of sheep that are even shorn, which came up from the washing; whereof every one bear twins, and none is barren among them. Thy lips are like a thread of scarlet, and thy speech is comely; thy temples are like a piece of a pomegranate within thy locks. Thy neck is like the tower of David builded for an armory, whereon there hang a thousand bucklers, all shields of mighty men. Thy two breasts are like two young roes that are twins, which feed among the lilies.

Until the day break, and the shadows flee away, I will get me to the mountain of myrrh, and to the hill of frankincense.

Thou are all fair, my love; there is no spot in thee.[4:1-7]

A garden inclosed is my sister, my spouse; a spring shut up, a fountain sealed.[4:12]

Awake, O north wind; and come, thou south; blow upon my garden, that the spices thereof may flow out. Let my beloved come into his garden, and eat his pleasant fruits.[4:16]

I sleep, but my heart waketh: it is the voice of my beloved that knocketh, saying, Open to me, my sister, my love, my dove, my undefiled.[5:2]

My beloved put in his hand by the hole of the door, and my bowels were moved for him. . . . I opened to my beloved; but my beloved had withdrawn himself, and was gone.

The watchmen that went about the city found me, they smote me, they wounded me; the keepers of the walls took away my veil from me.

I charge you, O daughters of Jerusalem, if ye find my beloved, that ye tell him, that I am sick of love.

What is thy beloved more than another beloved, O thou fairest among women?

My beloved is white and ruddy, the chiefest among ten thousand.[5:4-10]

His hands are as gold rings set with beryl: his belly is as bright ivory overlaid with sapphires: his legs are as pillars of marble, set upon sockets of fine gold: his countenance is as Lebanon, excellent as the cedars: his mouth is most sweet: yea, he is altogether lovely. This is my beloved, and this is my friend, O daughters of Jerusalem.[5:14-16]

THOU ART BEAUTIFUL, O MY LOVE

Thou art beautiful, O my love, as Tirzah, comely as Jerusalem, terrible as an army with banners.[6:4]

Who is she that looketh forth as the morning, fair as the moon, clear as the sun, and terrible as an army with banners?[6:10]

Return, return O Shulamite; return, return, that we may look upon thee.[6:13]

How beautiful are thy feet with shoes, O prince's daughter! ...

Thy navel is like a round goblet, which wanteth not liquor: thy belly is like a heap of wheat set about with lilies. Thy two breasts are like two young roes that are twins. Thy neck is as a tower of ivory; thine eyes like the fishpools in Heshbon, by the gate of Bath-rabbim: thy nose is as the tower of Lebanon which looketh toward Damascus.[7:1-4]

The roof of thy mouth like the best wine for my beloved, that goeth down sweetly, causing the lips of those that are asleep to speak.[7:9]

O that thou wert as my brother, that sucked the breasts of my mother! when I should find thee without, I would kiss thee; yea, I should not be despised. I would lead thee, and bring thee into my mother's house, who would instruct me.[8:1-2]

Set me as a seal upon thine heart ... for love is strong as death; jealousy is cruel as the grave. ... Many waters cannot quench love, neither can the floods drown it: if a man give all the substance of his house for love, it would utterly be contemned.[8:6-7]

We have a little sister, and she hath no breasts: what shall we do for our sister in the day when she shall be spoken for?[8:8]

Make haste, my beloved, and be thou like to a roe or to a young hart upon the mountains of spices.[8:14]

ISAIAH

After the death of king Azariah (also called Uzziah) of Judah, in a time of great uncertainty, of apostasy, and of impending doom, the word of the Lord comes to the prophet

Isaiah in a vision of overwhelming majesty and glory. He is commanded to carry the message of the Lord to the people —a message which will be heard but not understood, and warnings which will go unheeded.

Henceforth Isaiah's life is given to his mission: For Zion's sake will I not hold my peace, and for Jerusalem's sake I will not rest. . . . [62:1] *Warning, exhorting, comforting, commanding, he performs his ministry throughout the reigns of Jotham, Ahaz, and Hezekiah.*

This is the first of the prophetical books of the Bible. Isaiah himself, called "the Prophet of Faith," is regarded as the greatest of the Old Testament prophets. Following is a selection of the more famous passages of the book that bears his name:

THE LORD'S REBUKE TO JUDAH

Hear, O heavens, and give ear, O earth: for the Lord hath spoken; I have nourished and brought up children, and they have rebelled against me. The ox knoweth his owner, and the ass his master's crib: but Israel doth not know, my people doth not consider.

Ah sinful nation, a people laden with iniquity, a seed of evildoers, children that are corrupters: they have forsaken the Lord, they have provoked the Holy One of Israel unto anger, they are gone away backward. Why should ye be stricken any more? Ye will revolt more and more: the whole head is sick, and the whole heart faint.[1:2-5]

Your country is desolate, your cities are burned with fire.

And the daughter of Zion is left as a cottage in a vineyard, as a lodge in a garden of cucumbers. . . .[1:7-8]

Bring no more vain oblations; incense is an abomination unto me; the new moons and sabbaths, the calling of assemblies, I cannot away with; it is iniquity, even the solemn meeting. . . . Your appointed feasts my soul hateth: they are

a trouble unto me; I am weary to bear them. . . . Your
hands are full of blood. Wash ye, make you clean; put away
the evil of your doings from before mine eyes; cease to do
evil. Learn to do well; seek judgment, relieve the oppressed,
judge the fatherless, plead for the widow.

Come now, and let us reason together, saith the Lord:
though your sins be as scarlet, they shall be as white as snow.
. . . If ye be willing and obedient, ye shall eat the good of
the land.[1:13-19]

THE VISION OF ISAIAH

In the year that king Uzziah died I saw also the Lord
sitting upon a throne, high and lifted up, and his train filled
the temple. Above it stood the seraphim. . . . And one cried
unto another, and said, Holy, holy, holy, is the Lord of
hosts: the whole earth is full of his glory.

Then said I, Woe is me! for I am undone; because I am a
man of unclean lips, and I dwell in the midst of a people
of unclean lips: for mine eyes have seen the King, the Lord
of hosts.

Then flew one of the seraphim unto me, having a live
coal in his hand, which he had taken with the tongs from off
the altar: And he laid it upon my mouth, and said, Lo this
hath touched thy lips; and thine iniquity is taken away, and
thy sin purged.

Also I heard the voice of the Lord, saying, Whom shall
I send, and who will go for us? Then said I, Here am I; send
me.

And he said, Go, and tell this people, Hear ye indeed, but
understand not; and see ye indeed, but perceive not.

Then said I, Lord, how long? And he answered, Until the
cities be wasted without inhabitant, and the houses without
man, and the land be utterly desolate, and the Lord have

removed men far away, and there be a great forsaking in the midst of the land.

But yet in it shall be a tenth, and it shall return. . . . so the holy seed shall be the substance thereof.[6:1-13]

In the reign of king Ahaz of Judah, Syria and Israel together come up against Jerusalem. Isaiah brings the word of the Lord to Ahaz: the attack will fail. Moreover at this time Isaiah first speaks of the messianic hope of the world: The Lord himself shall give you a sign; Behold a virgin shall conceive, and bear a son, and shall call his name Immanuel. Butter and honey shall he eat, that he may know to refuse the evil, and choose the good.[7:14-15]

Prophesying an era of peace and righteousness, Isaiah sees a great light in the present darkness: For unto us a child is born.[9:6]

The people that walked in darkness have seen a great light: they that dwell in the land of the shadow of death, upon them hath the light shined.

Thou hast multiplied the nation, and not increased the joy: they joy before thee according to the joy in harvest, and as men rejoice when they divide the spoil. For thou hast broken the yoke of his burden. . . .

For every battle of the warrior is with confused noise, and garments rolled in blood; but this shall be with burning and fuel of fire.

For unto us a child is born, unto us a son is given: and the government shall be upon his shoulder: and his name shall be called Wonderful, Counselor, The mighty God, The everlasting Father, the Prince of Peace. Of the increase of his government and peace there shall be no end. . . . The zeal of the Lord of hosts will perform this.[9:2-7]

And there shall come forth a rod out of the stem of Jesse,

and a Branch shall grow out of his roots: And the Spirit of the Lord shall rest upon him, the spirit of wisdom and understanding, the spirit of counsel and might, the spirit of knowledge and of the fear of the Lord.[11:1-2]

The wolf also shall dwell with the lamb, and the leopard shall lie down with the kid; and the calf and the young lion and the fatling together; and a little child shall lead them.

The lion shall eat straw like the ox. And the suckling child shall play on the hole of the asp, and the weaned child shall put his hand in the cockatrice' den. They shall not hurt or destroy in all my holy mountain: for the earth shall be full of the knowledge of the Lord, as the waters cover the sea.[11:6-9]

Isaiah proclaims also the Doctrine of the Resurrection:

Thy dead men shall live, together with my dead body shall they arise. Awake and sing, ye that dwell in dust: for thy dew is as the dew of herbs, and the earth shall cast out the dead.

Come, my people, enter thou into thy chambers, and shut thy doors about thee: hide thyself as it were for a little moment, until the indignation be overpast. For, behold, the Lord cometh out of his place to punish the inhabitants of the earth for their iniquity: the earth also shall disclose her blood, and shall no more cover her slain.[26:19-21]

He warns the proud rulers of Judah of the Lord's wrath:

Hear the word of the Lord, ye scornful men, that rule this people which is in Jerusalem. Because ye have said, We have made a covenant with death, and with hell are we at agreement.

Therefore thus saith the Lord God, Behold I lay in Zion for a foundation a stone, a tried stone, a precious corner stone, a sure foundation: he that believeth shall not make haste. Judgment also will I lay to the line . . . and the hail shall sweep away the refuge of lies. . . . And your covenant with death shall be disannulled, and your agreement with hell shall not stand; when the overflowing scourge shall pass through, then ye shall be trodden down by it.[28:14-18]

THE VOICE IN THE WILDERNESS

Comfort ye, comfort ye my people, saith your God.

Speak ye comfortably to Jerusalem, and cry unto her, that her warfare is accomplished, that her iniquity is pardoned: for she hath received of the Lord's hand double for all her sins.

The voice of him that crieth in the wilderness, Prepare ye the way of the Lord, make straight in the desert a highway for our God.

Every valley shall be exalted, and every mountain and hill shall be made low: and the crooked shall be made straight, and the rough places plain. And the glory of the Lord shall be revealed. . . .[40:1-5]

The voice said, Cry. And he said, What shall I cry? All flesh is grass, and all the goodliness thereof is as the flower of the field: The grass withereth, the flower fadeth: because the spirit of the Lord bloweth upon it: surely the people is grass.

The grass withereth, the flower fadeth: but the word of our God shall stand for ever.[40:6-8]

He shall feed his flock like a shepherd: he shall gather the lambs with his arm, and carry them in his bosom, and shall gently lead those that are with young.[40:11]

Behold, the nations are as a drop of a bucket, and are counted as the small dust of the balance: behold, he taketh up the isles as a very little thing.[40:15]

Have ye not known? have ye not heard? Hath it not been told you from the beginning?[40:21]

They that wait upon the Lord shall renew their strength;

they shall mount up with wings as eagles; they shall run, and not be weary; and they shall walk, and not faint.⁴⁰:³¹

Isaiah delivers the Lord's message to the people: Israel will be restored and preserved. The Lord will send his Servant, the Redeemer, to comfort Israel and punish her oppressors:

Thus saith the Lord, the Redeemer of Israel, and his Holy One, to him whom man despiseth, to him whom the nation abhorreth, to a servant of rulers, Kings shall see and arise, princes also shall worship . . . and he shall choose thee.⁴⁹:⁷

Who hath believed our report? and to whom is the arm of the Lord revealed?

For he shall grow up before him as a tender plant. . . . He hath no form nor comeliness; and when we shall see him, there is no beauty that we should desire him. He is despised and rejected of men; a man of sorrows, and acquainted with grief: and we hid as it were our faces from him; he was despised, and we esteemed him not.

Surely he hath borne our griefs, and carried our sorrows.

But he was wounded for our transgressions, he was bruised for our iniquities: the chastisement of our peace was upon him; and with his stripes we are healed.

All we like sheep have gone astray; we have turned every one to his own way; and the Lord hath laid on him the iniquity of us all. He was oppressed, and he was afflicted, yet he opened not his mouth: he is brought as a lamb to the slaughter, and as a sheep before her shearers is dumb, so he opened not his mouth. . . . He was cut off out of the land of the living: for the transgression of my people was he stricken.⁵³:¹⁻⁸

He was numbered with the transgressors: and he bare the sin of many, and made intercession for the transgressors.[53:12]

Ho, every one that thirsteth, come ye to the waters, and he that hath no money; come ye, buy, and eat; yea, come, buy wine and milk without money and without price. Wherefore do ye spend money for that which is not bread? and your labor for that which satisfieth not? hearken diligently unto me, and eat ye that which is good, and let your soul delight itself in fatness.[55:1-2]

Let the wicked forsake his way, and the unrighteous man his thoughts: and let him return unto the Lord, and he will have mercy upon him; and to our God, for he will abundantly pardon.[55:7]

The Spirit of the Lord God is upon me; because the Lord hath anointed me to preach good tidings unto the meek; he hath sent me to bind up the brokenhearted, to proclaim liberty to the captives, and the opening of the prison to them that are bound; to proclaim the acceptable year of the Lord, and the day of vengeance of our God; to comfort all that mourn; . . . to give unto them beauty for ashes, the oil of joy for mourning, the garment of praise for the spirit of heaviness.[61:1-3]

JEREMIAH

The voice of another great prophet, Jeremiah, is raised in the time of king Josiah, and is heard in Judah until the people are carried away into Babylonian captivity. It is the fate of this prophet and patriot to watch while his nation, through its own sin and folly, rushes to its destruction.

JEREMIAH IS CHOSEN BY THE LORD

Then the word of the Lord came unto me, saying, Before I formed thee in the belly I knew thee; and before thou camest forth out of the womb I sanctified thee, and I ordained thee a prophet unto the nations.

Then said I, Ah, Lord God! behold, I cannot speak: for I am a child. But the Lord said unto me, Say not, I am a child: for thou shalt go to all that I shall send thee, and whatsoever I command thee thou shalt speak. Be not afraid of their faces: for I am with thee to deliver thee. . . .

Then the Lord put forth his hand, and touched my mouth. And the Lord said unto me, Behold, I have put my words in thy mouth.[1:4-9]

Go and cry in the ears of Jerusalem, saying, Thus saith the Lord; I remember thee, the kindness of thy youth, the love of thine espousals, when thou wentest after me in the wilderness, in a land that was not sown. Israel was holiness unto the Lord, and the firstfruits of his increase: all that devour him shall offend; evil shall come upon them, saith the Lord.[2:2-3]

Thus saith the Lord, What iniquity have your fathers found in me, that they are gone far from me, and have walked after vanity, and are become vain?[2:5]

Wherefore I will yet plead with you, saith the Lord, and with your children's children will I plead.[2:9]

Commanded by the Lord, Jeremiah comes forward to oppose the disastrous policies of both the king and the priests. His warnings are unwelcome; his prophecies cause him to be hated and denounced; his very life is threatened because of his pleas for reform.

In the reign of Jehoiakim, the son of Josiah, Jeremiah is put in prison. He sends for his disciple, Baruch, to whom he

dictates all the words of the Lord, saying, Go thou, and read
. . . in the ears of the people in the Lord's house upon the
fasting day.*[36:6] Baruch does this. When the matter comes to
the ears of the king, he burns the scroll and sends to seize
Baruch and Jeremiah; but the Lord hides them.*

THE RULERS OF JUDAH ARE WARNED

The Lord orders Jeremiah, Say unto the king and to the
queen, Humble yourselves, sit down: for your principalities
shall come down, even the crown of your glory. The cities
of the south shall be shut up, and none shall open them:
Judah shall be carried away captive all of it. . . .

Lift up your eyes, and behold them that come from the
north: where is the flock that was given thee, thy beautiful
flock?[13:18-20]

And if thou say in thine heart, Wherefore come these
things upon me? For the greatness of thine iniquity are thy
skirts discovered, and thy heels made bare. Can the Ethio-
pian change his skin, or the leopard his spots? then may ye
also do good, that are accustomed to do evil. [13:22-23]

*Thirty years after the death of king Josiah, in the reign of
his grandson, Jehoiachin, Jerusalem is besieged by the army
of Nebuchadnezzar, king of Babylon. Jehoiachin surrenders
the city. He is carried off prisoner to Babylon. Nebuchadnezzar puts a puppet king, Zedekiah, over Judah.*

*The prophet Jeremiah then goes to king Zedekiah with
a warning against a false ally, Egypt:* Thus saith the Lord
. . . Behold, Pharaoh's army, which is come forth to help
you, shall return to Egypt into their own land. And the
Chaldeans shall come again, and fight against this city, and
take it, and burn it with fire. . . .[37:7-8]

*But Jeremiah is cast into a dungeon: the king listens to
his false advisers; Nebuchadnezzar returns and takes Jeru-*

*salem. The city is destroyed, the king and thousands of the
people are carried off captives to Babylon.*

*Those who remain look toward Egypt for refuge, in spite
of Jeremiah's warnings. To them he says,* The Lord hath
said . . . O ye remnant of Judah; go ye not into Egypt; know
certainly that I have admonished you this day.[42:19] *To which
they reply,* Thou speakest falsely.[43:2]

*To his great sorrow, Jeremiah witnesses the fulfillment of
all his prophecies. The remnant of Judah, men, women, and
children, flee into Egypt—taking with them Jeremiah himself and Baruch the scribe.*

Then Jeremiah speaks to the exiles: Hear ye the word of
the Lord, all Judah that dwell in the land of Egypt. . . .
Behold, I will watch over them for evil, and not for good:
and all the men of Judah that are in the land of Egypt shall
be consumed by the sword and by the famine, until there be
an end of them. Yet a small number that escape the sword
shall return out of the land of Egypt into the land of Judah;
and all the remnant of Judah . . . shall know whose words
shall stand, mine, or theirs.[44:26-28]

LAMENTATIONS
(The Lamentations of Jeremiah)

Is this the city that men call The perfection of beauty, The
joy of the whole earth?[2:15]

*This book consists of five dirges for Jerusalem—songs of
sorrow and despair for the ruined city, in which the prophet
Jeremiah, in bitter grief, cries out for sympathy for Jerusalem, the pride of Judah, now conquered and humiliated:*
How doth the city sit solitary, that was full of people!
How is she become as a widow! she that was great among
nations, and princes among the provinces, how is she become a tributary![1:1]

Judah is gone into captivity because of affliction, and because of great servitude: she dwelleth among the heathen, she findeth no rest: all her persecutors overtook her between the straits.[1:3]

Her adversaries are the chief, her enemies prosper; for the Lord hath afflicted her for the multitude of her transgressions: her children are gone into captivity before the enemy.[1:5]

Is it nothing to you, all ye that pass by? behold, and see if there be any sorrow like unto my sorrow, which is done unto me, wherewith the Lord hath afflicted me in the day of his fierce anger.[1:12]

All that pass by clap their hands at thee; they hiss and wag their head at the daughter of Jerusalem. . . .[2:15]

Wherefore dost thou forget us for ever. . . . Turn thou us unto thee, O Lord, and we shall be turned; renew our days as of old.[5:20-21]

EZEKIEL

Son of man, I send thee to the children of Israel, to a rebellious nation that hath rebelled against me. . . . For they are impudent children and stiffhearted.[2:3-4]

It is largely due to Ezekiel ("God strengthens"), the Prophet of the Exile, that faith in the Lord survives among the Israelites in the years of their captivity. He is a priest in Jerusalem when king Jehoiachin is carried off to Babylon in the First Captivity; and Ezekiel is carried off with him. By means of exhortations, prophecies, and threats, he keeps before the exiles the memory of their transgressions; and at the same time he sustains in them hope for the restoration of the kingdom.

The Book of the Prophet Ezekiel is one of the most obscure and difficult in the Old Testament; for Ezekiel's prophecies come to him in fantastic visions, and by means of strange symbols:

Once, while in a trance, the prophet is handed a roll of a book in which are written words of lamentation and mourning and woe. *And a Voice says,* Son of man . . . eat this roll, and go speak unto the house of Israel.[3:1]

In a vision, Ezekiel is commanded to take a tile and portray upon it the city of Jerusalem; then to lay siege to the city; and to lie upon his side, first on the left and then on the right, bearing upon himself the iniquity of Israel and Judah for all the years of their iniquity—a day for each of the iniquitous years.

Ezekiel is then lifted up by a lock of his hair and transported from Babylon to Jerusalem, and back again.

He is shown the terrible Valley of Bones, where dry bones arise and become men again.

THE VISION OF GOD'S GLORY

Now it came to pass in the thirtieth year, in the fourth month, in the fifth day of the month, as I was among the captives by the river of Chebar, that the heavens were opened, and I saw visions of God.[1:1]

And I looked, and, behold, a whirlwind came out of the north, a great cloud, and a fire infolding itself, and a brightness was about it, and out of the midst thereof as the color of amber, out of the midst of the fire. Also out of the midst thereof came the likeness of four living creatures. And this was their appearance; they had the likeness of a man. And every one had four faces, and every one had four wings.[1:4-6]

As for the likeness of their faces, they four had the face of a man, and the face of a lion, on the right side: and they four had the face of an ox on the left side; they four also had the face of an eagle.[1:10]

The wings of these living creatures are stretched upward;

they move ever forward, without turning; as they run and return they are like a flash of lightning; and underneath them are wheels whose rims are full of eyes: For the spirit of the living creature was in the wheels.[1:21]

Above their heads is a platform, and upon this is a throne: and . . . the likeness as the appearance of a man above upon it. . . . I saw as it were the appearance of fire, and it had brightness round about.

As the appearance of the bow that is in the cloud in the day of rain, so was the appearance of the brightness round about. This was the appearance of the likeness of the glory of the Lord. And when I saw it, I fell upon my face, and I heard a voice of one that spake.[1:26-28]

And he said unto me, Son of man, I send thee to the children of Israel. . . .

And thou shalt say unto them, Thus saith the Lord God. And they, whether they will hear, or whether they will forbear (for they are a rebellious house), yet shall know that there hath been a prophet among them.[2:3-5]

THE SON SHALL NOT BEAR THE INIQUITY OF THE FATHER

Ezekiel sets forth the doctrine of personal responsibility: God will judge each man by his own deeds:

The Lord says to him, What mean ye, that ye use this proverb, concerning the land of Israel, saying, The fathers have eaten sour grapes, and the children's teeth are set on edge?

As I live, saith the Lord God, ye shall not have occasion any more to use this proverb in Israel. Behold, all souls are mine; as the soul of the father, so also the soul of the son is mine: the soul that sinneth, it shall die.[18:2-4]

The son shall not bear the iniquity of the father, neither shall the father bear the iniquity of the son: the righteousness of the righteous shall be upon him, and the wickedness of the wicked shall be upon him.[18:20]

Again, when the wicked man turneth away from his wickedness that he hath committed, and doeth that which is lawful and right, he shall save his soul alive.[18:27]

THE VALLEY OF DRY BONES

The hand of the Lord was upon me, and carried me out in the Spirit of the Lord, and set me down in the midst of the valley which was full of bones. . . . And he said unto me, Son of man, can these bones live? And I answered, O Lord God, thou knowest.

Again he said unto me, Prophesy upon these bones, and say unto them, O ye dry bones, hear the word of the Lord. . . . Behold, I will cause breath to enter into you, and ye shall live. And I will lay sinews upon you, and will bring up flesh upon you, and cover you with skin, and put breath in you, and ye shall live; and ye shall know that I am the Lord.[37:1-6]

So I prophesied as he commanded me, and the breath came into them, and they lived, and stood up upon their feet, an exceeding great army.

Then he said unto me, Son of man, these bones are the whole house of Israel: behold, they say, Our bones are dried, and our hope is lost: we are cut off for our parts.

Therefore prophesy and say unto them . . . Behold, O my people, I will open your graves . . . and bring you into the land of Israel. . . .[37:10-12]

And shall put my Spirit in you, and ye shall live, and I shall place you in your own land: then shall ye know that I the Lord have spoken it, and performed it. . . .[37:14]

I will take the children of Israel from among the heathen, whither they be gone, and will gather them on every side, and bring them into their own land: and I will make them one nation. . . .[37:21-22]

And David my servant shall be king over them; . . . they shall also walk in my judgments, and observe my statutes, and do them.[37:24]

My tabernacle also shall be with them: yea, I will be their God, and they shall be my people.[37:27]

DANIEL

O Daniel, a man greatly beloved, understand the words that I speak unto thee. . . .[10:11]

During the years of exile in Babylon, four young boys are chosen from among the Israelites to be trained for service in the king's palace. One of these boys is Daniel; at the palace his name is changed to Belteshazzar. To him, because of his wisdom in interpreting visions and dreams, king Nebuchadnezzar shows great favor. In time he becomes chief among the wise men, and governor of the province of Babylon.

The king sets up a great image of gold in the plain of Dura. At the dedication, a herald announces the royal decree: O people . . . at what time ye hear the sound of the cornet, flute, harp, sackbut, psaltery, dulcimer, and all kinds of music, ye fall down and worship the golden image that Nebuchadnezzar the king hath set up: And whoso falleth not down and worshippeth shall the same hour be cast into the midst of a burning fiery furnace.[3:4-6]

But this decree is ignored by Daniel's three friends, Shadrach, Meshach and Abed-nego.

Nebuchadnezzar is full of fury. He commands that the furnace shall be heated seven times more than it is wont to be heated.

Then these men were bound in their coats, their hose, and their hats, and their other garments, and were cast into the midst of the burning fiery furnace.[3:21]

Approaching the furnace, the king says in astonishment,
Lo, I see four men loose, walking in the midst of the fire, and
they have no hurt; and the form of the fourth is like the Son
of God. *He calls to the men in the furnace to come out:*
Then Shadrach, Meshach, and Abed-nego came forth of
the midst of the fire.[3:25-26]

The king says, Blessed be the God of Shadrach, Meshach,
and Abed-nego, who hath sent his engel, and delivered his
servants that trusted in him. . . .[3:28]

*Nebuchadnezzar, at the height of his power, has a fearful
dream, which Daniel is called upon to interpret. He says to
the king,* They shall drive thee from men, and thy dwelling
shall be with the beasts of the field . . . till thou know that
the most High ruleth in the kingdom of men. . . .[4:25] *The king
in his pride rejects this warning. Within the year he goes
mad, grazing with the cattle in the fields.*

At length he regains his sanity—as he himself testifies:
I Nebuchadnezzar lifted up mine eyes unto heaven, and
mine understanding returned unto me, and I blessed the
most High, and I praised and honored him that liveth
forever. . . .[4:34]

THE HANDWRITING ON THE WALL

*After the days of Nebuchadnezzar, Belshazzar is king in
Babylon. He gives a great feast, to which are brought the
sacred vessels of gold from the Temple in Jerusalem so that
the king, his princes, his wives and concubines may drink
from them.*

*Suddenly there appear the fingers of a man's hand, writing
on the plaster of the wall. Shaking with fright, the king calls
for his astrologers and wise men: none can read the writing.
Daniel is summoned, to whom the king says,* I have heard
of thee. . . . Now if thou canst read the writing, and make

known to me the interpretation thereof, thou shalt be clothed with scarlet, and . . . shalt be the third ruler in the kingdom. *Daniel replies,* Let thy gifts be to thyself, and give thy rewards to another; yet will I read the writing. . . .[5:16-17]

This is the writing on the wall: MENE, MENE, TEKEL, UPHARSIN.

This is Daniel's interpretation: God hath numbered thy kingdom, and finished it. Thou are weighed in the balances, and art found wanting. Thy kingdom is divided, and given to the Medes and Persians. [5:25-28]

In the night, king Belshazzar is slain. Darius the Mede becomes the new ruler of the kingdom.

DANIEL IN THE LIONS' DEN

Powerful enemies now conspire against Daniel, for Darius raises him to a very high station in the kingdom. The king is induced to sign a decree: Whosoever shall ask a petition of any God or man for thirty days, save of thee, O king, he shall be cast into the den of lions.[6:7]

Nevertheless Daniel continues to pray to the Lord:

His windows being open in his chamber toward Jerusalem, he kneeled upon his knees three times a day, and prayed, and gave thanks before his God, as he did aforetime.[6:10]

It is reported to the king, but he sees that he has been the tool of plotters. However, by the law of the Medes and the Persians he cannot alter his decree.

They brought Daniel, and cast him into the den of lions[6:16]

Early next morning, the king hurries to the den. He cries, O Daniel, servant of the living God, is thy God, whom thou servest continually, able to deliver thee from the lions? *Daniel replies,* My God hath sent his angel, and hath shut the lions' mouths, that they have not hurt me.

So Daniel was taken up out of the den, and no manner of hurt was found upon him, because he believed in his God.[6:20-23]

The life of Daniel is one of piety and of devoted service to his fellow-exiles in Babylon. The Lord grants him divine revelations and prophetic visions to give courage and hope to the children of Israel. And an angel of the Lord appears to Daniel and reveals the future:

. . . there shall be a time of trouble, such as never was since there was a nation. . . . And at that time thy people shall be delivered, every one that shall be found written in the book.

And many of them that sleep in the dust of the earth shall awake, some to everlasting life, and some to shame and everlasting contempt.

And they that be wise shall shine as the brightness of the firmament; and they that turn many to righteousness, as the stars for ever and ever.

But thou, O Daniel, shut up the words, and seal the book, even to the time of the end: many shall run to and fro, and knowledge shall be increased.[12:1-4]

Many shall be purified, and made white, and tried; but the wicked shall do wickedly: and none of the wicked shall understand; but the wise shall understand.[12:10]

Blessed is he that watcheth. . . . But go thou thy way till the end be: for thou shalt rest, and stand in thy lot at the end of the days.[12:12-13]

HOSEA

The prophecies of Hosea, "the prophet of the sorrowful heart," are in the form of parables which apparently spring from his own tragic experience in marriage. His love for his adulterous wife, Gomer, is thought by some scholars to symbolize the love of God for idolatrous Israel, and his compassion for her to reflect the prophet's faith in God's ultimate forgiveness of His erring people.

Hosea is the first of the "twelve prophets." His ministry takes place in Israel in the last decades before the fall of the kingdom.

The Lord said to Hosea, Go, take unto thee a wife of whoredoms and children of whoredoms: for the land hath committed great whoredom, departing from the Lord. So he went and took Gomer . . . which conceived, and bare him a son.[1:2-3]

The boy is named Jezreel, at the Lord's command: I will break the bow of Israel in the valley of Jezreel.[1:5] *A second child is named Lo-ruhamah (unpitied), for says the Lord,* I will no more have mercy upon the house of Israel[1:6] *A third child is named Lo-ammi (not my people):* Ye are not my people, and I will not be your God.[1:9]

Hosea speaks to his children: Plead with your mother, plead: for she is not my wife, neither am I her husband: let her therefore put away her whoredoms out of her sight, and her adulteries from between her breasts; lest I strip her naked, and set her as in the day that she was born, and make her as a wilderness, and set her like a dry land, and slay her with thirst.[2:2-3]

And I will not have mercy upon her children. . . . For their mother hath played the harlot: she that conceived them hath done shamefully. [2:4-5]

And she shall follow after her lovers, but she shall not overtake them. . . . Then shall she say, I will go and return to my first husband; for then was it better with me than now.[2:7]

And I will have mercy upon her that had not obtained mercy. . . .[2:23]

The Lord says, Rejoice not, O Israel, for joy, as other people: for thou hast gone a whoring from thy God, thou hast loved a reward upon every cornfloor.[9:1]

They have sown the wind, and they shall reap the whirlwind.[8:7]

Ye have plowed wickedness, ye have reaped iniquity.[10:13]

I drew them with cords of a man, with bands of love: and I was to them as they that take off the yoke of their jaws. . . .[11:4]

I have also spoken by the prophets, and I have multiplied visions and used similitudes, by the ministry of the prophets.[12:10]

O Israel, return unto the Lord thy God; for thou hast fallen by thine iniquity. Take with you words, and turn to the Lord: say unto him, Take away all iniquity, and receive us graciously. . . . [14:1-2]

I will heal their backsliding, I will love them freely: for mine anger is turned away. . . .[14:4]

JOEL

The prophet Joel appears in Jerusalem during a time of great affliction, when a plague of locusts is devastating the land. He warns the people that the scourge is upon them as a sign of God's wrath:

Sanctify ye a fast, call a solemn assembly, gather the elders and all the inhabitants of the land into the house of the Lord your God, and cry unto the Lord.[1:14]

That which the palmerworm hath left hath the locust eaten. . . . Awake, ye drunkards, and weep; and howl, all ye drinkers of wine, because . . . it is cut off from your mouth.[1:4-5]

The field is wasted, the land mourneth. . . . [1:10]

Let all the inhabitants of the land tremble: for the day of the Lord cometh, for it is nigh at hand.[2:1]

The Lord will forgive, says Joel; and He will restore the land: I will restore to you the years that the locust hath eaten. . . . And ye shall eat in plenty, and be satisfied, and praise the name of the Lord your God. . . .[2:25-26]

And it shall come to pass afterward, that I will pour out my spirit upon all flesh; and your sons and your daughters shall prophesy, your old men shall dream dreams, your young men shall see visions.[2:28]

Multitudes, multitudes in the valley of decision: for the day of the Lord is near in the valley of decision.[3:14]

Egypt shall be a desolation, and Edom shall be a desolate wilderness. . . . But Judah shall dwell for ever, and Jerusalem from generation to generation.[3:19-20]

AMOS

It is when Israel is powerful and prosperous, in the reign of Uzziah and of Jeroboam II, that Amos, a poor shepherd of Tekoa, arises to cry doom: The Lord took me as I followed the flock, and the Lord said unto me, Go, prophesy unto my people Israel.[7:15]

Thus saith the Lord; For three transgressions of Israel, and for four, I will not turn away the punishment thereof; because they sold the righteous for silver, and the poor for a pair of shoes.[2:6]

O children of Israel . . . you only have I known of all the

families of the earth: therefore I will punish you for all your iniquities. Can two walk together unless they be agreed?[3:1-3]

I will smite the winter house with the summer house; and the houses of ivory shall perish, and the great houses shall have an end.[3:15]

Ye were as a firebrand plucked out of the burning: yet have ye not returned unto me, saith the Lord.[4:11]

Woe to them that are at ease in Zion, and trust in the mountain of Samaria, which are named chief of the nations. . . .[6:1]

Amos says to the people, Behold, the Lord stood upon a wall made by a plumbline, with a plumbline in his hand. And the Lord said unto me, Amos, what seest thou? And I said, A plumbline. Then said the Lord, Behold, I will set a plumbline in the midst of my people Israel. . . . And the high places of Isaac shall be desolate, and the sanctuaries of Israel shall be laid waste; and I will rise against the house of Jeroboam with the sword. [7:7-9]

Behold, the eyes of the Lord God are upon the sinful kingdom, and I will destroy it from off the face of the earth; saving that I will not utterly destroy the house of Jacob, saith the Lord.[9:8]

OBADIAH

This is the shortest Book in the Old Testament. Its twenty-one verses comprise a denunciation of the kingdom of Edom, and a prophecy of the destruction of the kingdom for having participated with the Chaldeans in the sack of Jerusalem.

Thus saith the Lord God concerning Edom; We have heard a rumor from the Lord, and an ambassador is sent among the heathen, Arise ye, and let us rise against her in battle.

Behold, I have made thee small among the heathen; thou art greatly despised. The pride of thine heart hath deceived thee. . . .

Though thou exalt thyself as the eagle, and though thou set they nest among the stars, thence will I bring thee down, saith the Lord. [1:1-4]

For thy violence against they brother Jacob shame shall cover thee, and thou shalt be cut off for ever.[1:10]

JONAH

The word of the Lord comes to the prophet Jonah: Arise, go to Nineveh, that great city, and cry against it; for their wickedness is come before me.[1:2]

Instead, Jonah takes ship for Tarshish: for he fears that the wicked Ninevites, upon hearing his warning, may repent their sins and be forgiven, thereby turning aside his prophecy.

But the Lord sends a storm of such violence that the sailors of Jonah's ship are afraid. They say to each other, Let us cast lots, that we may know for whose cause this evil is upon us.

So they cast lots, and the lot fell upon Jonah.[1:7]

Jonah confesses that he is fleeing from the presence of God: they must cast him forth into the sea. They do so; and the sea at once grows calm.

Now the Lord had prepared a great fish to swallow up Jonah. And Jonah was in the belly of the fish three days and three nights.[1:17]

He prays to the Lord: I am cast out of thy sight; yet will I look again toward thy holy temple.[2:4] *The whale vomits him out on dry land.*

Again the word of the Lord comes to Jonah: now he obeys.

Walking through the streets of Nineveh, he cries aloud, Yet forty days, and Nineveh shall be overthrown.[3:4]

The Ninevites proclaim a fast. They put on sackcloth. They repent their evil ways. And God spares them His punishment.

But Jonah, waiting in vain for his prophecy to be fulfilled, is angry. He says to the Lord, Was not this my saying, when I was yet in my country? . . . for I knew that thou art a gracious God, and merciful . . . and repentest thee of the evil. Therefore now, O Lord, take, I beseech thee, my life from me; for it is better for me to die than to live.

The Lord says, Doest thou well to be angry?[4:2-4]

Then He causes a gourd to grow, comforting to the prophet where he sits in its shade. But the gourd dies; the sun beats down more mercilessly than ever; again Jonah longs for death.

The Lord says to him, Doest thou well to be angry for the gourd? *Jonah replies,* I do well to be angry, even unto death.

The Lord says, Thou hast had pity on the gourd, for the which thou hast not labored, neither madest it grow. . . . And should I not spare Nineveh, that great city, wherein are more than sixscore thousand persons that cannot discern between their right hand and their left hand; and also much cattle?[4:9-11]

MICAH

A contemporary of the prophet Isaiah, Micah performs his ministry in Judah in the reigns of Jotham, Ahaz, and Hezekiah.

*He prophesies the destruction of Samaria and of Jeru-
salem:* For, behold, the Lord cometh forth out of his place,
and will come down, and tread upon the high places of the
earth. And the mountains shall be molten under him, and
the valleys shall be cleft, as wax before fire. . . . For the
transgression of Jacob is all this, and for the sins of the
house of Israel.[1:3-5]

The prophet predicts world peace at last: They shall sit
every man under his vine and under his fig tree; and none
shall make them afraid. . . . For all people will walk every
one in the name of his god, and we will walk in the name of
the Lord our God for ever and ever.[4:4-5]

Like Isaiah, Micah too predicts the coming of a Messiah:
But thou, Bethlehem Ephratah, though thou be little among
the thousands of Judah, yet out of thee shall he come forth
unto me that is to be ruler in Israel; whose goings forth have
been from of old, from everlasting.[5:2]

Micah pleads with the people for the Lord, saying, He
hath showed thee, O man, what is good; and what doth the
Lord require of thee, but to do justly, and to love mercy,
and to walk humbly with thy God?[6:8]

NAHUM

*Nahum preaches in Judah in the reign of king Hezekiah.
He prophesies the destruction of Nineveh. Almost a century
later, the city is destroyed, exactly as Nahum foretold:*

Woe to the bloody city! It is all full of lies and rob-
bery. . . .[3:1]

Behold, I am against thee, saith the Lord of hosts . . . and
I will show the nations thy nakedness, and the kingdoms thy
shame.[3:5]

And it shall come to pass, that all they that look upon

thee shall flee from thee, and say, Nineveh is laid waste; who will bemoan her? whence shall I seek comforters for thee?[3:7]

Thy crowned are as the locusts, and thy captains as the great grasshoppers. . . . Thy shepherds slumber, O king of Assyria: thy nobles shall dwell in the dust: thy people is scattered upon the mountains, and no man gathereth them.

There is no healing of thy bruise; thy wound is grievous: all that hear the bruit of thee shall clap the hands over thee: for upon whom hath not thy wickedness passed continually?[3:17-19]

HABAKKUK

When the children of Israel are in bondage to Babylon, the prophet Habakkuk, like Job, cries out to the Lord against His seeming injustice:

O Lord, how long shall I cry, and thou wilt not hear! even cry out unto thee of violence, and thou wilt not save![1:2]

The Lord replies: His instrument of punishment is at hand. For, lo, I raise up the Chaldeans, that bitter and hasty nation, which shall march through the breadth of the land. . . .[1:6]

They shall come all for violence. . . . And they shall scoff at the kings, and the princes shall be a scorn unto them.[1:9-10]

Write the vision, and make it plain upon tables, that he may run that readeth it. For the vision is yet for an appointed time . . . though it tarry, wait for it; because it will surely come.[2:2-3]

The transgressor shall be punished; the just man shall live by his faith and shall have his reward in the end: The Lord is in his holy temple: let all the earth keep silence before him.[2:20]

ZEPHANIAH

The word of the Lord comes to Zephaniah in the days of Josiah, king of Judah. He prophesies against Judah and the surrounding nations; but he holds out promises of blessings to the meek and the righteous of the Lord's people.

I will utterly consume all things from off the land, saith the Lord. I will consume man and beast . . . and I will cut off man from off the land. . . . I will also stretch out mine hand upon Judah, and upon all the inhabitants of Jerusalem; and I will cut off the remnant of Baal from this place. . . .[1:2-4]

Seek ye the Lord, all ye meek of the earth, which have wrought his judgment; seek righteousness, seek meekness: it may be ye shall be hid in the day of the Lord's anger.[2:3]

The remnant of Israel shall not do iniquity, nor speak lies; neither shall a deceitful tongue be found in their mouth: for they shall feed and lie down, and none shall make them afraid.[3:13]

Behold, at that time I will undo all that afflict thee: and I will save her that halteth, and gather her that was driven out; and I will get them praise and fame in every land where they have been put to shame.[3:19]

HAGGAI

After the seventy years' captivity in Babylon, three prophets speak to the restored remnant in Jerusalem: Haggai, Zechariah, and Malachi. Haggai exhorts the people to finish the work of rebuilding the Temple.

It is in the second year of king Darius of Persia. In Jerusalem, the returned exiles are saying, The time is not come, the time that the Lord's house should be built.[1:2] *But the word of the Lord comes to Haggai the prophet:* Is it time for you, O ye, to dwell in your ceiled houses, and this house lie waste? . . . Consider your ways. Ye have sown much, and bring in little; ye eat, but ye have not enough; ye drink, but ye are not filled with drink; ye clothe you, but there is none warm; and he that earneth wages, earneth wages to put it into a bag with holes.

Go up to the mountain, and bring wood, and build the house; and I will take pleasure in it, and I will be glorified, saith the Lord.[1:4-8]

The Lord tells Haggai to speak to Zerubbabel, the governor, and to Joshua, the high priest, and to the people: Be strong, all ye people of the land, saith the Lord, and work: for I am with you. . . . My Spirit remaineth among you: fear ye not.[2:4-5]

ZECHARIAH

Zechariah brings a message of hope to the returned remnant in Jerusalem; and he, like Haggai, urges upon them the rebuilding of the Temple: Not by might, nor by power, but by my Spirit, saith the Lord of hosts.[4:6]

Zechariah says to the children of Israel: Thus saith the Lord of hosts; Turn ye unto me . . . and I will turn unto you. . . .[1:3]

Be ye not as your fathers, unto whom the former prophets have cried, saying . . . Turn ye now from your evil ways, and from your evil doings: but they did not hear, nor hearken unto me. . . .

Your fathers, where are they? and the prophets, do they live for ever? But my words and my statutes, which I commanded my servants the prophets, did they not take hold? . . .[1:4-6]

I have spread you abroad as the four winds of the heaven, saith the Lord.[2:6]

Rejoice greatly, O daughter of Zion. . . . Behold, thy King cometh unto thee: he is just, and having salvation; lowly, and riding upon an ass. . . .[9:9]

Turn you to the stronghold, ye prisoners of hope.[9:12]

One shall say unto him, What are these wounds in thine hands? Then he shall answer, Those with which I was wounded in the house of my friends.[13:6]

And the Lord shall be King over all the earth: in that day shall there be one Lord, and his name one.[14:9]

MALACHI

The last of the Old Testament prophets is anonymous: the word Malachi is translated "my messenger." The prophecy belongs to the time of Ezra and Nehemiah, in the early years of the restored remnant in Jerusalem. The Temple has now been rebuilt; but the people have lost heart: their lot is hard; droughts and famine afflict them; they are attacked by enemy nations. They ask, Where is the God of judgment?[2:17]

Malachi brings the people renewed assurance of God's love. Their sufferings are only caused by their own sinfulness:

Have we not all one father? hath not one God created us? why do we deal treacherously every man against his brother . . . ?[2:10]

The prophecy ends with the promise of the coming of a Prophet who will save the world from the Lord's curse:

For, behold, the day cometh, that shall burn as an oven;

and all the proud, yea, and all that do wickedly, shall be stubble. . . . But unto you that fear my name shall the Sun of righteousness arise with healing in his wings. . . .[4:1-2]

Behold, I will send you Elijah the prophet before the coming of the great and dreadful day of the Lord: And he shall turn the heart of the fathers to the children, and the heart of the children to their fathers, lest I come and smite the earth with a curse.[4:5-6]

The New Testament

ST. MATTHEW

The story of the birth and childhood of Jesus, his minis-try, his death and resurrection, is told in The Gospel According to St. Matthew. Here is given an account of His life, his teaching and his works; and here are recorded the utterances of Jesus: the discourses, the parables, the sermons, prayers and sayings.

The first Gospel begins with a genealogical table tracing the generations from Abraham to David, and through David to Joseph: the husband of Mary, of whom was born Jesus, who is called Christ.[1:16]

Now the birth of Jesus Christ was on this wise: When as his mother Mary was espoused to Joseph, before they came together, she was found with child of the Holy Ghost. Then Joseph her husband, being a just man, and not willing to make her a public example, was minded to put her away privily. But while he thought on these things, behold, the angel of the Lord appeared unto him in a dream, saying, Joseph, thou son of David, fear not to take unto thee Mary thy wife: for that which is conceived in her is of the Holy

Ghost. And she shall bring forth a son, and thou shalt call his name JESUS: for he shall save his people from their sins.

Now all this was done, that it might be fulfilled which was spoken of the Lord by the prophet, saying, Behold, a virgin shall be with child, and shall bring forth a son, and they shall call his name Emmanuel, which being interpreted is, God with us.

Then Joseph being raised from sleep did as the angel of the Lord had bidden him, and took unto him his wife: And knew her not till she had brought forth her firstborn son: and he called his name JESUS.[1:18-25]

Now when Jesus was born in Bethlehem of Judea in the days of Herod the king, behold, there came wise men from the east to Jerusalem, saying, Where is he that is born King of the Jews? for we have seen his star in the east, and are come to worship him.[2:1-2]

Herod is troubled: Bethlehem, according to prophecy, is to be the birthplace of Christ. He commands the wise men to go in search of the newborn child. They go; and the star in the east goes before them, until it is over the place where lies the baby.

When they were come into the house, they saw the young child with Mary his mother, and fell down, and worshipped him: and when they had opened their treasures, they presented unto him gifts; gold, and frankincense, and myrrh. And being warned of God in a dream that they should not return to Herod, they departed into their own country another way.[2:11-12]

The Angel of the Lord speaks to Joseph: Arise, and take the young child and his mother, and flee into Egypt . . . for Herod will seek the young child to destroy him.[2:13] *Joseph obeys.*

But Herod is enraged that they have escaped him. At his

command all the children of Bethlehem, up to the age of two years, are put to death.

It is the slaughter which Jeremiah prophesied of old, and when he saw Rachel weeping for her children, and would not be comforted, because they are not.[2:18]

Herod the king dies; and then Joseph takes Mary and the child to live in Galilee, in the city of Nazareth.

JOHN THE BAPTIST

In those days came John the Baptist, preaching in the wilderness of Judea, and saying, Repent ye: for the kingdom of heaven is at hand.

Thus a prophecy of Isaiah's is fulfilled: The voice of one crying in the wilderness, Prepare ye the way of the Lord, make his paths straight.

And the same John had his raiment of camel's hair, and a leathern girdle about his loins; and his meat was locusts and wild honey.[3:1-4]

All Judea comes to John to be baptized in the Jordan—including many Pharisees and Sadducees, to whom John says, O generation of vipers, who hath warned you to flee the wrath to come?[3:7]

I indeed baptize you with water unto repentance: but he that cometh after me is mightier than I, whose shoes I am not worthy to bear: he shall baptize you with the Holy Ghost, and with fire.[3:11]

Jesus comes from Galilee to be baptized; and John says, I have need to be baptized of thee, and comest thou to me? *Jesus replies,* Suffer it to be so now: for thus it becometh us to fulfil all righteousness.[3:14-15]

Jesus is baptized; and a voice is heard from heaven, saying, This is my beloved Son, in whom I am well pleased.[3:17]

Then was Jesus led up of the spirit into the wilderness to be tempted of the devil.[4:1]

He fasts for forty days and forty nights. Satan says to Him, If thou be the Son of God, command that these stones be made bread. *He replies,* It is written, Man shall not live by bread alone, but by every word that proceedeth out of the mouth of God.[4:3-4]

The devil takes Him to Jerusalem, to a high pinnacle of the Temple, and says, Cast thyself down: for it is written, He shall give his angels charge concerning thee. *Jesus replies,* It is written again, Thou shalt not tempt the Lord thy God. *Then He is promised* all the kingdoms of the world, and the glory of them, *if he will but fall down and worship Satan; and Jesus says,* It is written, Thou shalt worship the Lord thy God, and him only shalt thou serve. *Satan leaves Him.*

And, behold, angels came and ministered unto him.[4:6-11]

John the Baptist is thrown into prison. When Jesus learns this, he leaves Nazareth and goes to live in Capernaum, on the seacoast of Galilee. From this time He begins to preach, Repent: for the kingdom of heaven is a hand.[4:17]

He calls to two fishermen, Simon called Peter, and Simon's brother, Andrew, saying, Follow me, and I will make you fishers of men.[4:19] *These two and two others, James and John, the sons of a fisherman named Zebedee, accompany Jesus as he goes about Galilee, teaching in the synagogues, preaching the gospel of the kingdom, and healing the sick, the palsied, the lunatic, the possessed. His fame spreads. Great multitudes come to hear Him and be healed.*

THE SERMON ON THE MOUNT

And seeing the multitudes, he went up into a mountain: and when he was set, his disciples came unto him: And he opened his mouth, and taught them, saying,

Blessed are the poor in spirit: for theirs is the kingdom of heaven.

Blessed are they that mourn: for they shall be comforted.

Blessed are the meek: for they shall inherit the earth.

Blessed are they which do hunger and thirst after righteousness: for they shall be filled.

Blessed are the merciful: for they shall obtain mercy.

Blessed are the pure in heart: for they shall see God.

Blessed are the peacemakers: for they shall be called the children of God.

Blessed are they which are persecuted for righteousness' sake: for theirs is the kingdom of heaven.

Blessed are ye, when men shall revile you, and persecute you, and shall say all manner of evil against you falsely, for my sake.

Rejoice, and be exceeding glad: for great is your reward in heaven; for so persecuted they the prophets which were before you.

Ye are the salt of the earth: but if the salt have lost his savour, wherewith shall it be salted? It is thenceforth good for nothing, but to be cast out, and to be trodden under foot of men.

Ye are the light of the world. A city that is set on a hill cannot be hid.

Neither do men light a candle, and put it under a bushel, but on a candlestick; and it giveth light unto all that are in the house.

Let your light so shine before men, that they may see your good works, and glorify your Father which is in heaven. [5:1-16]

Think not that I am come to destroy the law, or the prophets: I am not come to destroy, but to fulfil.

For verily I say unto you, Till heaven and earth pass, one jot or one tittle shall in no wise pass from the law, till all be fulfilled.

Whosoever therefore shall break one of these least commandments, and shall teach men so, he shall be called the least in the kingdom of heaven: but whosoever shall do and teach them, the same shall be called great in the kingdom of heaven. For I say unto you, That except your righteousness shall exceed the righteousness of the scribes and Pharisees, ye shall in no case enter into the kingdom of heaven.

Ye have heard that it was said by them of old time, Thou shalt not kill; and whosoever shall kill shall be in danger of the judgment: But I say unto you, That whosoever is angry with his brother without a cause shall be in danger of the judgment: and whosoever shall say to his brother, Raca,* shall be in danger of the council: but whosoever shall say, Thou fool, shall be in danger of hell fire.

Therefore if thou bring thy gift to the altar, and there rememberest that thy brother hath aught against thee; leave there thy gift before the altar, and go thy way; first be reconciled to thy brother, and then come and offer thy gift.

Agree with thine adversary quickly, while thou are in the way with him; lest at any time the adversary deliver thee to the judge, and the judge deliver thee to the officer, and thou be cast into prison. Verily I say unto thee, thou shalt by no means come out thence, till thou hast paid the uttermost farthing.

Ye have heard that it was said by them of old time, Thou shalt not commit adultery: But I say unto you, that whosoever looketh on a woman to lust after her hath committed adultery with her already in his heart.

And if thy right eye offend thee, pluck it out, and cast it from thee: for it is profitable for thee that one of thy members should perish, and not that thy whole body should be cast into hell.

And if thy right hand offend thee, cut it off, and cast it from thee: for it is profitable for thee that one of thy members should perish, and not that thy whole body should be cast into hell.

---

* An expression of contempt.

OF MARRIAGE AND DIVORCE

It hath been said, Whosoever shall put away his wife, let him give her a writing of divorcement: But I say unto you, That whosoever shall put away his wife, saving for the cause of fornication, causeth her to commit adultery: and whosoever shall marry her that is divorced committeth adultery.

Again, ye have heard that it hath been said by them of old time, Thou shalt not forswear thyself, but shalt perform unto the Lord thine oaths: But I say unto you, Swear not at all; neither by heaven; for it is God's throne: nor by the earth; for it is his footstool: neither by Jerusalem; for it is the city of the great King. Neither shalt thou swear by thy head, because thou canst not make one hair white or black. But let your communication be, Yea, yea; Nay, nay: for whatsoever is more than these cometh of evil.

Ye have heard that it hath been said, An eye for an eye, and a tooth for a tooth: But I say unto you, that ye resist not evil: but whosoever shall smite thee on thy right cheek, turn to him the other also.

And if any man will sue thee at the law, and take away thy coat, let him have thy cloak also. And whosoever shall compel thee to go a mile, go with him twain.

Give to him that asketh thee, and from him that would borrow of thee turn not thou away.

Ye have heard that it hath been said, Thou shalt love thy neighbor, and hate thine enemy. But I say unto you, Love your enemies, bless them that curse you, do good to them that hate you, and pray for them which despitefully use you, and persecute you; that ye may be the children of your Father which is in heaven: for he maketh his sun to rise on the evil and on the good, and sendeth rain on the just and on the unjust. For if ye love them which love you, what reward have ye? do not even the publicans the same? And if ye salute your brethren only, what do ye more than others? do not even the publicans so?

Be ye therefore perfect, even as your Father which is in heaven is perfect.[5:17-48]

Take heed that ye do not your alms before men, to be seen of them: otherwise ye have no reward of your Father which is in heaven. Therefore when thou doest thine alms, do not sound a trumpet before thee, as the hypocrites do in the synagogues and in the streets, that they may have glory of men. Verily I say unto you, They have their reward. But when thou doest alms, let not thy left hand know what thy right hand doeth: That thine alms may be in secret: and thy Father which seeth in secret himself shall reward thee openly.

And when thou prayest, thou shalt not be as the hypocrites are: for they love to pray standing in the synagogues and in the corners of the streets, that they may be seen of men. Verily I say unto you, They have their reward. But thou, when thou prayest, enter into thy closet, and when thou hast shut thy door, pray to thy Father which is in secret; and thy Father which seeth in secret shall reward thee openly.

But when ye pray, use not vain repetitions, as the heathen do: for they think that they shall be heard for their much speaking. Be not ye therefore like unto them: for your Father knoweth what things ye have need of, before ye ask him.[6:1-8]

THE LORD'S PRAYER

After this manner therefore pray ye:
Our Father which art in heaven, Hallowed be thy name.
Thy kingdom come. Thy will be done in earth, as it is in heaven.
Give us this day our daily bread.
And forgive us our debts, as we forgive our debtors.
And lead us not into temptation, but deliver us from evil:

For thine is the kingdom, and the power, and the glory, for
ever. Amen.[6:9-13]

For if ye forgive men their trespasses, your heavenly
Father will also forgive you: But if ye forgive not men their
trespasses, neither will your Father forgive your trespasses.

Moreover when ye fast, be not, as the hypocrites, of a sad
countenance: for they disfigure their faces, that they may
appear unto men to fast. Verily I say unto you, They have
their reward. But thou, when thou fastest, anoint thine head,
and wash thy face; that thou appear not unto men to fast,
but unto thy Father which is in secret: and thy Father which
seeth in secret shall reward thee openly.

Lay not up for yourselves treasures upon earth, where
moth and rust doth corrupt, and where thieves break
through and steal: But lay up for yourselves treasures in
heaven, where neither moth nor rust doth corrupt, and
where thieves do not break through nor steal: For where
your treasure is, there will your heart be also.

The light of the body is the eye: if therefore thine eye be
single, thy whole body shall be full of light. But if thine
eye be evil, thy whole body shall be full of darkness. If
therefore the light that is in thee be darkness, how great
is that darkness!

No man can serve two masters: for either he will hate
the one, and love the other; or else he will hold to the
one, and despise the other. Ye cannot serve God and
mammon.[6:14-24]

THE CURE OF ANXIETY

Therefore I say unto you, Take no thought of your life,
what ye shall eat, or what ye shall drink; nor yet for your
body, what ye shall put on. Is not the life more than meat,
and the body than raiment?

Behold the fowls of the air: for they sow not, neither do they reap, nor gather into barns; yet your heavenly Father feedeth them. Are ye not much better than they?

Which of you by taking thought can add one cubit unto his stature?

And why take ye thought for raiment? Consider the lilies of the field, how they grow; they toil not, neither do they spin: And yet I say unto you, That even Solomon in all his glory was not arrayed like one of these.

Wherefore, if God so clothe the grass of the field, which today is, and tomorrow is cast into the oven, shall he not much more clothe you, O ye of little faith? Therefore take no thought, saying, What shall we eat? or, What shall we drink? or, Wherewithal shall we be clothed? (For after all these things do the Gentiles seek:) for your heavenly Father knoweth that ye have need of all these things.

But seek ye first the kingdom of God, and his righteousness; and all these things shall be added unto you.

Take therefore no thought for the morrow: for the morrow shall take thought for the things of itself. Sufficient unto the day is the evil thereof. 6:25-34

Judge not, that ye be not judged. For with what judgment ye judge, ye shall be judged: and with what measure ye mete, it shall be measured to you again. And why beholdest thou the mote that is in thy brother's eye, but considereth not the beam that is in thine own eye? Or how wilt thou say to thy brother, Let me pull out the mote of thine eye; and behold, a beam is in thine own eye? Thou hypocrite, first cast out the beam out of thine own eye; and then shalt thou see clearly to cast out the mote out of thy brother's eye.

Give not that which is holy unto the dogs, neither cast ye your pearls before swine, lest they trample them under their feet, and turn again and rend you.

Ask, and it shall be given you; seek, and ye shall find; knock, and it shall be opened unto you: For every one that asketh receiveth; and he that seeketh findeth; and to him that knocketh it shall be opened.

Or what man is there of you, whom if his son ask bread, will he give him a stone? Or if he ask a fish, will he give him a serpent? If ye then, being evil, know how to give good gifts unto your children, how much more shall your Father which is in heaven give good things to them that ask him?[7:1-11]

THE GOLDEN RULE

Therefore all things whatsoever ye would that men should do to you, do ye even so to them: for this is the law and the prophets.

Enter ye in at the strait gate: for wide is the gate, and broad is the way, that leadeth to destruction, and many there be which go in thereat: Because strait is the gate, and narrow is the way, which leadeth unto life, and few there be that find it.

Beware of false prophets, which come to you in sheep's clothing, but inwardly they are ravening wolves. Ye shall know them by their fruits. Do men gather grapes of thorns, or figs of thistles? Even so every good tree bringeth forth good fruit; but a corrupt tree bringeth forth evil fruit. A good tree cannot bring forth evil fruit, neither can a corrupt tree bring forth good fruit. Every tree that bringeth not forth good fruit is hewn down, and cast into the fire. Wherefore by their fruits ye shall know them.[7:12-20]

THE FIRM FOUNDATION

Not every one that saith unto me, Lord, Lord, shall enter into the kingdom of heaven; but he that doeth the will of my Father which is in heaven.

Men will say to me in that day, Lord, Lord, have we not prophesied in thy name? and in thy name have cast out devils? and in thy name done many wonderful works? And then will I profess unto them, I never knew you: depart from me, ye that work iniquity.

Therefore, whosoever heareth these sayings of mine, and doeth them, I will liken him unto a wise man, which built his house upon a rock: and the rain descended, and the floods came, and the winds blew, and beat upon that house; and it fell not: for it was founded upon a rock. And every one that heareth these sayings of mine, and doeth them not, shall be likened unto a foolish man, which built his house upon the sand: and the rain descended, and the floods came, and the winds blew, and beat upon that house; and it fell: and great was the fall of it.[7:21-27]

When Jesus had ended these sayings, the people were astonished at his doctrine: For he taught them as one having authority, and not as the scribes.[7:28-29]

THE MIRACLES

Great multitudes follow him when he descends from the mountain. The sick and afflicted who come to him are healed: it is as Isaiah prophesied, Himself took our infirmities, and bare our sicknesses.[8:17]

A leper is made clean by his touch; then Jesus says to him, See thou tell no man; but go thy way, show thyself to priest, and offer the gift that Moses commanded.*. . .*[8:4] *A centurion pleads for his sick servant:* Lord, I am not worthy thou shouldest come under my roof: but speak the word only, and my servant shall be healed.[8:8] *Jesus marvels at this saying,* I have not found so great faith, no, not in

---

* Leviticus 14:10-11

Israel.[8:10] *The centurion's servant is cured within the hour.*
Peter's mother-in-law, sick with a fever, arises and is well at
Jesus' touch upon her hand.

While He and the disciples are crossing the Sea of Galilee,
their ship is tossed about by a great tempest. The disciples
turn in their fear to Jesus, saying, Lord save us: we
perish.[8:25] *But He rebukes the winds and the waves, and*
they become calm.

They are met on the other side, in the country of the
Gergesenes, by two men possessed of fierce devils. Jesus
commands the devils, and they flee into a herd of swine:

And, behold, the whole herd of swine ran violently down
a steep place into the sea, and perished in the waters.[8:32]

This sight so terrifies the people of this place that they beg
Him to leave.

He returns with his disciples to Capernaum; and here he
sees a man, named Matthew, sitting at the receipt of custom,
to whom he says, Follow me; *and Matthew does so.*[9:9]

While they sit together at their meal, many publicans and
sinners come and sit with Jesus and the disciples. The Phari-
sees ask the disciples, Why eateth your Master with publicans and sinners? *Jesus answers,* They that be whole need
not a physician, but they that are sick. . . . I am not come
to call the righteous, but sinners to repentance.[9:11-13]

Jesus calls to himself twelve disciples: Simon called Peter;
Andrew his brother; James and John the sons of Zebedee;
Philip; Bartholomew; Thomas; Matthew the publican;
James the son of Alpheus; Lebbeus, whose surname is Thad-
deus; Simon the Canaanite (or Simon Zelotes); and Judas
Iscariot, who will one day betray Him.

As he sends them forth to preach, Jesus says to the twelve,
Go not into the way of the Gentiles, and into any city of
the Samaritans enter ye not: But go rather to the lost sheep

of the house of Israel.[10:5-6] *He gives them power to heal the sick, to cleanse the lepers, to raise the dead, to cast out devils:* Freely ye have received, freely give.[10:8]

And whosoever shall not receive you, nor hear your words, when ye depart out of that house or city, shake off the dust of your feet.[10:14] I send you forth as sheep in the midst of wolves: be ye therefore wise as serpents, and harmless as doves.[10:16]

They are warned against deceit and treachery: Ye shall be hated of all men for my name's sake: but he that endureth to the end shall be saved.[10:22]

Think not that I am come to send peace on earth: I came not to send peace, but a sword.[10:34]

He that findeth his life shall lose it: and he that loseth his life for my sake shall find it.[10:39]

From his prison, John the Baptist sends two of his disciples to inquire of Jesus, Art thou he that should come, or do we look for another?[11:3] *Jesus sends the men back to report to John the miracles of which they have heard and which they now see. When they have gone, He speaks to the people concerning John:*

What went ye out into the wilderness to see? A reed shaken with the wind? But what went ye out for to see? A man clothed in soft raiment? Behold, they that wear soft clothing are in kings' houses. But what went ye out for to see? A prophet? yea, I say unto you, and more than a prophet. For this is he, of whom it is written, Behold, I send my messenger before thy face, which shall prepare thy way before thee.

Verily I say unto you, Among them that are born of women, there hath not risen a greater than John the Baptist.[11:7-11]

He that hath ears to hear, let him hear.[11:15]

Then He says to the people, Come unto me, all ye that labor and are heavy laden, and I will give you rest. Take my yoke upon you, and learn of me; for I am meek and lowly in heart: and ye shall find rest unto your souls. For my yoke is easy, and my burden is light.[11:28-30]

THE PARABLES

He speaks in parables. And when his disciples ask him why he speaks to the people in parables, Jesus replies, Because it is given unto you to know the mysteries of the kingdom of heaven, but to them it is not given. For whosoever hath, to him shall be given, and he shall have more abundance: but whosoever hath not, from him shall be taken away even that he hath.[13:11-12]

THE PARABLE OF THE SOWER: Behold, a sower went forth to sow; and when he sowed, some seeds fell by the wayside, and the fowls came and devoured them up. *But some seeds fall upon stony places, and are scorched by the sun:* Because they had no root, they withered away. *Some seeds fall among thorns, and are choked.* But other fell into good ground, and brought forth fruit, some a hundredfold, some sixtyfold, some thirtyfold.[13:3-8]

He that received seed into the good ground is he that heareth the word, and understandeth it; which also beareth fruit, and bringeth forth. . . .[13:23]

THE PARABLE OF THE MUSTARD SEED: The kingdom of heaven is like to a grain of mustard seed, which a man took, and sowed in his field: which indeed is the least of all seeds: but when it is grown, it . . . becometh a tree, so that the birds of the air come and lodge in the branches thereof.[13:31-32]

THE PEARL OF GREAT PRICE: The kingdom of heaven is

like unto a merchant man, seeking goodly pearls: who, when he had found one pearl of great price, went and sold all that he had, and bought it.[13:45-46]

His words are received with astonishment by the people of Nazareth, His own people, who say, Is not this the carpenter's son? . . . Whence then hath this man all these things? *Jesus replies,* A prophet is not without honor, save in his own country, and in his own house.[13:55-57] *And His works are not done here, because of their unbelief.*

THE MARTYRDOM OF JOHN THE BAPTIST

On the birthday of Herod the king, his wife's young daughter dances before him, and so pleases Herod that he swears he will give her anything she may ask. Her mother, Herodias the queen, bitterly hates John the Baptist: she instructs her daughter to say to Herod, Give me here John Baptist's head in a charger.[14:8] *So John's head is brought to the maiden; and she gives it to her mother on a platter.*

When Jesus hears of this, he goes into the desert. A great number of people—some five thousand men, together with their women and children—follow Him on foot. There is no food for them, save five loaves and two fishes. Jesus takes these and blesses them; and the disciples distribute the food to the people:

And they did all eat, and were filled: and they took up of the fragments that remained twelve baskets full.[14:20]

Then He sends the people away; and the disciples he sends by ship to the land of Gennesaret, while he goes upon a mountain to pray. In the night, the disciples are frightened by a storm which tosses their ship about on the waves.

And in the fourth watch of the night Jesus went unto them, walking on the sea. . . . The disciples . . . were troubled, saying, It is a spirit. . . . But straightway Jesus spake unto them, saying, Be of good cheer, it is I; be not afraid.[14:25-27]

Peter says, Lord, if it be thou, bid me come unto thee on the water. And he said, Come.[14:28-29] *Peter leaves the ship. But he is afraid and begins to sink. Jesus stretches out his hand to him, saying,* O thou of little faith, wherefore didst thou doubt?[14:31] *They go aboard the ship, and the wind dies. Then they worship Jesus, saying,* Of a truth thou art the Son of God.[14:33]

When they reach land, people come from all the country round about only to touch the hem of His garment. But scribes and Pharisees from Jerusalem come and complain against the disciples: they do not wash their hands before eating, as the law commands. Jesus says, Hear, and understand: Not that which goeth into the mouth defileth a man; but that which cometh out of the mouth, this defileth a man.[15:10-11] *The Pharisees are offended at this. Jesus tells his disciples,* Let them alone: they be blind leaders of the blind. And if the blind lead the blind, both shall fall into the ditch.[15:14]

Whom do men say that I, the Son of man, am? *asks Jesus of his disciples.* Some say that thou art John the Baptist; some, Elias; and others, Jeremias, or one of the prophets, *they reply. He says,* But whom say ye that I am? *Simon called Peter answers and says,* Thou art the Christ, the Son of the living God. *Jesus blesses him, saying,* I say also unto thee, That thou art Peter, and upon this rock I will build my church; and the gates of hell shall not prevail against it. And I will give unto thee the keys of the kingdom of heaven.[16:13-19]

He charges them to tell no one that he is the Christ. From this time on, also, He begins to speak to them of his return to Jerusalem, *of the suffering he must undergo there, and of his death and resurrection.* If any man will come after me, let him deny himself, and take up his cross, and follow me. For whosoever will save his life shall lose it: and whosoever will lose his life for my sake shall find it. For what is a man profited, if he shall gain the whole world, and lose his own soul?[16:24-26]

Then Jesus takes Peter, James, and John up upon a high mountain; and he is transfigured before them: his face shines as the sun, and his clothing is white as the light; and Moses and Elijah appear, and talk with him.

Peter says, Lord, it is good for us to be here: if thou wilt, let us make here three tabernacles; one for thee, and one for Moses, and one for Elias. *A voice speaks from out of a cloud, saying,* This is my beloved Son, in whom I am well pleased; hear ye him.[17:4-5]

THE WORDS OF JESUS

He says to his disciples, If ye have faith as a grain of mustard seed, ye shall say unto this mountain, Remove hence to yonder place; and it shall remove: and nothing shall be impossible unto you.[17:20]

Who is the greatest in the kingdom of heaven?[18:1] *ask his disciples. Jesus answers,* Except ye be converted, and become as little children, ye shall not enter into the kingdom of heaven. Whosoever therefore shall humble himself as this little child, the same is greatest in the kingdom of heaven. And whoso shall receive one such little child in my name receiveth me. But whoso shall offend one of these little ones which believe in me, it were better for him that a millstone were hanged about his neck, and that he were drowned in the depth of the sea.

Woe unto the world because of offenses! for it must needs

be that offenses come; but woe to that man by whom the offense cometh.[18:3-7]

Again I say unto you, That if two of you shall agree on earth as touching anything that they shall ask, it shall be done for them of my Father which is in heaven. For where two or three are gathered together in my name, there am I in the midst of them.[18:19-20]

The Pharisees ask of Him, Is it lawful for a man to put away his wife for every cause?[19:3] *Jesus replies,* . . . they are no more twain, but one flesh. What therefore God hath joined together, let not man put asunder. [19:6]

He says to His disciples, who rebuke some children brought to him for his blessing, Suffer little children, and forbid them not, to come unto me; for of such is the kingdom of heaven.[19:14]

A rich young man comes asking what he shall do to have eternal life. Jesus says, Keep the commandments. . . .[19:17] *Then He says to the young man,* If thou wilt be perfect, go and sell that thou hast, and give to the poor, and thou shalt have treasure in heaven: and come and follow me. *But the young man goes sorrowfully away:* for he had great possessions.[19:21-22]

Jesus then says to his disciples, It is easier for a camel to go through the eye of a needle, than for a rich man to enter into the kingdom of God. *When the disciples ask,* Who then can be saved? *He replies,* With men this is impossible; but with God all things are possible.[19:24-26]

The kingdom of heaven is likened to the owner of a vineyard: In the morning he hires laborers for a penny a day; later he hires others, and later still others. In the evening, the laborers are given their hire, every man receiving a penny. The first laborers complain, saying, thou hast made them equal unto us, which have borne the burden and

heat of the day. *The vineyard owner says,* Friend, I do thee
no wrong. . . . Take that thine is, and go thy way: I will
give unto this last, even as unto thee. Is it not lawful for me
to do what I will with mine own? Is thine eye evil, because
I am good?

So the last shall be first, and the first last: for many be
called, but few chosen.[20:12-16]

THE CLEANSING OF THE TEMPLE

They enter Jerusalem.

And Jesus went into the temple of God, and cast out all
them that sold and bought in the temple, and overthrew the
tables of the money changers. . . . And said unto them, It is
written, My house shall be called the house of prayer; but
ye have made it a den of thieves.[21:12-13]

Seeking to entangle Him, the Pharisees ask, Is it lawful
to give tribute unto Caesar, or not?[22:17] *He says,* Show me
the tribute money. . . . Whose is this image and superscrip-
tion? *They say it is Caesar's. He replies:* Render therefore
unto Caesar the things which are Caesar's; and unto God
the things that are God's.[22:19-21]

He denounces the Pharisees: Woe unto you, scribes and
Pharisees, hypocrites! for ye pay tithe of mint and anise
and cummin, and have omitted the weightier matters of the
law, judgment, mercy, and faith. . . . Ye blind guides, which
strain at a gnat, and swallow a camel. [23:23-24] Woe unto
you, scribes and Pharisees, hypocrites! for ye are like unto
whited sepulchres, which indeed appear beautiful outward,
but are within full of dead men's bones and of all uncleanness.[23:27]

O Jerusalem, Jerusalem, thou that killest the prophets,
and stonest them which are sent unto thee, how often would
I have gathered thy children together, even as a hen gathereth her chickens under her wings, and ye would not![23:37]

THE OLIVET DISCOURSE

Upon being shown the buildings of the Temple, Jesus says to his disciples, Verily I say unto you, There shall not be left here one stone upon another, that shall not be thrown down.[24:2]

They sit upon the mount of Olives. His disciples ask, Tell us, when shall these things be? and what shall be the sign of thy coming, and of the end of the world? *Jesus replies,* Take heed that no man deceive you. For many shall come in my name. . . . And ye shall hear of wars and rumors of wars: see that ye be not troubled: for all these things must come to pass, but the end is not yet.

For nation shall rise against nation, and kingdom against kingdom: and there shall be famines, and pestilences, and earthquakes. . . .

All these are the beginning of sorrows. Then shall they deliver you up to be afflicted, and shall kill you: and ye shall be hated of all nations for my name's sake.[24:3-9]

But he that shall endure unto the end, the same shall be saved.[24:13]

Heaven and earth shall pass away, but my words shall not pass away. But of that day and hour knoweth no man, not the angels of heaven, but my Father only.[24:35-36]

Again, He likens the kingdom of heaven to ten virgins, which took their lamps, and went forth to meet the bridegroom. And five of them were wise, and five were foolish. They that were foolish . . . took no oil with them: but the wise took oil in their vessels. . . .[25:1-4]

At midnight there is a cry, Behold the bridegroom cometh.[25:6] *The foolish virgins say to the wise,* Give us of your oil.[25:8] *They are refused; and while they go to buy oil, the bridegroom arrives, the marriage begins, the door is shut; and the foolish virgins are turned away.*

Watch therefore, for ye know neither the day nor the hour wherein the Son of man cometh.[25:13]

THE LAST JUDGMENT

Jesus says to his disciples, When the Son of man shall come in his glory, and all the holy angels with him, then shall he sit upon the throne of his glory: And before him shall be gathered all nations: and he shall separate them one from another, as a shepherd divideth his sheep from the goats. . . .

Then shall the King say unto them on his right hand, Come, ye blessed of my Father, inherit the kingdom prepared for you from the foundation of the world: For I was ahungered and ye gave me meat: I was thirsty, and ye gave me drink: I was a stranger, and ye took me in. Naked, and ye clothed me: I was sick, and ye visited me: I was in prison, and ye came unto me. Then shall the righteous answer him, saying, Lord, when saw we thee ahungered . . . or thirsty . . . a stranger . . . or naked? . . . Or when saw we thee sick, or in prison? . . . And the king shall answer . . . Verily, I say unto you, inasmuch as ye have done it unto one of the least of these my brethren, ye have done it unto me.

Then shall he say also unto them on the left hand. . . .[25:31-41]

Verily I say unto you, Inasmuch as ye did it not to one of the least of these, ye did it not to me. And these shall go away into everlasting punishment: but the righteous into life eternal.[25:45-46]

THE DEATH AND THE RESURRECTION

The chief priests, the scribes, and the elders of Jerusalem assemble in the palace of the high priest, Caiaphas, to plot how they may take Jesus, and kill him. Then Judas Iscariot comes to them and says, What will ye give me, and I will deliver him unto you?

And they covenanted with him for thirty pieces of silver.[26:15]

On the first day of the Passover, Jesus says to his disciples, Go into the city to such a man, and say unto him, The Master saith, My time is at hand; I will keep the passover at thy house with my disciples.[26:18]

In the evening they sit down at the table together. Jesus says, Verily I say unto you, that one of you shall betray me.

Each says sorrowfully, Lord, is it I?[26:21-22] *Jesus replies,* The Son of man goeth as it is written of him: but woe unto that man by whom the Son of man is betrayed! it had been good for that man if he had not been born. *Judas Iscariot says,* Master, is it I? *And He answers,* Thou hast said.

And as they were eating, Jesus took bread, and blessed it, and brake it, and gave it to the disciples, and said, Take, eat; this is my body. And he took the cup, and gave thanks, and gave it to them, saying, Drink ye all of it; for this is my blood of the new testament, which is shed for many for the remission of sins.[26:24-28]

He says, All ye shall be offended because of me this night. . . . But after I am risen again, I will go before you into Galilee. *Peter protests this: and Jesus says to him,* This night, before the cock crow, thou shalt deny me thrice.

Though I should die with thee, *says Peter,* yet will I not deny thee.[26:31-35]

They are together in a place called Gethsemane. Jesus goes apart to pray: O my Father, if it be possible, let this cup pass from me: nevertheless, not as I will, but as thou wilt.

The disciples have meanwhile fallen asleep. Jesus says, What, could ye not watch with me one hour? Watch and pray, that ye enter not into temptation: the spirit indeed is willing, but the flesh is weak.[26:39-41]

While He speaks to them, saying, the hour is at hand, and

the Son of man is betrayed into the hands of sinners,[26:45] *Judas appears, and says to the multitude, carrying swords and staves, who accompany him,* Whomsoever I shall kiss, that same is he. . . .

And forthwith he came to Jesus, and said, Hail, Master; and kissed him.

Jesus says, Friend, wherefore art thou come? *Then He is seized. One of the disciples strikes with his sword at a servant of the High Priest, and cuts off the man's ear. Jesus says,* Put up again thy sword . . . for all they that take the sword shall perish with the sword. Thinkest thou that I cannot now pray to my Father? . . .[26:48-53]

He is brought before the High Priest, Caiaphas, who says, I adjure thee by the living God, that thou tell us whether thou be the Christ, the Son of God, *Jesus replies,* Thou hast said.[26:63-64] *Accused of blasphemy, mocked, buffeted, spit upon, He holds his peace.*

Meanwhile Peter, waiting outside, is twice recognized to be a follower of Jesus. Twice he denies it. The third time he begins to curse and swear, saying, I know not the man.

And immediately the cock crew.[26:74]

Remembering Jesus' words, Peter weeps bitterly.

Judas repents his act of betrayal; but the thirty pieces of silver, which he tries to return, are refused. Throwing them down in the Temple, he goes away and hangs himself.

Standing before Pontius Pilate, the governor, Jesus, again asked Art thou the King of the Jews? *once more replies,* Thou sayest.[27:11] *Silent before their accusations, His only advocate is Pilate's wife, from whom comes a message to the governor:* Have nothing to do with that just man.[27:19] *Pilate gives the people their choice: either Jesus' life, or that of Barabbas, a notorious criminal. They condemn Jesus, shouting,* Let him be crucified.[27:22]

When Pilate saw that he could prevail nothing . . . he took water, and washed his hands before the multitude, saying, I am innocent of the blood of this just person: see ye to it. Then answered all the people, and said, His blood be on us, and on our children.[27:24-25]

Jesus is taken by the soldiers; He is stripped, and dressed in a scarlet robe; a crown of thorns is put on his head, and a reed in his right hand; he is mocked, and spit upon, and struck on the head.

He is taken to a place called Golgotha, that is to say, a place of a skull.[27:33] *Here they crucify Him. Over His head they write,* THIS IS JESUS THE KING OF THE JEWS.[27:37]

Two thieves are crucified on either side of Him. The chief priests, the scribes and the elders come to mock Him: He saved others; himself he cannot save.[27:42] *There is darkness over all the land.*

At about the ninth hour Jesus cries, Eli, Eli, lama sabachthani? . . . My God, My God, why hast thou forsaken me?[27:46] *He dies.*

And behold, the veil of the temple was rent in twain from the top to the bottom; and the earth did quake, and the rocks rent. . . .[27:51]

And those watching say, Truly this was the Son of God.[27:54]

In the evening Joseph, a rich man of Arimathea, with the consent of Pilate, lays the body of Jesus in his own tomb, rolling a great stone against the door. Here Mary Magdalene, and Mary the mother of James and Joses, keep watch.

At the end of the sabbath, toward dawn, the Angel of the Lord descends, amidst a great earthquake, and rolls back the stone from the sepulchre, saying to the women, Go quickly, and tell his disciples that he is risen from the dead.[28:7]

Some report of this reaches the ears of the elders in Jerusalem; who thereupon bribe the soldiers on guard to say that His disciples came and stole away his body.

The eleven disciples go into Galilee. Here, at an appointed place, He comes and speaks to them:

All power is given unto me in heaven and earth.

Go ye therefore, and teach all nations, baptizing them in the name of the Father, and of the Son, and of the Holy Ghost: teaching them to observe all things whatsoever I have commanded you: and, lo, I am with you always, even unto the end of the world. Amen.^{28:18-20}

ST. MARK

The Gospel According to St. Mark* is essentially the same story as that told in the first Gospel; but Mark contains additional biographical details of the life of Jesus, while both Matthew and Luke contain a higher proportion of His works and teaching.

Beginning with the story of John the Baptist, The voice of one crying in the wilderness,^{1:3} *The Gospel of Mark recounts the baptism of Jesus; his temptation by Satan in the wilderness; his ministry in Galilee; the calling of his disciples; the healing of the sick and the casting out of demons;*

---

* Though second in canonical order, the Gospel of Mark is regarded by most biblical scholars as the earliest of the four Gospels and as the probable source material of Matthew and Luke. "Of the 661 verses contained in the authentic text of Mark, it has been calculated that more than 600 are reproduced or represented in substance in Matthew, and about 350 in Luke."—*Encyclopaedia Britannica.*

As most of the events, parables, discourses, and sayings recorded by both Mark and Luke are found in Matthew, for the sake of brevity these will not be repeated in this or in the succeeding Gospel synopsis.

*his parables; his rejection by his own people in Nazareth;
the Olivet discourse; the transfiguration on the mountain,
and Jesus' prediction of his death and resurrection.*

*Mark also presents a second account of the Last Supper,
of the agony of our Lord in the garden at Gethsemane, of
His trial before the high priest and before Pilate. Finally,
it records the Crucifixion and the Resurrection.*

In this book, Jesus makes his entry into Galilee, saying,
The time is fulfilled, and the kingdom of God is at hand:
repent ye, and believe the gospel.[1:15]

*These are passages and sayings from the Gospel of Mark
which do not appear in Matthew:*

The sabbath was made for man, and not man for the
sabbath.[2:27]

If a house be divided against itself, that house cannot
stand.[3:25]

With what measure ye mete, it shall be measured to
you.[4:24]

So is the kingdom of God, as if a man should cast seed
into the ground; and should sleep, and rise night and day,
and the seed should spring and grow up, he knoweth not
how. For the earth bringeth forth fruit of herself; first the
blade, then the ear, after that the full corn in the ear.[4:26-28]

*Jesus sees how the people cast money into the treasury of
the synagogue:*

And there came a certain poor widow, and she threw in
two mites, which make a farthing. And he called unto him
his disciples, and saith unto them, Verily I say unto you,
That this poor widow hath cast more in, than all they which
have cast into the treasury: For all they did cast in of their
abundance; but she of her want did cast in all that she
had. . . .[12:42-44]

Beware of the scribes, which love . . . salutations in the
marketplaces, and the chief seats in the synagogues, and

the uppermost rooms at the feasts: which devour widows' houses, and for a pretense make long prayers: these shall receive greater damnation.[12:38-40]

THE RESURRECTION

Now when Jesus was risen early the first day of the week, he appeared first to Mary Magdalene, out of whom he had cast seven devils.[16:9]

Afterward he appeared unto the eleven as they sat at meat. . . . And he said unto them, Go ye into all the world, and preach the gospel to every creature. He that believeth and is baptized shall be saved; but he that believeth not shall be damned.[16:14-16]

So then, after the Lord had spoken unto them, he was received up into heaven, and sat on the right hand of God.[16:19]

ST. LUKE

Luke "the beloved physician" (Colossians 4:14), the friend and fellow-worker of the apostle Paul and his companion on missionary journeys, here undertakes to set forth the facts, as he has had them from eye-witnesses, concerning the life of Jesus and the beginning of the Christian faith. The Gospel According to St. Luke is addressed to a friend of Luke's, otherwise unknown, whose name is Theophilus:

It seemed good to me also, having had perfect understanding of all things from the very first, to write unto thee in order, most excellent Theophilus, that thou mightest know the certainty of those things, wherein thou hast been instructed.[1:3-4]

Although Luke's account parallels those of Matthew and

Mark, the early life of Jesus is most fully told in this third Gospel, which contains as well a number of incidents, parables and utterances that are peculiar to it.

THE BIRTH OF JESUS

In Judea, in the reign of Herod, there is an elderly priest named Zacharias to whom one day the angel Gabriel appears, and says to him, thy wife Elisabeth shall bear thee a son, and thou shalt call his name John.[1:13]

Six months later, in the city of Nazareth in Galilee, Gabriel appears to a virgin named Mary, and says, Hail, thou that are highly favored, the Lord is with thee: blessed art thou among women.[1:28]

Behold, thou shalt conceive in thy womb, and bring forth a son, and shalt call his name JESUS. He shall be great, and shall be called the Son of the Highest. . . . And of his kingdom there shall be no end.

Mary says to the angel, How shall this be, seeing I know not a man? *He replies,* The Holy Ghost shall come upon thee, and the power of the Highest shall overshadow thee: therefore also that holy thing which shall be born of thee shall be called the Son of God.[1:31-35]

Mary hurries to the home of Elisabeth who, inspired by the Holy Ghost, greets her in a loud voice: Blessed art thou among women, and blessed is the fruit of thy womb.[1:42]

Mary answers, My soul doth magnify the Lord, and my spirit hath rejoiced in God my Saviour. For he hath regarded the low estate of his handmaiden: for, behold, from henceforth all generations shall call me blessed.

He hath showed strength with his arm; he hath scattered the proud in the imagination of their hearts. He hath put down the mighty from their seats, and exalted them of low degree. He hath filled the hungry with good things; and the rich he hath sent empty away.[1:46-53]

Mary stays with Elisabeth for about three months; then she returns to Nazareth.

As the angel has promised, Elisabeth, though well advanced in years, gives birth to a son, who is named John. Zacharias prophesies and says, Thou, child, shalt be called the prophet of the Highest: for thou shalt go before the face of the Lord to prepare his ways. . . .[1:76]

To give light to them that sit in darkness and in the shadow of death, to guide our feet into the way of peace.[1:79]

And it came to pass in those days, that there went out a decree from Caesar Augustus, that all the world should be taxed.[2:1]

Each man, for this purpose, must go to his native city. So Joseph, with Mary his wife, goes to his own city of Bethlehem in Judea. Here the time of Mary's delivery arrives:

And she brought forth her firstborn son, and wrapped him in swaddling clothes, and laid him in a manger; because there was no room for them in the inn.

And there were in the same country shepherds abiding in the field, keeping watch over their flock by night. And, lo, the angel of the Lord came upon them, and the glory of the Lord shone round about them: and they were sore afraid.

The angel says, Fear not: for, behold, I bring you good tidings of great joy, which shall be to all people. For unto you is born this day in the city of David a Saviour, which is Christ the Lord. And this shall be a sign unto you; Ye shall find the babe wrapped in swaddling clothes, lying in a manger.

Suddenly, with the angel, there is a heavenly host, praising God, and saying, Glory to God in the highest, and on earth peace, good will toward men.[2:7-14]

The shepherds hasten to find Mary and Joseph, and the

*baby lying in the manger. They spread the story, to the
wonder of all who hear it.*

And the child grew, and waxed strong in spirit, filled with
wisdom: and the grace of God was upon him.[2:40]

*When he is twelve years old, Jesus is taken by his par-
ents to Jerusalem for the feast of the Passover. Afterwards
Joseph and Mary turn their steps homeward; but the boy
Jesus, without their knowledge, remains behind. They find
him, after three days, sitting among the doctors in the
Temple, listening and asking questions, astonishing every-
one by his knowledge and understanding. When Mary reproaches him for causing them anxiety, he says,* How is it
that ye sought me? Wist ye not that I must be about my
Father's business?[2:49]

His parents do not understand his meaning.

But his mother kept all these things in her heart. And
Jesus increased in wisdom and stature, and in favor with
God and man.[2:51-52]

*In the fifteenth year of the reign of Tiberius Caesar in
Rome, Pontius Pilate is the Roman governor of Judea;
Herod is tetrarch of Galilee; his brother Philip is tetrarch
of Iturea and the region of Trachonitis; Annas and Caiaphas
are the high priests.*

*Jesus, having been baptized by John, the Spirit of the
Lord having descended upon him, is teaching in the synagogues of Galilee. Although he is rejected by his own people in Nazareth, his fame spreads throughout the region.*

*As he sits at table in the house of a Pharisee named
Simon, in Capernaum, a woman of the city comes weeping.
She washes his feet with her tears, kisses them and anoints
them. Privately, Simon scorns this: If Jesus is a prophet, he
should know that the woman is a sinner. Jesus says,* Simon,

I have somewhat to say unto thee; and Simon says, Master, say on.

Jesus says, There was a certain creditor which had two debtors: the one owed five hundred pence, and the other fifty. And when they had nothing to pay, he frankly forgave them both. Tell me therefore, which of them will love him most? *Simon replies,* I suppose that he, to whom he forgave most. *Jesus says,* Thou hast rightly judged.[7:40-43]

Wherefore I say unto thee, Her sins, which are many, are forgiven; for she loved much: but to whom little is forgiven, the same loveth little.[7:47]

THE GOOD SAMARITAN

Thou shalt love . . . thy neighbor as thyself.[10:27]
Who is my neighbor? a lawyer inquires of Jesus.
He replies, A certain man went down from Jerusalem to Jericho, and fell among thieves, which stripped him of his raiment, and wounded him, and departed, leaving him half dead. And by chance there came down a certain priest that way: and when he saw him, he passed by on the other side. And likewise a Levite. . . .

But a certain Samaritan . . . had compassion on him, and went to him, and bound up his wounds . . . and brought him to an inn, and took care of him. And on the morrow when he departed, he took out two pence, and gave them to the host, and said unto him, Take care of him; and whatsoever thou spendest more, when I come again, I will repay thee.

Which of these three, asks Jesus, was neighbor unto him that fell among the thieves? *The lawyer says,* He that showed mercy on him. *Jesus says,* Go, and do thou likewise.[10:30-37]

In his journeying, Jesus is received into the home of two sisters, Mary and Martha. Mary sits at His feet, listening to his words.

But Martha was cumbered about much serving, *and complains that her sister has left her to serve alone. But Jesus says,* Martha, Martha, thou art careful and troubled about many things: But one thing is needed: and Mary hath chosen that good part, which shall not be taken away from her.[10:40-42]

THE PRODIGAL SON

There are murmurs against Jesus among the Pharisees and scribes, that he receives sinners, and eats with them. He answers, saying, What man of you, having a hundred sheep, if he lose one of them, doth not leave the ninety and nine in the wilderness, and go after that which is lost, until he find it? And when he hath found it, he layeth it on his shoulders, rejoicing. . . . I say unto you, that likewise joy shall be in heaven over one sinner that repenteth, more than over ninety and nine just persons which need no repentance.[15:4-7]

He tells of a man with two sons, who divides his possessions between them. The younger son leaves his home and wastes his substance in riotous living. Starving, he says to himself, I will arise and go to my father, and will say unto him, Father, I have sinned against heaven, and before thee, and am no more worthy to be called thy son: make me as one of thy hired servants.[15:18-19]

But when his father sees him he falls on his neck, and kisses him, and calls to his servants, Bring hither the fatted calf, and kill it; and let us eat, and be merry: For this my son was dead, and is alive again; he was lost, and is found.[15:23-24]

The elder son angrily reproaches his father: These many years do I serve thee, neither transgressed I at any time thy commandment; and yet thou never gavest me a kid. . . . But as soon as this thy son was come, which hath devoured thy living with harlots, thou hast killed for him the fatted calf.

The father replies, Son, thou art ever with me, and all that I have is thine. It was meet that we should make merry, and be glad: for this thy brother was dead, and is alive again; and was lost, and is found.[15:29-32]

Jesus, when the Pharisees deride him, speaks to them of a certain rich man clothed in purple and fine linen, dining sumptuously every day; and of a miserable beggar named Lazarus lying at the rich man's gate, begging only the crumbs from his table.

The beggar died, and was carried by the angels into Abraham's bosom.[16:22]

The rich man also dies. Being tormented in hell, he raises his eyes, and sees Lazarus; upon which he cried out to Abraham to send Lazarus to him, that he may dip the tip of his finger in water, and cool my tongue. . . . *Abraham says,* Son, remember that thou in thy lifetime receivedst thy good things, and likewise Lazarus evil things. . . . And besides all this, between us and you there is a great gulf fixed. . . .

At least, pleads the rich man, if Abraham will send Lazarus to save the rich man's brothers: if one went unto them from the dead, they will repent. *Says father Abraham,* If they hear not Moses and the prophets, neither will they be persuaded, though one rose from the dead.[16:24-31]

FATHER, FORGIVE THEM

When He has been sentenced by Pilate, Jesus is led away.

And there followed him a great company of people, and of women, which also bewailed and lamented him. But Jesus turning unto them said, Daughters of Jerusalem, weep not for me, but weep for yourselves, and for your children. . . .[23:27-28]

And when they were come to the place, which is called Calvary, there they crucified him, and the malefactors, one on the right hand, and the other on the left.

Jesus says, Father, forgive them; for they know not what they do.[23:33-34]

One of the two malefactors rails at Him: If thou be Christ, save thyself and us. *But the other rebukes him, saying,* Dost not thou fear God? . . . We received the due rewards of our deeds: but this man hath done nothing amiss. *To Jesus he says,* Lord, remember me when thou comest into thy kingdom. *Jesus says to him,* Today shalt thou be with me in paradise.[23:39-43]

And when Jesus had cried with a loud voice, he said, Father, into thy hands I commend my spirit: and having said thus, he gave up the ghost.[23:46]

ST. JOHN

The fourth Gospel takes for granted a familiarity with the people and events of the first three. While these three (called the Synoptic Gospels) record the earthly events in the life of Jesus, the Gospel according to St. John is principally concerned with the spiritual meaning of His ministry. The theme is set forth in the opening verses:

In the beginning was the Word, and the Word was with God, and the Word was God. . . .

All things were made by him; and without him was not any thing made that was made. In him was life; and the life was the light of men. And the light shineth in darkness; and the darkness comprehended it not.

There was a man sent from God, whose name was John

. . . to bear witness of the Light, that all men through him might believe. He was not that Light, but was sent to bear witness of that Light.

That was the true Light, which lighteth every man that cometh into the world. He was in the world, and the world was made by him, and the world knew him not. He came unto his own, and his own received him not. But as many as received him, to them gave he power to become the sons of God. . . .

And the Word was made flesh, and dwelt among us . . . full of grace and truth.[1:1-14]

For the law was given by Moses, but grace and truth came by Jesus Christ.[1:17]

The following passages are peculiar to the Gospel of John, and are not found in the other Gospels:

THE MARRIAGE AT CANA

The first miracle performed by Jesus in Galilee, manifesting his glory, takes place at a marriage in Cana, when Mary, his mother, says to him, They have no wine. *Jesus says to her,* Woman, what have I to do with thee? mine hour is not yet come.[2:3-4] *But he tells the servants to fill the waterpots. The steward of the feast, tasting the water, says to the bridegroom,* Thou hast kept the good wine until now.[2:10]

Except a man be born again, he cannot see the kingdom of God.[3:3]

Nicodemus, a Pharisee, a ruler of the Jews, wonders at this saying of Jesus. Jesus says to him, Marvel not that I said unto thee, Ye must be born again. The wind bloweth where it listeth, and thou hearest the sound thereof, but canst not tell whence it cometh, and whither it goeth: so is every one that is born of the Spirit.[3:7-8]

And no man hath ascended up to heaven, but he that came down from heaven, even the Son of man. . . .[3:13]

For God so loved the world, that he gave his only begotten Son, that whosoever believeth in him should not perish, but have everlasting life.[3:16]

And this is the condemnation, that light is come into the world, and men loved darkness rather than light, because their deeds were evil.[3:19]

As Jesus is teaching in the Temple, the scribes and Pharisees bring before him a woman taken in adultery. To trap him, they ask if, in accordance with the law of Moses, she shall be stoned. Jesus says, He that is without sin among you, let him first cast a stone at her.[8:7] *They leave, one by one. Left alone with the woman, Jesus says to her,* Neither do I condemn thee: go, and sin no more.[8:11]

THE RAISING OF LAZARUS

Lazarus of Bethany, and his sisters, Mary and Martha, are greatly beloved by Jesus. Lazarus falls very sick; and his sisters send to Jesus for help. When He arrives in Bethany, Lazarus is four days dead; but Jesus says to Martha, Thy brother shall rise again. *She replies,* I know that he shall rise again in the resurrection at the last day. *But He says,* I am the resurrection, and the life: he that believeth in me, though he were dead, yet shall he live: and whosoever liveth and believeth in me shall never die.[11:23-26]

He is taken to the tomb in which lies Lazarus. Jesus weeps. He cries, Lazarus, come forth.

And he that was dead came forth. . . .[11:43-44]

When this becomes known, the priests and the Pharisees meet to consider what shall be done to Jesus: If we let him thus alone, all men will believe on him: and the Romans shall come and take away both our place and nation. *The high priest, Caiaphas, speaks the decisive word:* It is expedient for us, that one man should die for the people, and that the whole nation perish not.[11:48-50]

THE LAST SUPPER

The Passover feast is finished, when Jesus says to Judas Iscariot, That thou doest, do quickly.[13:27] *Judas quickly leaves.*

Then He speaks to the others:

Little children, yet a little while I am with you. Ye shall seek me. . . . Whither I go, ye cannot come; so now I say to you.

A new commandment I give unto you, That ye love one another; as I have loved you, that ye also love one another. By this shall all men know that ye are my disciples. . . .[13:33-35]

Let not your heart be troubled: ye believe in God, believe also in me. In my Father's house are many mansions: if it were not so, I would have told you. I go to prepare a place for you. And if I go and prepare a place for you, I will come again, and receive you unto myself; that where I am there ye may be also.[14:1-3]

I am the way, the truth, and the life: no man cometh unto the Father, but by me.[14:6]

Philip, His disciple, says, Lord, show us the Father, and it sufficeth us. *Jesus replies,* Have I been so long time with you, and yet hast thou not known me, Philip? he that hath seen me hath seen the Father. . . . Believest thou not that I am in the Father, and the Father in me?[14:8-10]

I will not leave you comfortless: I will come to you. Yet a little while, and the world seeth me no more; but ye see me: because I live, ye shall live also.[14:18-19]

Peace I leave with you, my peace I give unto you. . . .[14:27]

Greater love hath no man than this, that a man lay down his life for his friends. Ye are my friends, if ye do whatsoever I command you. . . .

Ye have not chosen me, but I have chosen you, and ordained you, that ye should go and bring forth fruit . . . that whatsoever ye shall ask of the Father in my name, he may give it you.[15:13-16]

It is expedient for you that I go away: for if I go not away, the Comforter will not come unto me; but if I depart, I will send him unto you. And when he is come, he will reprove the world of sin, and of righteousness, and of judgment.[16:7-8]

I have yet many things to say unto you, but ye cannot bear them now.[16:12]

A little while, and ye shall not see me: and again, a little while, and ye shall see me, because I go to the Father.[16:16]

These things I have spoken unto you, that in me ye might have peace. In the world ye shall have tribulation: but be of good cheer; I have overcome the world.[16:33]

GOLGOTHA

Jesus is on trial before Pilate. He says, To this end was I born, for this cause came I into the world, that I should bear witness unto the truth. . . .

Pilate replies, What is truth? *Then he says to the Jews,* I find in him no fault at all. . . . Will ye therefore that I release unto you the King of the Jews? *But they cry,* Not this man, but Barabbas.

Now Barabbas was a robber.[18:37-40]

From his cross, Jesus looks down upon Mary, his mother, and upon a beloved disciple standing nearby. He says to his mother, Woman, behold thy son! *And to the disciple,* Behold thy mother![19:26-27] *From this time on, the disciple takes His mother into his own home.*

On the day of His resurrection, in the evening, Jesus comes and stands among his disciples, and breathes on them, saying, Receive ye the Holy Ghost.[20:22]

But one of the disciples, Thomas, is not with them at the time; and when he is told by the others, We have seen the Lord, *he says,* Except I shall see in his hands the print of the nails, and put my finger into the print of the nails, and thrust my hand into his side, I will not believe.[20:25]

After eight days, Jesus again appears to them, and says to Thomas, Reach hither thy finger, and behold my hands; and reach hither thy hand, and thrust it into my side: and be not faithless, but believing. *Thomas answers,* My Lord and my God.

Jesus says to him, Thomas, because thou hast seen me, thou hast believed: blessed are they that have not seen, and yet have believed.[20:27-29]

THE ACTS OF THE APOSTLES

This book continues the history of Christianity begun in the third Gospel. The two books are part of the same work by St. Luke. The Gospel of Luke records the life and works of Jesus. The Acts of the Apostles, beginning with His reincarnation and ascension, goes on to tell of the descent of the Holy Spirit at Pentecost, the ministry of Peter, the martyrdom of Stephen, the conversion of Paul, the founding of the Christian church, the missionary journeys of the apostles.

As in the third Gospel, the Book of the Acts opens with a dedication to one Theophilus:

The former treatise have I made, O Theophilus, of all that Jesus began both to do and teach, until the day in which he was taken up, after that he through the Holy Ghost had given commandments unto the apostles whom he had chosen: To whom also he showed himself alive after his passion by many infallible proofs, being seen of them forty days, and speaking of the things pertaining to the kingdom of God:

And, being assembled together with them, commanded them that they should not depart from Jerusalem, but wait for the promise of the Father, which, saith he, ye have heard of me. For . . . ye shall be baptized with the Holy Ghost not many days hence.[1:1-5]

When Jesus has finished speaking, continues Luke, He is taken up out of their sight. While they look toward heaven, two men clad in white stand by them, saying, Ye men of Galilee, why stand ye gazing up into heaven? this same Jesus, which is taken up from you into heaven, shall so come in like manner as ye have seen him go into heaven.[1:11]

THE DAY OF PENTECOST

The little band of believers now number about a hundred and twenty persons: the eleven apostles, the women (among them Mary the mother of Jesus), and the other disciples. Having sought guidance in prayer, they appoint Matthias to fill the place of Judas Iscariot.

They are gathered together on the day of Pentecost:

Suddenly there came a sound from heaven as of a rushing mighty wind. . . . And there appeared unto them cloven tongues like as of fire . . . And they were all filled with the Holy Ghost, and began to speak with other tongues, as the Spirit gave them utterance.[2:2-4]

People come from everywhere to hear them. Jews and proselytes from every nation say in amazement to each other. We do hear them speak in our tongues the wonderful works of God. . . . What meaneth this?[2:11-12] *The twelve apostles stand up before them, and Peter speaks:* Ye men of Israel, hear these words; Jesus of Nazareth, a man approved of God among you by miracles and wonders and signs, which God did by him in the midst of you, as ye yourselves also know.[2:22]

This Jesus hath God raised up, whereof we all are witnesses.

Therefore being by the right hand of God exalted . . . he hath shed forth this, which ye now see and hear.[2:32-33]

Repent, and be baptized every one of you in the name of Jesus Christ for the remission of sins, and ye shall receive the gift of the Holy Ghost.[2:38]

About three thousand are baptized on this day.

Many wonders and signs are wrought by the apostles.

And all that believed were together, and had all things in common; and sold their possessions and goods, and parted them to all men, as every man had need. And they . . . did eat their meat with gladness and singleness of heart, praising God, and having favor with all the people. And the Lord added to the church daily such as should be saved.[2:44-47]

As Peter and John are entering the Temple one day at the hour of prayer, a lame man asks alms of them. Peter says to him. Silver and gold have I none; but such as I have give I thee: In the name of Jesus Christ of Nazareth, rise up and walk.[3:6]

The man leaps to his feet. He enters the Temple, praising God, filling the people with wonder and amazement. Peter speaks to them: Ye denied the Holy One and the Just, and desired a murderer to be granted unto you: And killed the Prince of life, whom God hath raised from the dead; whereof we are witnesses. And his name, through faith in his name, hath made this man strong. . . .[3:14-16] Repent ye therefore, and be converted, that your sins may be blotted out. . . .[3:19]

From this time the apostles are forbidden by the High Priest to speak or teach in the name of Jesus. Nevertheless they continue to preach in His name. They continue to perform signs and wonders. They are thrown into prison; but upon being released by the Angel of the Lord, they immediately go to teach again in the Temple. Questioned by the

High Priest, they say, We ought to obey God rather than men.[5:29]

It is decided by the council to put them to death. But Gamaliel, a Pharisee, a noted doctor of law, urges caution: For if this counsel or this work be of men, it will come to nought: But if it be of God, ye cannot overthrow it; lest haply ye be found even to fight against God.[5:38-39]

The apostles are beaten, and then released—rejoicing that they were counted worthy to suffer shame for His name.[5:41]

The disciple Stephen, full of faith and power, performing many miracles among the people, is charged with blasphemy, confronted by false witness, driven out of the city, and stoned to death.

His martyrdom is witnessed by a young man named Saul: And Saul was consenting unto his death.[8:1]

Afterwards there is a great persecution of the disciples. They scatter abroad—all but the apostles, who remain in Jerusalem.

Saul, a Jew of Tarsus but a Roman citizen by birth, leads in the persecution in Jerusalem, entering every house, carrying men and women off to prison, breathing out threatenings and slaughter.[9:1] *With authority from the high priest, he sets out for Damascus to bring back in chains the disciples who have fled there.*

Suddenly, as he nears Damascus, a light from heaven shines upon him. A voice says, Saul, Saul, why persecutest thou me? *Falling to the earth, Saul says,* Who art thou, Lord? *The voice replies,* I am Jesus whom thou persecutest: it is hard for thee to kick against the pricks. . . . Arise, and go into the city, and it shall be told thee what thou must do.[9:4-6]

Saul arises, blind. He is led into Damascus. For three days he neither eats nor drinks. Then, at the word of the Lord, a disciple named Ananias goes to Saul, in the street which is called Straight,[9:11] *and, laying his hands upon him, causes the scales to fall from Saul's eyes. He is baptized; and immediately he begins to preach Christ in the synagogues. So boldly does he preach, that the disciples, for his own safety, smuggle him out of Damascus and send him on his way to Jerusalem.*

THE MISSIONARY JOURNEYS

The churches are now established throughout Judea, Galilee, and Samaria. Peter, journeying from one to the other, comes upon a man named Eneas sick of the palsy, and says to him, Eneas, Jesus Christ maketh thee whole.[9:34] *Eneas, bedridden for eight years, arises and is cured.*

Tabitha, a woman full of good works,[9:36] *lying dead upon her bier, opens her eyes and sits up when Peter kneels and prays at her side.*

Though it is unlawful for a Jew to seek the company of Gentiles, Peter goes to the house of a centurion named Cornelius in Caesarea, because, he says, God hath showed me that I should not call any man common or unclean.[10:28] *Cornelius, a good and devout man, has been told in a vision to send for Peter:* who, when he cometh, shall speak unto thee.[10:32] *Upon hearing this, Peter says,* I perceive that God is no respecter of persons: But in every nation he that feareth him, and worketh righteousness, is accepted with him.[10:34-35]

He preaches to Cornelius and his assembled kin the remission of sin through faith in Jesus:

While Peter yet spake these words, the Holy Ghost fell on all them which heard the word. And they of the circumcision which believed were astonished, as many as came with Peter, because that on the Gentiles also was poured out the gift of the Holy Ghost. For they heard them speak with tongues, and magnify God.[10:44-46]

And Peter orders these Gentiles to be baptized in the name of the Lord.

Fleeing persecution, some of the disciples journey as far as Antioch, in northern Syria. They preach not only in the synagogues but to the Greeks as well, and a great number are converted.

When word of this reaches the church in Jerusalem, Barnabas is sent to look into the matter. What he finds at Antioch makes him rejoice. He fetches Saul from Tarsus, and they remain in Antioch for a year. The work prospers. Many people are converted and turn to the Lord. It is here in Antioch that the disciples are first called Christians.

Being warned by a prophet named Agabus of a coming famine, the church at Antioch determines to send relief, every man according to his ability,[11:29] *to the brethren in Judea. Barnabas and Saul go to Jerusalem on this mission. When they return to Antioch, they bring with them Mark, a cousin of Barnabas.*

A new wave of persecution now breaks over the disciples in Jerusalem. James the son of Zebedee is killed. Peter is imprisoned. Constant prayer is made for him by the brethren; and on the night before he is to be brought to trial the Angel of the Lord appears and sets him free.

Shortly afterwards Herod, seated on his throne, makes an oration to the people, who shout, It is the voice of a god, and not of a man.[12:22] *Immediately he is smitten:*

And he was eaten of worms, and gave up the ghost.

But the word of God grew and multiplied.[12:23-24]

At Antioch the prophets and teachers of the church, by divine command, send forth Barnabas and Saul to preach the word of God. They sail from the port of Seleucia to Cyprus, where they preach as Salamis and at Paphos; and afterwards to Perga in Pamphylia, where Mark, who has accompanied them this far, leaves them and returns to Jerusalem.

In Pisidian Antioch, Barnabas and Saul (who also is called Paul[13:9]), *angrily rejected by the Jews, preach to the Gentiles:*

Seeing ye . . . judge yourselves unworthy of everlasting life, lo, we turn to the Gentiles. For so hath the Lord commanded us, saying, I have set thee to be a light of the Gentiles. . . .[13:47]

They are expelled from here; and also from Iconium, where they next preach, and where the Jews stir up the people against them.

In Lystra a miracle is wrought. Paul causes a lame man, who has never before stood up, to leap to his feet and walk. A cry goes up from the bystanders: The gods are come down to us in the likeness of men.[14:11] *Barnabas is called Jupiter; and Paul, Mercury. Sacrifices to them are made ready. Paul and Barnabas plead with the people, saying,* Sirs, why do ye these things? We also are men of like passions with you. . . . Turn from these vanities unto the living God. . . .[14:15]

But then there arrive certain of the Jews of Pisidian Antioch and Iconium, who incite the people against Paul. They stone him and throw him out of the city.

Nevertheless, on their return journey to Antioch, Paul and Barnabas retrace their steps through Lystra, Iconium, and Pisidian Antioch, and through Pamphylia: Confirming the souls of the disciples, and exhorting them to continue in the faith, and that we must through much tribulation enter into the kingdom of God.

And when they had ordained them elders in every church,

and had prayed with fasting, they commended them to the Lord, on whom they believed.[14:22-23]

THE LETTERS TO THE GENTILES

Dissension arises at Antioch: Is it required that Gentile converts be circumcised in accordance with the law of Moses?

Paul and Barnabas, returned from their journey, are sent to the mother church in Jerusalem about this question. They find division among the apostles and elders of the church. Some say it is necessary that all be circumcised. But Peter says, Ye know how that a good while ago God made choice among us, that the Gentiles by my mouth should hear the word of the gospel, and believe. And God, which knoweth the hearts . . . put no difference between us and them, purifying their hearts by faith.[15:7-9]

James then speaks: My sentence is, that we trouble not them, which from among the Gentiles are turned to God.[15:19]

The decision is made to send two men, Judas Barsabas and Silas, to Antioch with Paul and Barnabas, and to send letters by them which read, in part, as follows:

Greetings unto the brethren which are of the Gentiles in Antioch and Syria and Cilicia: Forasmuch as we have heard, that certain which went out from us have troubled you with words, subverting your souls, saying, Ye must be circumcised, and keep the law: to whom we gave no such commandment: It seemed good unto us . . . to send chosen men unto you with our beloved Barnabas and Paul, men that have hazarded their lives for the name of our Lord Jesus Christ.[15:23-26]

For it seemed good to the Holy Ghost, and to us, to lay upon you no greater burden than these necessary things;

that ye abstain from meats offered to idols, and from blood, and from things strangled, and from fornication: from which if ye keep yourselves, ye shall do well. Fare ye well.[15:28-29]

Once more in Antioch, Paul one day proposes to Barnabas that they revisit the cities where they have preached.

Barnabas is determined to take along Mark; but Paul, because Mark left them at Pamphylia during the first journey, opposes this. So Barnabas, with Mark, sails for Cyprus; while Paul, taking Silas, goes to Syria, Cilicia, and Lystra. At Lystra a disciple named Timotheus, the son of a Greek father and a Jewish mother, is added to their party.

Paul journeys throughout Phrygia and Galatia, confirming the churches, delivering the decrees ordained by the apostles and elders in Jerusalem.

And so were the churches established in the faith, and increased in number daily.[16:5]

PAUL IN ATHENS

In Philippi, chief city of Macedonia, Paul makes the first European convert: a certain woman named Lydia, a seller of purple. . . .[16:14]

But here also the people rise against them, they are beaten and imprisoned, their feet are fastened in the stocks, and only the miracle of an earthquake which breaks open the prison saves their lives.

When they come to Thessalonica, where there is a synagogue, a cry is set up by certain lewd fellows of the baser sort[17:5] *that* these that have turned the world upside down are come hither also.[17:6] *They are forced to flee Thessalonica in the night.*

Leaving Silas and Timotheus in nearby Berea, Paul goes on to Athens, where philosophers of the Epicureans and Stoics ask each other, What will this babbler say?[17:18]

(For all the Athenians, and strangers which were there,

spent their time in nothing else, but either to tell or to hear some new thing.)

Then Paul stood in the midst of Mars' hill, and said, Ye men of Athens, I perceive that in all things ye are too superstitious. For as I passed by, and beheld your devotions, I found an altar with this inscription. TO THE UNKNOWN GOD. Whom therefore ye ignorantly worship, him declare I unto you.

God that made the world and all things therein, seeing that he is Lord of heaven and earth, dwelleth not in temples made with hands. . . .[17:21-24]

Seek the Lord. . . . For in him we live, and move, and have our being; as certain also of your own poets have said. . . .[17:27-28]

And the times of . . . ignorance God winked at; but now commandeth all men every where to repent: Because he hath appointed a day, in the which he will judge the world in righteousness by that man whom he hath ordained; whereof he hath given assurance unto all men, in that he hath raised him from the dead.[17:30-31]

Some of his listeners mock; but others believe. Among the latter are Dionysius the Areopagite, and a woman named Damaris, and others.

From Athens, Paul goes to Corinth, where he remains for a year and a half. Silas and Timotheus come from Macedonia. With them, and with the help of a Jew named Aquila and his wife Priscilla, who are tent-makers, the work goes forward in spite of opposition from the Jews of the synagogue. Many converts are made. The church at Corinth is founded.

After this Paul sails to Syria, and comes to Ephesus, where there are disciples who know only the baptism of John, and who say to Paul, We have not so much as heard whether there be any Holy Ghost.[19:2] *These he baptizes in the name of Jesus.*

He is in Ephesus for two years:

So that all they which dwelt in Asia heard the word of the Lord Jesus, both Jews and Greeks: And God wrought special miracles by the hands of Paul.[19:10-11]

PAUL'S RETURN TO JERUSALEM

Sending for the elders of the church at Ephesus, Paul says to them, Behold, I go bound in the spirit unto Jerusalem, not knowing the things that shall befall me there.[20:22]

Neither count I my life dear unto myself, so that I might finish my course with joy, and the ministry, which I have received of the Lord Jesus, to testify the gospel of the grace of God. . . .

I know that ye all, among whom I have gone preaching the kingdom of God, shall see my face no more.[20:24-25]

Take heed therefore unto yourselves, and to all the flock, over the which the Holy Ghost hath made you overseers. . . .[20:28]

I have showed you all things, how that so laboring ye ought to support the weak, and to remember the words of the Lord Jesus, how he said, It is more blessed to give than to receive.[20:35]

He sails from Ephesus for Jerusalem.

The brethren receive him gladly. But as he enters the Temple he is seized by an angry crowd stirred up by zealots, and is only saved from death by a band of soldiers who carry him off in chains to the garrison.

As he is being led into the garrison, Paul says, I am a man which am a Jew of Tarsus, a city in Cilicia, a citizen of no mean city: and, I beseech thee, suffer me to speak unto the people.[21:39]

*Given leave, standing on the stairs, Paul speaks in He-
brew:* Men, brethren, and fathers, hear ye my defense. . . .
I am verily a man which am a Jew, born in Tarsus . . . , yet
brought up in this city at the feet of Gamaliel, and taught
according to the perfect manner of the law. . . .[22:1-3]

*He tells of his persecution of the disciples, of the miracle
on the road to Damascus, of his conversion to faith in the
Lord. But at the end the people demand his punishment.
He is ordered to be scourged; but he says,* Is it lawful
for you to scourge a man that is a Roman, and uncon-
demned?[22:25] *The captain of the garrison asks,* Art thou a
Roman? *When Paul answers,* Yea, *the captain retorts,* With
a great sum obtained I this freedom. *Paul says,* But I was
freeborn.[22:27-28]

*He is unbound. For his own safety he is sent to Caesarea,
to be heard by the governor of Judea. But it is two years
before he comes before Festus, the governor, to whom he
says,* I stand at Caesar's judgment seat, where I ought to be
judged: to the Jews have I done no wrong. . . . I appeal
unto Caesar. *Festus replies,* Hast thou appealed unto Caesar? unto Caesar shalt thou go.[25:10-12]

*But the king of Judea, Agrippa, happening at this time to
be in Caesarea, asks to see Paul. Brought before him, Paul
says,* I think myself happy, king Agrippa, because I shall
answer for myself this day before thee. . . .[26:2] *He states his
cause so eloquently that Agrippa says,* Almost thou per-
suadest me to be a Christian.[26:28]

PAUL IN ROME

*He is placed aboard a ship for Italy. The story of the voy-
age is one of storm and shipwreck; of miraculous escape
from death; and of the adventures of the shipload of sur-
vivors cast away on the island of Melita (Malta), where they
gain the confidence of the natives only through Paul's mi-*

raculous power of healing, and are rescued at last by a ship which carries them to Italy.

In Rome, Paul is allowed to live by himself, with only a soldier to guard him. He calls together the leaders of the Jews, to whom he tells his story.

He expounded and testified the kingdom of God, persuading them concerning Jesus, both out of the law of Moses, and out of the prophets. . . .[28:23]

When he sees that some believe his words, and some do not, he quotes the prophet Isaiah:

Hearing ye shall hear, and shall not understand; and seeing ye shall see, and not perceive. For the heart of this people is waxed gross, and their ears dull of hearing, and their eyes have they closed. . . .

Paul says, Be it known therefore unto you, that the salvation of God is sent unto the Gentiles, and that they will hear it.[28:26-28]

The Jews leave, having great argument among themselves.

And Paul dwelt two whole years in his own hired house, and received all that came in unto him, preaching the kingdom of God, and teaching those things which concern the Lord Jesus Christ, with all confidence, no man forbidding him.[28:30-31]

ROMANS

The teaching of St. Paul, "the apostle to the Gentiles," was carried on not only through his missionary labors but also by means of his great Epistles to the Gentile churches. These letters were written in ceaseless effort to fortify, instruct and correct the members of the various Christian communities. They develop the Christian doctrine. They define the nature, purpose and function of the Church at

*the same time as they reveal the many-sided mind and per-
sonality of Paul.*

*There are thirteen Epistles of Paul in the New Testa-
ment, written, it seems probable, between 50 and 70* A.D.
*Quoted below are some of the more famous passages and
those that seem best to convey the essence of Paul's teaching.*

*The Epistle to the Romans, although first in canonical
order, appears actually to be the sixth in chronological
order, which is generally believed to be as follows: I and II
Thessalonians, I and II Corinthians, Galatians, Romans,
Philemon, Colossians, Ephesians, Philippians, I Timothy,
Titus and II Timothy. Romans was written from Corinth
during Paul's third visit to that city:*

To all that be in Rome, beloved of God, called to be
saints: Grace to you and peace from God our Father, and
the Lord Jesus Christ.[1:7]

Without ceasing I make mention of you always in my
prayers.[1:9]

As much as in me is, I am ready to preach the gospel to
you that are at Rome. . . . For I am not ashamed of the
gospel of Christ: for it is the power of God unto salvation
to every one that believeth; to the Jew first, and also to the
Greek. For therein is the righteousness of God revealed
from faith to faith: as it is written, The just shall live by
faith.[1:15-17]

SIN AND THE LAW

For there is no respect of persons with God.

For as many as have sinned without law shall also perish
without law; and as many as have sinned in the law shall
be judged by the law. . . .

For when the Gentiles, which have not the law, do by
nature the things contained in the law, these, having not

the law, are a law unto themselves: which show the work of the law written in their hearts. . . .[2:11-15]

We conclude that a man is justified by faith without the deeds of the law. Is he the God of the Jews only: is he not also of the Gentiles? Yes, of the Gentiles also: seeing it is one God, which shall justify the circumcision by faith, and the uncircumcision through faith. Do we then make void the law through faith? God forbid: yea, we establish the law.[3:28-31]

Because the law worketh wrath: for where no law is, there is no transgression.[4:15]

Now if we be dead with Christ, we believe that we shall also live with him: knowing that Christ being raised from the dead dieth no more; death hath no more dominion over him. For in that he died, he died unto sin once: but in that he liveth, he liveth unto God. Likewise reckon ye also your-selves to be dead indeed unto sin, but alive unto God through Jesus Christ our Lord.[6:8-11]

I speak after the manner of men because of the infirmity of your flesh.[6:19]

For the wages of sin is death; but the gift of God is eternal life through Jesus Christ our Lord.[6:23]

Is the law sin? God forbid. Nay, I had not known sin, but by the law.[7:7]

If then I do that which I would not, I consent unto the law that it is good. Now then it is no more I that do it, but sin that dwelleth in me. For I know that in me (that is, in my flesh,) dwelleth no good thing: for to will is present with me; but how to perform that which is good I find not. For the good that I would, I do not: but the evil which I would not, that I do.[7:16-19]

I find then a law, that, when I would do good, evil is present with me. . . .

O wretched man that I am! who shall deliver me from the body of this death?

I thank God through Jesus Christ our Lord. So then with the mind I myself serve the law of God; but with the flesh the law of sin.[7:21-25]

THE FLESH AND THE SPIRIT

For they that are after the flesh do mind the things of the flesh; but they that are after the Spirit, the things of the Spirit. For to be carnally minded is death; but to be spiritually minded is life and peace.[8:5-6]

We know that all things work together for good to them that love God.[8:28]

For I am persuaded, that neither death, nor life, nor angels, nor principalities, nor powers, nor things present, nor things to come, nor height, nor depth, nor any other creature, shall be able to separate us from the love of God, which is in Christ Jesus our Lord.[8:38-39]

I beseech you therefore, brethren, by the mercies of God, that ye present your bodies a living sacrifice, holy, acceptable unto God. . . .[12:1]

Let love be without dissimulation. Abhor that which is evil; cleave to that which is good. Be kindly affectioned one to another with brotherly love; in honor preferring one another; not slothful in business; fervent in spirit; serving the Lord. . . .[12:9-11]

Rejoice with them that do rejoice, and weep with them that weep.

Mind not high things, but condescend to men of low estate. Be not wise in your own conceits. Recompense to no man evil for evil. . . . If it be possible, as much as lieth in you, live peaceably with all men.

Dearly beloved, avenge not yourselves. . . . Vengeance is

mine; I will repay, saith the Lord. Therefore if thine enemy hunger, feed him; if he thirst, give him drink; for in so doing thou shalt heap coals of fire on his head.

Be not overcome of evil, but overcome evil with good.[12:15-21]

Love is the fulfilling of the law.[13:10]

Now it is high time to awake out of sleep: for now is our salvation nearer than we believed. The night is far spent, the day is at hand: let us therefore cast off the works of darkness, and let us put on the armor of light.[13:11-12]

Put ye on the Lord Jesus Christ, and make not provision for the flesh, to fulfil the lusts thereof.[13:14]

Salute one another with a holy kiss. The churches of Christ salute you.[16:16]

I CORINTHIANS

The first Epistle of Paul to the church at Corinth:

I beseech you, brethren, by the name of our Lord Jesus Christ, that ye all speak the same thing, and that there be no divisions among you. . . .[1:10]

God hath chosen the foolish things of the world to confound the wise; and God hath chosen the weak things of the world to confound the things which are mighty. . . .[1:27]

Your glorying is not good. Know ye not that a little leaven leaveneth the whole lump? Purge out therefore the old leaven, that ye may be a new lump. . . . For even Christ our passover is sacrificed for us: Therefore let us keep the feast, not with old leaven, neither with the leaven of malice and wickedness; but with the unleavened bread of sincerity and truth.[5:6-8]

I would that all men were even as I myself. But every man hath his proper gift of God. . . . I say therefore to the unmarried and widows, it is good for them if they abide even as I. But if they cannot contain, let them marry: for it is better to marry than to burn.[7:7-9]

I am made all things to all men, that I might by all means save some.[9:22]

Know ye not that they which run in a race run all, but one receiveth the prize? . . .

Now they do it to obtain a corruptible crown; but we an incorruptible. I therefore so run, not as uncertainly; so fight I, not as one that beateth the air: But I keep under my body, and bring it into subjection: lest that by any means, when I have preached to others, I myself should be a castaway.[9:24-27]

Though I speak with the tongues of men and of angels, and have not charity, I am become as sounding brass, or a tinkling cymbal. And though I have the gift of prophecy, and understand all mysteries, and all knowledge; and though I have all faith, so that I could remove mountains, and have not charity, I am nothing. And though I bestow all my goods to feed the poor . . . and have not charity, it profiteth me nothing. Charity suffereth long, and is kind; charity envieth not; charity vaunteth not itself, is not puffed up. . . .[13:1-4]

Charity never faileth: but whether there be prophecies, they shall fail; whether there be tongues, they shall cease; whether there be knowledge, it shall vanish away. For we know in part, and we prophesy in part. But when that which is perfect is come, then that which is in part shall be done away.

When I was a child, I spake as a child, I understood as a child, I thought as a child: but when I became a man, I put away childish things. For now we see through a glass, darkly; but then face to face: now I know in part; but then shall I know even as also I am known.

And now abideth faith, hope, charity, these three: but the greatest of these is charity.[13:8-13]

If in this life only we have hope in Christ, we are of all men most miserable. But now is Christ risen from the dead, and become the firstfruits of them that slept. For since by man came death, by man came also the resurrection of the dead. For as in Adam all die, even so in Christ shall all be made alive.[15:19-22]

The last enemy that shall be destroyed is death.[15:26]

The first man is of the earth, earthy: the second man is the Lord from heaven.[15:47]

Behold, I show you a mystery; We shall not all sleep, but we shall all be changed, in a moment, in the twinkling of an eye, at the last trump: for the trumpet shall sound, and the dead shall be raised incorruptible. . . .

For this corruptible must put on incorruption, and this mortal must put on immortality. . . .

Then shall be brought to pass the saying that is written, Death is swallowed up in victory.

O death, where is thy sting? O grave, where is thy victory?[15:51-55]

II CORINTHIANS

The second Epistle of Paul to the church at Corinth:

I speak as concerning reproach, as though we had been weak. Howbeit, whereinsoever any is bold, (I speak foolishly,) I am bold also. Are they Hebrews? so am I. Are they Israelites? so am I. Are they the seed of Abraham? so am I. Are they ministers of Christ? (I speak as a fool,) I am more. . . .

Of the Jews five times received I forty stripes save one. Thrice was I beaten with rods, once was I stoned, thrice I suffered shipwreck, a night and a day have I been in the deep. In journeyings often, in perils of waters, in perils of robbers, in perils by mine own countrymen, in perils by the heathen, in perils in the city, in perils in the wilderness, in perils in the sea, in perils among false brethren; in weariness and painfulness . . . in hunger and thirst. . . .[11:21-27]

It is not expedient for me doubtless to glory. . . .

I knew a man in Christ above fourteen years ago (whether in the body, I cannot tell; or whether out of the body, I cannot tell: God knoweth;) such a one caught up to the third heaven.[12:1-2]

And heard unspeakable words, which it is not lawful for a man to utter.

Of such a one will I glory: yet of myself I will not glory, but in mine infirmities.[12:4-5]

GALATIANS

The Epistle of Paul to the churches in Galatia:

O foolish Galatians, who hath bewitched you, that ye should not obey the truth, before whose eyes Jesus Christ hath been evidently set forth, crucified among you? This only would I learn of you, Received ye the Spirit by the works of the law, or by the hearing of faith? Are ye so foolish? having begun in the Spirit, are ye now made perfect by the flesh? Have ye suffered so many things in vain?[3:1-4]

Ye are all the children of God by faith in Christ Jesus. For as many of you as have been baptized into Christ have put on Christ. There is neither Jew nor Greek, there is neither bond nor free, there is neither male nor female: for ye are all one in Christ Jesus.[3:26-28]

This I say then, Walk in the Spirit, and ye shall not fulfil the lust of the flesh. For the flesh lusteth against the Spirit, and the Spirit against the flesh: and these are contrary the one to the other; so that ye cannot do the things that ye would.[5:16-17]

Now the works of the flesh are manifest, which are these; Adultery, fornication, uncleanness, lasciviousness . . . envyings, murders, drunkenness, revelings, and such like. . . . But the fruit of the Spirit is love, joy, peace, long-suffering, gentleness, goodness, faith, meekness, temperance.[5:19-23]

Be not deceived; God is not mocked: for whatsoever a man soweth, that shall he also reap.[6:7]

And let us not be weary in well doing: for in due season we shall reap, if we faith not.[6:9]

EPHESIANS

The Epistle of Paul to the church at Ephesus:

You hath he quickened, who were dead in trespasses and sins. . . .[2:1]

I therefore, the prisoner of the Lord, beseech you that ye walk worthy of the vocation wherewith ye are called. . . .[4:1]

That we henceforth be no more children, tossed to and fro, and carried about with every wind of doctrine. . . .

But speaking the truth in love, may grow up into him in all things, which is the head, even Christ.[4:14-15]

Wherefore putting away lying, speak every man truth with his neighbor: for we are members one of another. Be ye angry, and sin not: let not the sun go down upon your wrath.[4:25-26]

Let no man deceive you with vain words: for because of these things cometh the wrath of God upon the children of disobedience.[5:6]

Put on the whole armor of God, that ye may be able to stand against the wiles of the devil. For we wrestle not against flesh and blood, but against principalities, against powers, against the rulers of the darkness of this world, against spiritual wickedness in high places. Wherefore take unto you the whole armor of God, that ye may be able to withstand in the evil day, and having done all, to stand.[6:11-13]

Your feet shod with the preparation of the gospel of peace; above all, taking the shield of faith, wherewith ye shall be able to quench all the fiery darts of the wicked.[6:15-16]

PHILIPPIANS

The Epistle of Paul to the church at Philippi:

I would ye should understand, brethren, that the things which happened unto me have fallen out rather unto the furtherance of the gospel.[1:12]

For to me to live is Christ, and to die is gain.[1:21]

For I am in a strait betwixt two, having a desire to depart, and to be with Christ; which is far better: Nevertheless to abide in the flesh is more needful for you.[1:23-24]

Brethren, be followers together of me, and mark them which walk so as ye have us for an ensample. (For many walk of whom I have told you often . . . whose end is destruction, whose God is their belly, and whose glory is in their shame, who mind earthly things.)[3:17-19]

Rejoice in the Lord always: and again I say, Rejoice.[4:4]

And the peace of God, which passeth all understanding, shall keep your hearts and minds through Christ Jesus.

Finally, brethren, whatsoever things are true, whatsoever things are honest, whatsoever things are just, whatsoever things are pure, whatsoever things are lovely, whatsoever things are of good report; if there be any virtue, and if there be any praise, think on these things.[4:7-8]

I can do all things through Christ which strengtheneth me.[4:13]

COLOSSIANS

The Epistle of Paul to the church at Colosse:

Beware lest any man spoil you through philosophy and vain deceit, after the tradition of men, after the rudiments of the world, and not after Christ.[2:8]

Set your affection on things above, not on things on the earth.[3:2]

Also put off all these: anger, wrath, malice, blasphemy, filthy communications out of your mouth. Lie not one to another, seeing that ye have put off the old man with his deeds; and have put on the new man, which is renewed in knowledge after the image of him that created him: Where there is neither Greek nor Jew, circumcision nor uncircumcision, Barbarian, Scythian, bond nor free: but Christ is all, and in all.[3:8-11]

Let your speech be always with grace, seasoned with salt, that ye may know how ye ought to answer every man.[4:6]

I THESSALONIANS

The first Epistle of Paul to the church at Thessalonica:

Remembering without ceasing your work of faith, and labor of love, and patience of hope in our Lord Jesus Christ, in the sight of God and our Father.[1:3]

We beseech you, brethren, that ye increase more and more; and that ye study to be quiet, and to do your own business, and to work with your own hands, as we commanded you; That ye may walk honestly toward them that are without, and that ye may have lack of nothing.[4:10-12]

Let us, who are of the day, be sober, putting on the

breastplate of faith and love; and for a helmet, the hope of salvation.[5:8]

Be at peace among yourselves. . . . Warn them that are unruly, comfort the feebleminded, support the weak, be patient toward all men.[5:13-14]

Pray without ceasing.[5:17]

Prove all things; hold fast that which is good.[5:21]

II THESSALONIANS

The second Epistle of Paul to the church at Thessalonica:

We are bound to thank God always for you, brethren, as it is meet, because that your faith groweth exceedingly, and the charity of every one of you all toward each other aboundeth; So that we ourselves glory in you in the churches of God for your patience and faith in all your persecutions and tribulations that ye endure.[1:3-4]

When we were with you, this we commanded you, that if any would not work, neither should he eat. For we hear that there are some which walk among you disorderly, working not at all, but are busybodies. Now them that are such we command and exhort by our Lord Jesus Christ, that with quietness they work, and eat their own bread.

But ye, brethren, be not weary in well doing.[3:10-13]

Now the Lord of peace himself give you peace always by all means. The Lord be with you all.[3:16]

I TIMOTHY

The first Epistle of Paul to Timothy, his friend and fellow worker, at Ephesus:

This is a faithful saying, and worthy of all acceptation, that Christ Jesus came into the world to save sinners; of whom I am chief.[1:15]

This is a true saying, If a man desire the office of a bishop, he desireth a good work. A bishop then must be blameless, the husband of one wife, vigilant, sober, of good behavior, given to hospitality, apt to teach; not given to wine, no striker, not greedy of filthy lucre; but patient, not a brawler, not covetous; one that ruleth well his own house, having his children in subjection with all gravity; (for if a man know not how to rule his own house, how shall he take care of the church of God?)[3:1-5]

Godliness with contentment is great gain. For we brought nothing into this world, and it is certain we can carry nothing out.[6:6-7]

The love of money is the root of all evil.[6:10]

Fight the good fight of faith, lay hold on eternal life. . . .[6:12]

O Timothy, keep that which is committed to thy trust, avoiding profane and vain babblings, and oppositions of science falsely so called; which some professing have erred concerning the faith.[6:20-21]

II TIMOTHY

Paul's second Epistle to Timothy, who had been ordained the first bishop of the church of the Ephesians, was written from Rome shortly before Paul's second appearance before Nero. It contains the last recorded words of the apostle:

To Timothy, my dearly beloved son.[1:2]

I put thee in remembrance, that thou stir up the gift of God, which is in thee by the putting on of my hands. For God hath not given us the spirit of fear; but of power, and of love, and of a sound mind.[1:6-7]

From a child thou hast known the holy Scriptures. . . .[3:15]

I charge thee therefore before God . . . preach the word,

be instant in season, out of season; reprove, rebuke, exhort with all long-suffering and doctrine.[4:1-2]

For I am now ready to be offered, and the time of my departure is at hand. I have fought a good fight, I have finished my course, I have kept the faith.[4:6-7]

Do thy diligence to come shortly unto me: for Demas hath forsaken me, having loved this present world. . . .

Only Luke is with me. Take Mark, and bring him with thee: for he is profitable to me for the ministry.[4:9-11]

Alexander the coppersmith did me much evil: the Lord reward him according to his works: of whom be thou ware also; for he hath greatly withstood our words.[4:14-15]

TITUS

The Epistle of Paul to Titus, first bishop of the church of Crete:

Unto the pure all things are pure: but unto them that are defiled and unbelieving is nothing pure; but even their mind and conscience is defiled.[1:15]

But speak thou the things which become sound doctrine.[2:1]

Put them in mind to be subject to principalities and powers, to obey magistrates, to be ready to every good work, to speak evil of no man, to be no brawlers, but gentle, showing all meekness unto all men.

For we ourselves also were sometimes foolish, disobedient, deceived, serving divers lusts and pleasures, living in malice and envy, hateful, and hating one another.

But after that the kindness and love of God our Saviour toward man appeared, not by works of righteousness which we have done, but according to his mercy he saved us, by the washing of regeneration, and renewing of the Holy

Ghost; which he shed on us abundantly through Jesus Christ our Saviour.[3:1-6]

PHILEMON

Onesimus, a slave belonging to the Christian convert Philemon, robbed his master and fled to Rome. Paul, convinced of the man's conversion and repentance, sent him back to Philemon with this letter:

I beseech thee for my son Onesimus, whom I have begotten in my bonds: which in time past was to thee unprofitable, but now profitable to thee and to me: Whom I have sent again: thou therefore receive him, that is, mine own bowels: Whom I would have retained with me, that in thy stead he might have ministered unto me in the bonds of the gospel: but without thy mind would I do nothing; that thy benefit should not be as it were of necessity, but willingly.

For perhaps he therefore departed for a season, that thou shouldest receive him for ever; not now as a servant, but above a servant, a brother beloved, specially to me, but how much more unto thee, both in the flesh, and in the Lord?

If thou count me therefore a partner, receive him as myself. If he hath wronged thee, or oweth thee aught, put that on mine account; I Paul have written it with mine own hand, I will repay it.[1:10-19]

HEBREWS

It is not certain who the author was of the Epistle to the Hebrews, nor to whom it was addressed. But the point of view is generally agreed to be that of St. Paul; and the contents of the letter make it seem probable that it was intended for the Jewish Christians, to confirm them in their faith in the Saviour:

God, who at sundry times and in divers manners spake in times past unto the fathers by the prophets, hath in these last days spoken unto us by his Son, whom he hath appointed heir of all things, by whom also he made the worlds; who being the brightness of his glory, and the express image of his person, and upholding all things by the word of his power, when he had by himself purged our sins, sat down on the right hand of the Majesty on high; being made so much better than the angels. . . . For unto which of the angels said he at any time, Thou art my Son, this day have I begotten thee?[1:1-5]

Seeing we also are compassed about with so great a cloud of witnesses, let us lay aside every weight, and the sin which doth so easily beset us, and let us run with patience the race that is set before us, looking unto Jesus the author and finisher of our faith.[12:1-2]

Let brotherly love continue. Be not forgetful to entertain strangers: for thereby some have entertained angels unawares.[13:1-2]

So that we may boldly say, The Lord is my helper, and I will not fear what man shall do unto me. . . .

Jesus Christ the same yesterday, and today, and for ever.[13:6-8]

JAMES

The author of the general Epistle of James, it is generally agreed among scholars, was the brother of our Lord, to whom he appeared after his resurrection: After that he was seen of James; then of all the apostles. (I Corinthians, 15:7)

To the twelve tribes which are scattered abroad, greeting.[1:1]

The trying of your faith worketh patience. But let patience have her perfect work, that ye may be perfect and entire, wanting nothing.

If any of you lack wisdom, let him ask of God, that giveth to all men liberally, and upbraideth not. . . .[1:3-5]

Every good gift and every perfect gift is from above, and cometh down from the Father of lights, with whom is no variableness, neither shadow of turning.[1:17]

Wherefore, my beloved brethren, let every man be swift to hear, slow to speak, slow to wrath: for the wrath of man worketh not the righteousness of God.[1:19-20]

Be ye doers of the word, and not hearers only, deceiving your own selves. For if any be a hearer of the word, and not a doer, he is like unto a man beholding his natural face in a glass: For he beholdeth himself, and goeth his way, and straightway forgetteth what manner of man he was. But whoso looketh into the perfect law of liberty, and continueth therein . . . this man shall be blessed in his deed.[1:22-25]

If any man among you seem to be religious, and bridleth not his tongue, but deceiveth his own heart, this man's religion is vain.

Pure religion and undefiled before God and the Father is this, To visit the fatherless and widows in their affliction, and to keep himself unspotted from the world.[1:26-27]

But wilt thou know, O vain man, that faith without works is dead?[2:20]

The tongue can no man tame; it is an unruly evil, full of deadly poison.[3:8]

This wisdom descendeth not from above, but is earthly, sensual, devilish.[3:15]

Submit yourselves therefore to God. Resist the devil, and he will flee from you.[4:7]

Ye know not what shall be on the morrow. For what is your life? It is even a vapor, that appeareth for a little time, and then vanisheth away.[4:14]

Behold, we count them happy which endure. Ye have heard of the patience of Job, and have seen the end of the Lord; that the Lord is very pitiful, and of tender mercy.[5:11]

The effectual fervent prayer of a righteous man availeth much.[5:16]

I PETER

The first general Epistle of Peter was, it is thought probable, written in Rome. It is addressed to his fellow-believers dispersed over the world:

See that ye love one another with a pure heart fervently:

For all flesh is as grass, and all the glory of man as the flower of grass. The grass withereth, and the flower thereof falleth away: But the word of the Lord endureth for ever.[1:22-25]

Ye are a chosen generation, a royal priesthood, a holy nation, a peculiar people; that ye should show forth the praises of him who hath called you out of darkness into his marvelous light.[2:9]

Dearly beloved, I beseech you as strangers and pilgrims, abstain from fleshy lusts, which war against the soul.[2:11]

Honor all men. Love the brotherhood. Fear God. Honor the king.[2:17]

For what glory is it, if, when ye be buffeted for your faults, ye shall take it patiently? but if, when ye do well, and suffer for it, ye take it patiently, this is acceptable with God.[2:20]

The end of all things is at hand: be ye therefore sober, and watch unto prayer. And above all things have fervent charity among yourselves: for charity shall cover the multitude of sins.[4:7-8]

Be sober, be vigilant; because your adversary the devil,

as a roaring lion, walketh about, seeking whom he may devour.[5:8]

II PETER

The second general Epistle of Peter was presumably written by the apostle in the knowledge that martyrdom was near: Knowing that shortly I must put off this my tabernacle, even as our Lord Jesus Christ hath showed me.[1:14]

This second epistle, beloved, I now write unto you; in both which I stir up your pure minds by way of remembrance:

That ye may be mindful of the words which were spoken before by the holy prophets, and of the commandment of us the apostles of the Lord and Saviour: Knowing this first, that there shall come in the last days scoffers, walking after their own lusts, and saying, Where is the promise of his coming?[3:1-4]

But, beloved, be not ignorant of this one thing, that one day is with the Lord as a thousand years, and a thousand years as one day.[3:8]

Wherefore, beloved . . . be diligent that ye may be found of him in peace, without spot, and blameless.[3:14]

I JOHN

The three general Epistles of John are without signature; but the tradition, which most biblical scholars accept, is that they were written by the apostle John, the author of the fourth Gospel.

My little children, these things write I unto thee, that ye sin not.[2:1]

If we say that we have no sin, we deceive ourselves, and the truth is not in us.

If we confess our sins, he is faithful and just to forgive us our sins, and to cleanse us from all unrighteousness.[1:8-9]

But whoso hath this world's good, and seeth his brother have need, and shutteth up his bowels of compassion from him, how dwelleth the love of God in him? My little children, let us not love in word, neither in tongue; but in deed and in truth.[3:17-18]

He that loveth not, knoweth not God; for God is love.[4:8]

There is no fear in love; but perfect love casteth out fear.[4:18]

If a man say, I love God, and hateth his brother, he is a liar: for he that loveth not his brother whom he hath seen, how can he love God whom he hath not seen?[4:20]

II JOHN

The second Epistle of John:

The elder unto the elect lady and her children, whom I love in the truth. . . .[1:1]

I beseech thee, lady, not as though I wrote a new commandment unto thee, but that which we had from the beginning, that we love one another. And this is love, that we walk after his commandments.[1:5-6]

Look to yourselves, that we lose not those things which we have wrought, but that we receive a full reward.[1:8]

Having many things to write unto you, I would not write with paper and ink: but I trust to come unto you, and speak face to face, that our joy may be full.[1:12]

III JOHN

The third Epistle of John is a personal letter from "the elder" to his faithful friend, Gaius:

I rejoiced greatly, when the brethren came and testified of the truth that is in thee.[1:3]

Beloved, thou doest faithfully whatsoever thou doest to the brethren, and to strangers: which have borne witness of thy charity before the church.[1:5-6]

But I trust I shall shortly see thee, and we shall speak face to face. Peace be to thee.[1:14]

JUDE

The author of this brief Epistle, who describes himself as "the brother of James," is customarily identified with the Apostle Judas (Luke 6:16)—not of course Judas Iscariot. It is also thought possible that the letter was by Judas, a brother of Jesus (Matthew 13:55).

Jude, the servant of Jesus Christ, and brother of James, to them that are sanctified by God the Father, and preserved in Jesus Christ, and called.[1:1]

It was needful for me to write unto you, and exhort you. . . .

For there are certain men crept in unawares . . . ungodly men, turning the grace of our God into lasciviousness, and denying the only Lord God, and our Lord Jesus Christ.[3-4]

These are spots in your feasts of charity . . . clouds they are without water, carried about of winds. . . .

Raging waves of the sea, foaming out their own shame; wandering stars, to whom is reserved the blackness of darkness for ever.[12-13]

REVELATION

Belonging to the class of apocalyptic writings (like parts of Isaiah, Ezekiel, and Daniel), this last book of the New Testament is its most difficult. Its author was John, a prophet of Ephesus exiled to the island of Patmos. It is generally agreed that it was written toward the end of the reign of the Roman Emperor Domitian—about A.D. 96; and, as this was a time of fierce persecution of the Christians, that John purposely obscured the meaning of his book to make it unintelligible to pagans.

In prophetic visions of epic grandeur, by means of mystical symbols and strange and terrible allegories, John was shown the destiny of this world: the struggle between God and Satan for the soul of man; and God's final victory over all evil.

The book is addressed to the seven churches which are in Asia:[1:4]

I John, who also am your brother, and companion in tribulation, and in the kingdom and patience of Jesus Christ, was in the isle that is called Patmos, for the word of God, and for the testimony of Jesus Christ.

I was in the Spirit on the Lord's day, and heard behind me a great voice, as of a trumpet, saying, I am Alpha and Omega, the first and the last: and, What thou seest, write in a book, and send it unto the seven churches which are in Asia. . . .

And I turned to see the voice that spake with me. And . . . I saw seven golden candlesticks: And in the midst of the seven candlesticks one like unto the Son of man, clothed with a garment down to the foot, and girt about the paps with a golden girdle.

His head and his hairs were white like wool, as white as snow; and his eyes were as a flame of fire; and his feet like unto fine brass, as if they burned in a furnace; and his voice as the sound of many waters. And he had in his right hand seven stars: and out of his mouth went a sharp two-edged sword: and his countenance was as the sun shineth in his strength.

And when I saw him, I fell at his feet as dead. And he laid his right hand upon me, saying unto me, Fear not; I am the first and the last: I am he that liveth, and was dead; and, behold, I am alive for evermore, Amen; and have the keys of hell and of death.[1:9-18]

Fear none of those things which thou shalt suffer. . . . be thou faithful unto death, and I will give thee a crown of life.[2:10]

Behold, I stand at the door, and knock: if any man hear my voice, and open the door, I will come in to him, and will sup with him, and he with me.[3:20]

And, behold, a throne was set in heaven, and one sat on the throne. And he that sat was to look upon like a jasper and a sardine stone: and there was a rainbow round about the throne, in sight like unto an emerald.[4:2-3]

And out of the throne proceeded lightnings and thunderings and voices. . . .

And before the throne there was a sea of glass like unto crystal: and in the midst of the throne, and round about the throne, were four beasts full of eyes before and behind.[4:5-6]

And they were full of eyes within: and they rest not day and night, saying, Holy, holy, holy, Lord God Almighty, which was, and is, and is to come.[4:8]

And I saw a strong angel proclaiming with a loud voice, Who is worthy to open the book, and to loose the seals thereof?[5:2]

And lo, in the midst of the throne and of the four beasts . . . stood a Lamb as it had been slain, having seven horns and seven eyes, which are the seven Spirits of God sent forth into all the earth.[5:6]

And they sang a new song, saying, Thou art worthy to take the book, and to open the seals thereof: for thou wast slain, and hast redeemed us to God. . . .[5:9]

And I looked, and behold a pale horse: and his name that sat on him was Death, and Hell followed with him. . . .

I saw under the altar the souls of them that were slain for the word of God, and for the testimony which they held: And they cried with a loud voice, saying, How long, O Lord, holy and true, dost thou not judge and avenge our blood on them that dwell on the earth?[6:8-10]

After this I beheld, and, lo, a great multitude, which no man could number, of all nations, and kindreds, and people, and tongues. . . . and cried . . . Salvation to our God which sitteth upon the throne, and unto the Lamb.[7:9-10]

And one of the elders answered, saying unto me, What are these which are arrayed in white robes? . . . And I said unto him, Sir, thou knowest. And he said to me, These are they which came out of great tribulation, and have washed their robes, and made them white in the blood of the Lamb. Therefore are they before the throne of God. . . . They shall hunger no more, neither thirst any more; neither shall the sun light on them, nor any heat. . . . God shall wipe away all tears from their eye.[7:13-17]

THE BOTTOMLESS PIT

And he opened the bottomless pit; and there arose a smoke. . . . And there came out of the smoke locusts upon the earth. . . .

And it was commanded them that they should not hurt the grass . . . but only those men which have not the seal of God in their foreheads. . . . and their torment was as the torment of a scorpion, when he striketh a man. And in those days shall men seek death, and shall not find it; and shall desire to die, and death shall flee from them.[9:2-6]

And there was war in heaven: Michael and his angels fought against the dragon; and the dragon fought and his angels, and prevailed not. . . .[12:7-8]

And I saw heaven opened, and behold a white horse; and he that sat upon him was called Faithful and True, and in righteousness he doth judge and make war.[19:11]

And he hath on his vesture and on his thigh a name written, KING OF KINGS, AND LORD OF LORDS.[19:16]

And I saw an angel come down from heaven, having the key of the bottomless pit. . . . And he laid hold on the dragon, that old serpent, which is the Devil, and Satan, and bound him a thousand years, and cast him into the bottomless pit, and shut him up. . . . [20:1-3]

THE NEW JERUSALEM

And I saw a new heaven and a new earth: for the first heaven and the first earth were passed away; and there was no more sea.

And I John saw the holy city, new Jerusalem, coming down from God out of heaven, prepared as a bride adorned for her husband. And I heard a great voice out of heaven saying, Behold, the tabernacle of God is with men. . . .

And God shall wipe away all tears from their eyes; and there shall be no more death, neither sorrow, nor crying, neither shall there be any more pain: for the former things are passed away. And he that sat upon the throne said, Behold, I make all things new. And he said unto me, Write: for these words are true and faithful. . . . It is done. I am Alpha and Omega, the beginning and the end. I will give unto him that is athirst of the fountain of the water of life freely.[21:1-6]

And there came unto me one of the seven angels. . . . And he carried me away . . . and showed me that great city, the holy Jerusalem, descending out of heaven from God. . . .[21:9-10]

The city was pure gold, like unto clear glass. And the foundations of the wall of the city were garnished with all manner of precious stones. The first foundation was jasper; the second, sapphire; the third, a chalcedony; the fourth, an emerald; the fifth sardonyx; the sixth, sardius; the seventh, chrysolite; the eighth, beryl; the ninth, a topaz; the tenth, a chrysoprasus; the eleventh, a jacinth; the twelfth, an amethyst.

And the twelve gates were twelve pearls; . . . the street of the city was pure gold, as it were transparent glass.

I saw no temple therein: for the Lord God Almighty and the Lamb are the temple of it. And the city had no need of the sun, neither of the moon, to shine in it: for the glory of God did lighten it, and the Lamb is the light thereof.[21:18-23]

And he showed me a pure river of water of life, clear as crystal, proceeding out of the throne of God and of the Lamb. In the midst of the street of it . . . was there the tree of life . . . and the leaves of the tree were for the healing of the nations.[22:1-2]

And I John saw these things, and heard them.[22:8]

And he saith unto me . . . the time is at hand.[22:10]

I am the root and the offspring of David, and the bright and morning star. And the Spirit and the bride say, Come. And let him that heareth say, Come. And let him that is athirst come. And whosoever will, let him take the water of life freely.[22:16-17]

He which testifieth these things saith, Surely I come quickly. Amen. Even so, come, Lord Jesus.

The grace of our Lord Jesus Christ be with you all.[22:20-21]

Appendix

Additional Quotations

1. GENESIS

The Lord God formed man of the dust of the ground and breathed into his nostrils the breath of life; and man became a living soul. 2:7

There were giants in the earth in those days. 6:4

Mighty men which were of old, men of renown. 6:4

Nimrod the mighty hunter before the Lord. 10:9

In a good old age. 15:15

2. EXODUS

He hardened Pharaoh's heart, that he hearkened not. 7:13

Your lamb shall be without blemish. 12:5

Let not God speak with us, lest we die. 20:19

Behold, I send an Angel before thee, to keep thee in the way. 23:20

There shall no man see me, and live. 33:20

3. LEVITICUS

Let him go for a scapegoat into the wilderness. 16:10

The land shall not be sold for ever: for the land is mine; for ye are strangers and sojourners with me. 25:23

4. NUMBERS

The giants, the sons of Anak. 13:33

God is not a man, that he should lie. 23:19

Be sure your sin will find you out. 32:23

5. DEUTERONOMY

The Lord thy God hath chosen thee to be a special people unto Himself, above all people that are upon the face of the earth. 7:6

A dreamer of dreams. 13.1

The wife of thy bosom. 13:6

6. JOSHUA

The place whereon thou standest is holy. 5:15

Let them be hewers of wood and drawers of water. 9:21

I am going the way of all the earth. 23:14

7. JUDGES

I arose a mother in Israel. 5:7

She brought forth butter in a lordly dish. 5:25

Why tarry the wheels of his chariots? 5:28

Out of the eater came forth meat, and out of the strong came forth sweetness. 14:14

If ye had not plowed with my heifer, ye had not found out my riddle. 14:18

All the people arose as one man. 20:8

9. I SAMUEL

Be strong, and quit yourselves like men. 4:9

Is Saul also among the prophets? 10:11

A man after his own heart. 13:14

I know thy pride, and the naughtiness of thine heart. 17:28

10. II SAMUEL

Smote him under the fifth rib. 2:23

Tarry at Jericho until your beards be grown. 10:5

For we must needs die, and are as water spilt on the ground, which cannot be gathered up again. 14:14

David the son of Jesse . . . the sweet psalmist of Israel. 23:1

11. I KINGS

A proverb and a byword among all people. 9:7

A little cloud out of the sea, like a man's hand. 18:44

He girded up his loins. 18:46

12. II KINGS

O thou man of God, there is death in the pot. 4:40

Is not the sound of his master's feet behind him? 6:32

Is thy servant a dog, that he should do this great thing? 8:13

Set thine house in order; for thou shalt die. 20:1

18. JOB

In thoughts from the visions of the night, when deep sleep falleth on men. 4:13

Then a spirit passed before my face; the hair of my flesh stood up. 4:15

Shall mortal man be more just than God? shall a man be more pure than his maker? 4:17

He shall return no more to his house, neither shall his place know him any more. 7:10

I would not live alway. 7:16

Clearer than the noonday. 11:17

Speak to the earth, and it shall teach thee. 12:8

With the ancient is wisdom; and in length of days understanding. 12:12

If a man die, shall he live again? 14:14

The king of terrors. 18:14

Seeing the root of the matter is found in me. 19:28

The price of wisdom is above rubies. 28:18

When the ear heard me, then it blessed me; and when the eye saw me, it gave witness to me. 29:11

I caused the widow's heart to sing for joy. 29:13

I was eyes to the blind, and feet was I to the lame. 29:15

The house appointed for all living. 30:23

A companion to owls. 30:29

One among a thousand. 33:23

Far be it from God, that he should do wickedness; and from the Almighty, that he should commit iniquity. 34:10

He multiplieth words without knowledge. 35:16

Hard as a piece of the nether millstone. 41:24

He maketh the deep to boil like a pot. 41:31

21. ECCLESIASTES

A threefold cord is not quickly broken. 4:12

The sleep of a laboring man is sweet. 5:12

A man hath no better thing under the sun than to eat, and to drink, and to be merry. 8:15

All things come alike to all. 9:2

He that diggeth a pit shall fall into it. 10:8

Wine maketh merry: but money answereth all things. 10:19

My son, be admonished: of making many books there is no end: and much study is a weariness of the flesh. Let us hear the conclusion of the whole matter: Fear God, and keep his commandments: for this is the whole duty of man. 12:12-13

23. ISAIAH

They shall beat their swords into plowshares, and their spears into pruninghooks: nation shall not lift up sword against nation, neither shall they learn war any more. 2:4

Cease ye from man, whose breath is in his nostrils: for wherein is he to be accounted of? 2:22

The daughters of Zion are haughty, and walk with stretched forth necks and wanton eyes, walking and mincing as they go, and making a tinkling with their feet. 3:16

In that day seven women shall take hold of one man. 4:1

He looked for judgment, but behold oppression; for righteousness, but behold a cry. 5:7

Woe unto them that rise up early in the morning, that they may follow strong drink. 5:11

Woe unto them that draw iniquity with cords of vanity, and sin as it were with a cart rope. 5:18

Woe unto them that call evil good, and good evil. 5:20

The ancient and honorable. 9:15

How art thou fallen from heaven, O Lucifer, son of the morning! 14:12

Is this the man that made the earth to tremble, that did shake kingdoms? 14:16

Like the rushing of mighty waters. 17:12

Babylon is fallen, is fallen. 21:9

Watchman, what of the night?

Watchman, what of the night? The watchman said, the morning cometh, and also the night. 21:11-12

Let us eat and drink; for tomorrow we shall die. 22:13

The crowning city, whose merchants are princes, whose traffickers are the honorable of the earth. 23:8

Howl, ye ships of Tarshish. 23:14

He will swallow up death in victory; and the Lord God will wipe away tears from off all faces. 25:8

Thou wilt keep him in perfect peace, whose mind is stayed on thee. 26:3

Leviathan that crooked serpent. 27:1

For precept must be upon precept, precept upon precept; line upon line, line upon line; here a little, and there a little. 28:10

It shall be a vexation only to understand the report. 28:19

They are drunken, but not with wine; they stagger, but not with strong drink. 29:9

Their strength is to sit still. 30:7

In quietness and in confidence shall be your strength. 30:15

The bread of adversity, and the water of affliction. 30:20

And a man shall be as a hiding place from the wind, and a covert from the tempest; as rivers of water in a dry place, as the shadow of a great rock in a weary land. 32:2

The wilderness and the solitary place shall be glad for them; and the desert shall rejoice, and blossom as the rose. 35:1

Then the eyes of the blind shall be opened, and the ears of the deaf shall be unstopped. Then shall the lame man leap as a hart, and the tongue of the dumb sing: for in the wilderness shall waters break out, and streams in the desert. 35:5-6

Sorrow and sighing shall flee away. 35:10

Lo, thou trustest in the staff of this broken reed, on Egypt. 36:6

I shall go softly all my years in the bitterness of my soul. 38:15

He warmeth himself, and saith, Aha, I am warm, I have seen the fire. 44:16

Shall the clay say to him that fashioneth it, What makest thou? 45:9

Can woman forget her sucking child, that she should not have compassion on the son of her womb? yea, they may forget, yet will I not forget thee. 49:15

How beautiful upon the mountains are the feet of him that bringeth good tidings, that publisheth peace. 52:7

My thoughts are not your thoughts, neither are your ways my ways, saith the Lord. 55:8

Arise, shine; for thy light is come, and the glory of the Lord is risen upon thee. 60:1

A little one shall become a thousand, and a small one a strong nation. 60:22

I have trodden the winepress alone. 63:3

We are all as an unclean thing, and all our righteousnesses are as filthy rags; and we all do fade as a leaf. 64:6

I am holier than thou. 65:5

As one whom his mother comforteth, so will I comfort you. 66:13

24. JEREMIAH

Saying, Peace, peace; when there is no peace. 6:14

Stand ye in the ways, and see, and ask for the old paths, where is the good way, and walk therein, and ye shall find rest for your souls. 6:16

The harvest is past, the summer is ended, and we are not saved. 8:20

Is there no balm in Gilead? Is there no physician there? 8:22

Oh that I had in the wilderness a lodging place of wayfaring men; that I might leave my people, and go from them! 9:2

She hath given up the ghost; her sun is gone down while it was yet day. 15:9

A man of strife and a man of contention to the whole earth! 15:10

Written with a pen of iron, and with the point of a diamond. 17:1

The heart is deceitful above all things, and desperately wicked: who can know it? 17:9

Thou art my hope in the day of evil. 17:17

He shall be buried with the burial of an ass. 22:19

O earth, earth, earth, hear the word of the Lord. 22:29

25. LAMENTATIONS

My strength and my hope is perished from the Lord: Remembering mine affliction and my misery, the wormwood and the gall. 3:18-19

It is good that a man should both hope and quietly wait for the salvation of the Lord. It is good for a man that he bear the yoke in his youth. 3:26-27

27. DANIEL

His legs of iron, his feet part of iron and part of clay. 2:33

The Ancient of days. 7:13

28. HOSEA

Like people, like priest. 4:9

38. ZECHARIAH

I have spread you abroad as the four winds of the heaven. 2:6

Who hath despised the day of small things. 4:10

The eyes of the Lord, which run to and fro through the whole earth. 4:10

40. ST. MATTHEW

The children of the kingdom shall be cast out into outer darkness: there shall be weeping and gnashing of teeth. 8:12

The foxes have holes, and the birds of the air have nests; but the Son of man hath not where to lay his head. 8:20

Let the dead bury their dead. 8:22

Neither do men put new wine into old bottles. 9:17

The harvest truly is plenteous, but the laborers are few. 9:37

The disciple is not above his master, nor the servant above his lord. 10:24

A friend of publicans and sinners. 11:19

Wisdom is justified of her children. 11:19

He that is not with me is against me. 12:30

The tree is known by his fruit. 12:33

Out of the abundance of the heart the mouth speaketh. 12:34

Get thee behind me, Satan. 16:23

In the resurrection they neither marry, nor are given in marriage, but are as the angels of God in heaven. 22:30

Whosoever shall exalt himself shall be abased; and he that shall humble himself shall be exalted. 23:12

Abomination of desolation. 24:15

Wheresoever the carcass is, there will the eagles be gathered together. 24:28

Well done, thou good and faithful servant: . . . enter thou into the joy of thy lord. 25:21

I knew thee that thou art a hard man, reaping where thou hast not sown, and gathering where thou hast not strewed. 25:24

A woman having an alabaster box of very precious ointment. 26:7

To what purpose is this waste? 26:8

The potter's field, to bury strangers in. 27:7

41. ST. MARK

What manner of man is this, that even the wind and the sea obey him? 4:41

My name is Legion: for we are many. 5:9

Clothed, and in his right mind. 5:15

A certain woman . . . had suffered many things of many physicians, and had spent all that she had, and was nothing bettered, but rather grew worse. 5:25-26

Knowing in himself that virtue had gone out of him. 5:30

Lord, I believe; help thou mine unbelief. 9:24

Where their worm dieth not, and the fire is not quenched. 9:44

42. ST. LUKE

Lord, now lettest thou thy servant depart in peace. 2:29

A light to lighten the Gentiles, and the glory of thy people Israel. 2:32

Physician, heal thyself. 4:23

Woe unto you, when all men shall speak well of you! 6:26

Nothing is secret, that shall not be made manifest. 8:17

No man, having put his hand to the plow, and looking back, is fit for the kingdom of God. 9:62

Woe unto you, lawyers! for ye have taken away the key of knowledge: ye entered not in yourselves, and them that were entering in ye hindered. 11:52

Soul, thou hast much goods laid up for many years; take thine ease, eat, drink, and be merry. 12:19

Thou fool, this night thy soul shall be required of thee: then whose shall those things be? 12:20

Let your loins be girded about, and your lights burning. 12:35

Bring in hither the poor, and the maimed, and the halt, and the blind. 14:21

The lord commended the unjust steward, because he had done wisely: for the children of this world are in their generation wiser than the children of light. 16:8

Out of thine own mouth will I judge thee. 19:22

This do in remembrance of me. 22:19

Why seek ye the living among the dead? 24:5

Their words seemed to them as idle tales. 24:11

43. ST. JOHN

Can there any good thing come out of Nazareth? 1:46

Make not my Father's house a house of merchandise. 2:16

Rise, take up thy bed, and walk. 5:8

I am the bread of life: he that cometh to me shall never hunger. 6:35

Judge not according to the appearance. 7:24

I am the light of the world: he that followeth me shall not walk in darkness, but shall have the light of life. 8:12

Ye shall know the truth, and the truth shall make you free. 8:32

There is no truth in him. . . . He is a liar, and the father of it. 8:44

The night cometh, when no man can work. 9:4

Whether he be a sinner or no, I know not: one thing I know, that, whereas I was blind, now I see. 9:25

I am the door: by me if any man enter in, he shall be saved. 10:9

I am the good shepherd: the good shepherd giveth his life for the sheep. 10:11

The hireling fleeth, because he is a hireling and careth not for the sheep. 10:13

The poor always ye have with you; but me ye have not always. 12:8

Walk while ye have the light, lest darkness come upon you. 12:35

Put up thy sword into the sheath. 18:11

Behold the man! 19:5

What I have written I have written. 19:22

Simon Peter saith unto them, I go a fishing. 21:3

Feed my lambs. 21:15

Feed my sheep. 21:16

Lord, thou knowest all things; thou knowest that I love thee. 21:17

When thou wast young, thou girdest thyself, and walkest whither thou wouldest: but when thou shalt be old, thou shalt stretch forth thy hands, and another shall gird thee, and carry thee whither thou wouldest not. 21:18

44. ACTS

I wot that through ignorance ye did it. 3:17

They took knowledge of them, that they had been with Jesus. 4:13

It is not reason that we should leave the word of God, and serve tables. 6:2

Thy money perish with thee, because thou hast thought that the gift of God may be purchased with money. 8:20

Thy heart is not right in the sight of God. 8:21

Thou art in the gall of bitterness, and in the bond of iniquity. 8:23

Understandest thou what thou readest? 8:30

One Simon a tanner. 9:43

What God hath cleansed, that call not thou common. 10:15

We also are men of like passions with you. 14:15

A certain damsel possessed with a spirit of divination. 16:16

Gallio cared for none of those things. 18:17

An eloquent man, and mighty in the Scriptures. 18:24

Demetrius, a silversmith. 19:24

Some therefore cried one thing, and some another: for the assembly was confused; and the more part knew not wherefore they were come together. 19:32

God shall smite thee, thou whited wall. 23:3

To have always a conscience void of offense toward God, and toward men. 24:16

After the most straitest sect of our religion I lived a Pharisee. 26:5

This thing was not done in a corner. 26:26

They cast four anchors out of the stern, and wished for the day. 27:29

45. ROMANS

Who changed the truth of God into a lie, and worshipped and served the creature more than the Creator. 1:25

By patient continuance in well doing seek for glory and honor and immortality. 2:7

Let God be true, but every man a liar. 3:4

Not rather, (as we be slanderously reported. . .) Let us do evil, that good may come? whose damnation is just. 3:8

For all have sinned, and come short of the glory of God. 3:23

Who against hope believed in hope. 4:18

Hope maketh not ashamed. 5:5

Where sin abounded, grace did much more abound. 5:20

Shall we continue in sin, that grace may abound? God forbid. 6:1-2

Ye have not received the spirit of bondage again to fear; but ye have received the Spirit of adoption, whereby we cry, Abba, Father. 8:15

We are the children of God: and if the children, then heirs; heirs of God, and joint-heirs with Christ. 8:16-17

We know that the whole creation groaneth and travaileth in pain together until now. 8:22

If God be for us, who can be against us? 8:31

They are not all Israel, which are of Israel. 9:6

Hath not the potter power over the clay, of the same lump to make one vessel unto honor, and another unto dishonor? 9:21

They have a zeal of God, but not according to knowledge. 10:2

Let every soul be subject unto the higher powers. For there is no power but of God: the powers that be are ordained of God. 13:1

Rulers are not a terror to good works, but to the evil. 13:3

Render therefore to all their dues: tribute to whom tribute is due; custom to whom custom; fear to whom fear; honor to whom honor. Owe no man any thing, but to love one another; for he that loveth another hath fulfilled the law. 13:7-8

Make not provision for the flesh, to fulfil the lusts thereof. 13:14

Him that is weak in the faith receive ye, but not to doubtful disputations. 14:1

Let every man be fully persuaded in his own mind. 14:5

None of us liveth to himself, and no man dieth to himself. 14:7

We then that are strong ought to bear the infirmities of the weak, and not to please ourselves. 15:1

46. I CORINTHIANS

Eye hath not seen, nor ear heard, neither have entered into the heart of man, the things which God hath prepared for them that love him. 2:9

I have planted, Apollos watered; but God gave the increase. 3:6

We are made a spectacle unto the world, and to angels, and to men. 4:9

Absent in body, but present in spirit. 5:3

Your body is the temple of the Holy Ghost which is in you. 6:19

The unbelieving husband is sanctified by the wife. 7:14

The fashion of this world passeth away. 7:31

Knowledge puffeth up, but charity edifieth. 8:1

Who goeth a warfare any time at his own charges? who planteth a vineyard, and eateth not of the fruit thereof? 9:7

All things are lawful for me, but all things are not expedient: all things are lawful for me, but all things edify not. 10:23

The earth is the Lord's, and the fullness thereof. 10:26

If the trumpet give an uncertain sound, who shall prepare himself to the battle? 14:8

Let your women keep silence in the churches: for it is not permitted unto them to speak. . . . And if they will learn any thing, let them ask their husbands at home: for it is a shame for women to speak in the church. 14:34-35

Let all things be done decently and in order. 14:40

By the grace of God I am what I am. . . . But I labored more abundantly than they all: yet not I, but the grace of God which was with me. 15:10

If after the manner of men I have fought with beasts at Ephesus, what advantageth it me, if the dead rise not? let us eat and drink; for tomorrow we die. 15:32

Be not deceived: evil communications corrupt good manners. 15:33

There is one glory of the sun, and another glory of the moon, and another glory of the stars: for one star differeth from another star in glory. 15:41

It is sown in corruption; it is raised in incorruption. 15:42

If any man love not the Lord Jesus Christ, let him be Anathema, Maranatha. 16:22

47. II CORINTHIANS

Not in tables of stone, but in fleshly tables of the heart. 3:3

Able ministers of the new testament; not of the letter, but of the spirit: for the letter killeth, but the spirit giveth life. 3:6

Things which are seen are temporal; but the things which are not seen are eternal. 4:18

We have a building of God, a house not made with hands, eternal in the heavens. 5:1

We walk by faith, not by sight. 5:7

God loveth a cheerful giver. 9:7

For ye suffer fools gladly, seeing ye yourselves are wise. 11:19

There was given to me a thorn in the flesh, the messenger of Satan to buffet me, lest I should be exalted above measure. 12:7

My strength is made perfect in weakness. 12:9

48. GALATIANS

How turn ye again to the weak and beggarly elements? 4:9

It is good to be zealously affected always in a good thing. 4:18

49. EPHESIANS

That I should preach among the Gentiles the unsearchable riches of Christ. 3:8

To be strengthened with might by his Spirit in the inner man. 3:16

To know the love of Christ, which passeth knowledge. 3:19

Redeeming the time, because the days are evil. 5:16

Wives, submit yourselves unto your own husbands, as unto the Lord. 5:22

Honor thy father and mother; which is the first commandment with promise. 6:2

Ye fathers, provoke not your children to wrath. 6:4

50. PHILIPPIANS

Who, being in the form of God . . . made himself of no reputation, and took upon him the form of a servant, and was made in the likeness of men. 2:6-7

Wherefore God also hath highly exalted him, and given him a name which is above every name: That at the name of Jesus every knee should bow. 2:9-10

Work out your own salvation with fear and trembling. 2:12

What things were gain to me, those I counted loss for Christ. 3:7

This one thing I do, forgetting those things which are behind, and reaching forth unto those things which are before. 3:13

I have learned, in whatsoever state I am, therewith to be content. 4:11

51. COLOSSIANS

Touch not; taste not; handle not. 2:21

Husbands, love your wives, and be not bitter against them. 3:19

54. I TIMOTHY

Neither give heed to fables and endless genealogies. 1:4

I obtained mercy, because I did it ignorantly in unbelief. 1:13

Every creature of God is good, and nothing to be refused, if it be received with thanksgiving. 4:4

Refuse profane and old wives' fables. 4:7

Drink no longer water, but use a little wine for thy stomach's sake and thine often infirmities. 5:23

55. II TIMOTHY

Hold fast the form of sound words. 1:13

A workman that needeth not to be ashamed, rightly dividing the word of truth. 2:15

58. HEBREWS

The word of God is quick, and powerful, and sharper than any two-edged sword, piercing even to the dividing asunder of soul and spirit. 4:12

They crucify to themselves the Son of God afresh, and put him to an open shame. 6:6

It is a fearful thing to fall into the hands of the living God. 10:31

Faith is the substance of things hoped for, the evidence of things not seen. 11:1

He looked for a city which hath foundations, whose builder and maker is God. 11:10

These all died in faith, not having received the promises, but having seen them afar off. 11:13

Esteeming the reproach of Christ greater riches than the treasures in Egypt. 11:26

Of whom the world was not worthy. 11:38

Whom the Lord loveth he chasteneth. 12:6

He found no place of repentance though he sought it carefully with tears. 12:17

To God the Judge of all, and to the spirits of just men made perfect. 12:23

59. JAMES

Blessed is the man that endureth temptation: for when he is tried, he shall receive the crown of life. 1:12

How great a matter a little fire kindleth! 3:5

Doth a fountain send forth at the same place sweet water and bitter? 3:11

60. I PETER

As newborn babes, desire the sincere milk of the word, that ye may grow thereby. 2:2

Ye were as sheep, going astray; but are now returned unto the Shepherd and Bishop of your souls. 2:25

The ornament of a meek and quiet spirit, which is in the sight of God of great price. 3:4

Giving honor unto the wife, as unto the weaker vessel. 3:7

61. II PETER

Take heed, as unto a light that shineth in a dark place, until the dav dawn, and the day star arise in your hearts. 1:19

The dog is turned to his own vomit again; and the sow that was washed to her wallowing in the mire. 2:22

65. JUDE

Michael the archangel, when contending with the devil he disputed about the body of Moses, durst not bring against him a railing accusation, but said, The Lord rebuke thee. 1:9

66. REVELATION

To him that overcometh will I give to eat of the hidden manna, and will give him a white stone, and in the stone a new name written, which no man knoweth saving he that receiveth it. 2:17

I will write upon him my new name. 3:12

I know thy works, that thou art neither cold nor hot: I would thou wert cold or hot. So then because thou art lukewarm, and neither cold nor hot, I will spew thee out of my mouth. 3:15-16

O Lord . . . thou hast created all things, and for thy pleasure they are and were created. 4:11

Golden vials full of odors, which are the prayers of saints. 5:8

He went forth conquering, and to conquer. 6:2

A measure of wheat for a penny, and three measures of barley for a penny; and see thou hurt not the oil and the wine. 6:6

And the stars of heaven fell unto the earth, even as a fig tree casteth her untimely figs, when she is shaken of a mighty wind. 6:13

And said to the mountains and rocks, Fall on us, and hide us from the face of him that sitteth on the throne, and from the wrath of the Lamb. 6:16

There was silence in heaven about the space of half an hour. 8:1

It was in my mouth sweet as honey: and as soon as I had eaten it, my belly was bitter. 10:10

The kingdoms of this world are become the kingdoms of our Lord, and of his Christ; and he shall reign for ever and ever. 11:15

There appeared a great wonder in heaven; a women clothed with the sun, and the moon under her feet, and upon her head a crown of twelve stars. 12:1

The devil is come down unto you, having great wrath, because he knoweth that he hath but a short time. 12:12

And they worshipped the beast, saying, Who is like unto the beast? who is able to make war with him? 13:4

That no man might buy or sell, save he that had the mark, or the name of the beast, or the number of his name. . . . Let him that hath understanding count the number of the beast: for it is the number of a man; and his number is Six hundred threescore and six. 13:17-18

In their mouth was found no guile: for they are without fault before the throne of God. 14:5

Blessed are the dead which die in the Lord from henceforth: Yea, saith the Spirit, that they may rest from their labors; and their works do follow them. 14:13

I saw as it were a sea of glass mingled with fire. 15:2

Behold, I come as a thief. 16:15

He gathered them together into a place called in the Hebrew tongue Armageddon. 16:16

I will show unto thee the judgment of the great whore that sitteth upon many waters. 17:1

And upon her forehead was a name written, MYSTERY, BABY-

LON THE GREAT, THE MOTHER OF HARLOTS AND ABOMINATIONS OF THE EARTH. And I saw the woman drunken with the blood of the saints. 17:5-6

And a mighty angel took up a stone like a great millstone, and cast it into the sea, saying, Thus with violence shall that great city Babylon be thrown down, and shall be found no more at all. 18:21

Blessed are they which are called unto the marriage supper of the Lamb. 19:9

And I fell at his feet to worship him. And he said unto me, See thou do it not: I am thy fellow servant. 19:10

And I saw the dead, small and great, stand before God; and the books were opened: and another book was opened, which is the book of life: and the dead were judged out of those things which were written in the books. 20:12

Without are dogs, and sorcerers, and whoremongers, and murderers, and idolators, and whosoever loveth and maketh a lie. 22:15

I testify unto every man that heareth the prophecy of this book, If any man shall add unto these things, God shall add unto him the plagues that are written in this book: And if any man shall take away from the words of the book of this prophecy, God shall take away his part out of the book of life, and out of the holy city, and from the things which are written in this book. 22:18-19

Bibliography

As explained in the Preface, all the quotations in this book are from the King James Version of the Bible. These have been taken not only because they are by far the most familiar, but because the King James translation, in its sonorous beauty and power, is irreplaceable. In certain Books and passages—for example in Proverbs, Ecclesiastes, the Song of Solomon—some of the later versions are both clearer and more accurate. But I decided that it would be confusing to quote from more than one translation.

Since the King James Bible of 1611 (known also as the Authorized Version), there have been numerous translations of the Bible, among them the English Revised Version of 1881-1885; the American Revised Version of 1901; the Revised Standard Version of 1946-1952. There have been an increasing number of translations by individuals and by small groups. Edgar J. Goodspeed's New Testament translation of 1923, combined with the Old Testament translation edited by J. M. Powis Smith, was published in 1931 as *The Bible: An American Translation*. A translation by James Moffatt of the complete Bible was published in 1924; and one by J. B. Phillips of the New Testament alone, *The New Testament in Modern English,* came out in 1958. The Jewish Publication Society of America, together with the Central Conference of American Rabbis, published a new version of the Old Testament in 1917. The traditional Bible for English-reading Catholics is the Douai Version, a rendering from the Latin Vulgate (1582-1610). An outstanding Catholic Bible, newly translated from the Latin Vulgate by the Right Reverend Monsignor Ronald A. Knox, was published in 1944-1948. Monsignor Knox has also described his labors in this undertaking in his entertaining *Trials of a Translator* (Sheed & Ward, 1949).

In March of 1961, the Oxford and Cambridge University Presses brought out *The New English Bible,* the work of a representative group of British biblical scholars under the direction of Dr. C. H. Dodd of Cambridge.

In reading either the Bible itself or the present condensation, it may be helpful to have at hand an authoritative commentary or a good Bible handbook. In working on *The Concise Bible* I found extremely useful *The New Bible Commentary,* edited by Francis Davidson (Wm. B. Eerdmans Publishing Co., Grand Rapids, Michigan, 1953). Another standard work is *A Commentary on the Holy Bible,* by various writers, edited by The Reverend J. R. Dummelow of Queens College, Cambridge (Macmillan, 1958).

How to Read the Bible, by Edgar J. Goodspeed (John C. Winston Co., Phila., 1946), *Modern Reader's Guide to the Bible,* by Harold H. Watt (Harper, 1959), *Life and Language in the Old Testament,* by Mary Ellen Chase (Norton, 1955), and *The Bible and the Common Reader,* also by Mary Ellen Chase (Macmillan 1944), are books for supplementary Bible reading.

Bible History Digest, by Elmer W. K. Mould (Exposition Press, N.Y., 1950), is a concise and richly informative account of biblical history. For the history of the Book itself, Joseph C. Swain's *Where Our Bible Came From* (Reflection Books, 1960), and F. Bratton's *History of the Bible* (Beacon, 1959), can be recommended.

Index

Aaron, 35, 36, 40
  death of, 48
  sons of, 42–43
Abel, 19, 20
Abiathar, 72
Abigail, 66
Abner, 68
Abraham (Abram), 22–26, 32, 34, 90,
  159, 192
Achish, 66
Acts of the Apostles, Book of the, 198–
  210
Adam, 18–20
Agag, 64
Ahab, 77, 78
  death of, 79
  end of house of, 83, 84
Ahasuerus, 95, 98
Amos, Book of, 147–48
Andrew, Apostle, 162, 171
Annunciation to Mary, 187
Antioch (in Pisidia), 204
Antioch (of Syria), 203, 205, 206
Apocalypse. *See* Revelation, Book of
Apostles, 171, 198–99
  See also Disciples
Ararat, mount, 21
Ark, Noah's, 20, 21
Ark of the Covenant, 41, 46, 54, 63, 68,
  89
Ascension of Jesus, 186, 197, 199
Asenath, 30
Atonement, Day of, 44

Baal, 59, 77, 78, 79, 84, 153
Babel, Tower of, 22

Babylon, 85, 88, 90, 152, 153
Balaam, 48–49
Balak, 48, 49
Baptism of disciples, 186, 196, 197, 200
Baptism of Jesus, 161, 184
Barabbas, 182, 197
Barak, 57–58
Barnabas, 203, 204, 205, 206
Bartholomew, Apostle, 171
Bath-sheba, 69–70, 72
Beatitudes, 162–63
Belshazzar, 142–43
Benjamin:
  son of Jacob named, 29, 31
  tribe of, 60, 63, 91
Bethany, 195
Beth-el, 29
Bethlehem, 29, 61, 151, 160, 188
  star of, 160
Bildad, 100, 101
Boaz, 61–62

Caiaphas, 180, 182, 189, 196
Cain, 19, 20
Caleb, 47, 50
Calvary. *See* Golgatha
Canaan, 22, 23, 29, 32, 38, 55
  conquest of, 55–56
  division of, 56
Cana, marriage at, 194
Carmel, mount, 78
Children of Israel. *See* Israelites
Christ. *See* Jesus
Chronicles, First Book of, 89–90
Chronicles, Second Book of, 90

Church, Christian, 176, 198–200, 203, 204, 205, 206, 207, 208
Colossians, Epistle of Paul to, 220
Commandment, new, 196
Commandments, Ten, 38–39, 50
Corinth, 207
Corinthians, First Epistle of Paul to, 214–16
Corinthians, Second Epistle of Paul to, 216–17
Covenant of God with Israel, 50–53, 56, 85
Creation, 15–17, 89
Crucifixion, 180, 183, 193, 197
Cyrus, 91

Damascus, 79, 82, 201
Daniel, Book of, 141–44
  fiery furnace, 141–42
  handwriting on wall, 142–43
  lions' den, 143–44
Darius, 92, 143, 153
David, 62, 65–71, 72, 75, 159
  song of thanksgiving of, 71
Deborah, 57–58
Delilah, 60
Demas, 223
Deuteronomy, Book of, 50–53
Devil. *See* Satan
Dietary laws, 43
Disciples, 171, 176, 179, 209
  names of twelve, 171
  See also Apostles

Ecclesiastes, Book of, 119–23
Eden, Garden of, 17–19
Edom, 48, 49, 81, 82, 147, 148
Egypt, 29–36, 75, 88, 135, 136, 160
Eleazar, 48
Eli, 62–63
Eliab, 64
Elijah, 77–79, 80, 156, 176
  ascension of, 81
Eliphaz, 100, 101, 106
Elisabeth, 187–88
Elisha, 79, 81, 82, 83
Enoch (Cain's son), 20
Enoch (Seth's descendant), 20
Ephesians, Epistle of Paul to, 218–19

Ephraim (son of Joseph), 30
Esau, 27, 29, 38
Esther, Book of, 95–98
Eve, 18, 19, 20
Exodus, Book of, 32–42
Ezekiel, Book of, 137–41
Ezra, Book of, 91–92
Ezra the priest, 92, 94

Fall of man, 18–19
Flood, 20–21

Gabriel, Angel, 187
Gad, 71
Galatians, Epistle of Paul to, 217–18
Galilee, 161, 162, 181, 194
Gamaliel, 201, 209
Garden of Eden. *See* Eden, Garden of
Gath, 66–67
Gaza, 60
Genesis, Book of, 15–32
Gentiles, 171, 202, 210, 211–12
  epistles to, 205, 210
Gibeon, 55, 60
Gideon, 59
Gilgal, 54, 64
Golden calf, 40–41
Golden Rule, 169
Goliath, 65–66
Gomorrah, 23, 24, 25
Goshen, 35, 36
Gospels, four, 159–98

Habakkuk, Book of, 152
Hagar, 24–25
Haggai, Book of, 153–54
Ham, 20, 22
Haman, 95–97
Handwriting on wall, 142–43
Hannah, 62
Haran, 22, 27
Hazael, 79, 82
Heaven, 27, 163, 165, 166, 234
Heber, 58
Hebrews, Epistle to, 224–25
Hell, 164, 233
Herod, 160, 187, 203
Hezekiah, 86–87
Holiness Code, 42, 45–46

Holy Ghost, 59, 130, 133, 154, 159,
    187, 189, 198, 199, 200, 202, 213,
    217, 218, 231
  Father, Son and, 184
Hor, mount, 48
Horeb, mount. *See* Sinai, mount
Hosea, Book of, 144–46

Immanuel, 129, 160
  See also Promised Land
Isaac, 25–26, 27, 29, 32, 34, 90
Isaiah, Book of, 126–33
Ishbosheth, 68
Ishmael, 24, 26
Israel
  Isaac's son named. *See* Jacob
  land of, 32, 56. *See also* Promised
    Land
Israelites, 49, 64, 65, 67, 85, 144, 147,
    172. *See also* Jews

Jabin, 57
Jacob (Israel), 27–29, 34, 49, 90, 149
Jael, 58
James, Apostle (son of Alpheus), 171
James, Apostle (son of Zebedee), 162,
    171, 203
James, Epistle of, 225–27
Japheth, 20, 22
Jehoshaphat, 79–80
Jehu, 79, 83, 84
Jephthah, 59, 60
  daughter of, 59
Jeremiah, Book of, 133–36
Jericho, 54–55
Jeroboam, 75, 76
Jerusalem, 68, 74, 134, 178, 208
  entry of Jesus into, 178
  last days of, 85–89, 151
  New, 234
  rebuilding of, 93–94
Jesse, 62, 64, 65, 129
Jesus, 159-98
  ascension of, 186, 197, 199
  baptism of, 161, 184
  betrayal of, 180–81
  birth of, 159–61, 187–89
  calling of disciples by, 171
  crucifixion of, 183, 185, 193, 197

Jesus—*cont.*
  entry of, into Jerusalem, 178
  Last Supper instituted by, 181, 185,
    196
  miracles of, 170–71, 194, 195
  parables of, 173–74, 177–78, 179,
    190–92
  resurrection of, 130, 183–84, 186,
    197–98, 216
  Sermon on Mount given by, 162–70
  temptation of, by Satan, 161–62
  transfiguration of, 176, 185
  trial of, 182–83, 197
Jews, 182, 183, 204, 209, 210, 211,
    212, 217, 220. *See also* Israelites
Jezebel, 78, 79, 80, 83
Joab, 68, 69, 72
Job, Book of, 98–107
Joel, Book of, 146–47
John, Apostle, 162, 171, 197
John, First Epistle of, 228–29
John, Gospel According to, 193–98
John, Revelation of. *See* Revelation,
    Book of
John, Second Epistle of, 229
John the Baptist, 161–62, 172, 174,
    175, 184, 187, 188, 193, 194, 207
John, Third Epistle of, 229–30
Jonah, Book of, 149–50
Jonathan, 64, 65, 67
  David's lament for, 67
Joseph (husband of Mary), 159–61,
    188–89
Joseph (son of Jacob), 29–32
Joseph of Arimathea, 183
Joshua, 47, 50, 53, 55, 56
Joshua, Book of, 53–56
Josiah, 87–88
Judah
  end of kingdom of, 87–89
  kingdom of, 76, 85, 91, 136
  rebuke of God to, 127–28
  son of Jacob named, 32
Judas Iscariot, 171, 180, 182, 196, 199
Jude, Epistle of, 230
Judges, Book of, 57–61
Judgment, Last, 180

Kings, First Book of, 72–80
Kings, Second Book of, 80–89

Laban, 28
Lamentations, Book of, 136–37
Last Supper, 181, 185, 196
Laws and commandments. *See* Moses,
　judgments, laws, and statutes of
Lazarus of Bethany, 195
Leah, 28
Levi, 32
Leviticus, Book of, 42–46
Lord's Prayer, 166–67
Lot, 22–23, 24–25
　wife of, 25
Love
　one another, 196
　thy neighbor, 190
　your enemies, 165
Luke, Gospel According to, 186–93

Malachi, Book of, 155–56
Manasseh (son of Joseph), 30
Manna, 37–38, 46, 51
Mark, 206, 223
Mark, Gospel According to, 184–86
Martha, 190–91, 195
Mary (mother of Jesus), 159–61, 187–
　89, 197, 199
Mary (sister to Martha), 190–91, 195
Mary Magdalene, 183, 186
Matthew, Apostle, 171
Matthew, Gospel According to, 159–84
Matthias, Apostle, 199
Mephibosheth, 69
Messiah, 129. *See also* Jesus
Methuselah, 20
Micah, Book of, 150–51
Micaiah, 80
Michael, Archangel, 233
Miracles of Jesus. *See* Jesus, miracles
　of
Mizpah, 28, 63
Moab, land of, 48, 53, 61, 62, 81
Mordecai, 95–98
Moriah, mount, 25
Moses, 32–53, 107, 176, 194
　birth of, 32–33
　death of, 52–53
　flight from Egypt of, 37
　Holiness Code given by, 42, 45–46
　judgments, laws, and statutes of, 39–
　　40, 42–46, 51–52

Moses—*cont.*
　pilgrimage to Sinai led by, 37–38
　Ten Commandments delivered by,
　　38–39, 50
　voice of God to, 34
　wilderness journey led by, 46–48

Naaman, 82
Nabal, 66
Naboth, 79, 83
Nahum, Book of, 151–52
Naomi, 61–62
Nathan, 69–70
Nazareth, 161, 174, 185, 187–89
Nebuchadnezzar, 88–89, 91, 135, 141–
　42
Nehemiah, Book of, 93–94
New Testament, 157–235
Nicodemus, 194
Ninevah, 86, 149, 150, 151–52
Noah, 20–21, 22
Numbers, Book of, 46–50

Obadiah, Book of, 148–49
Obed, 62
Old Testament, 13–156
Olivet (mount of Olives), 179, 185
Onesimus, 224

Parables. *See* Jesus, parables of
Paul, Apostle, 201–2, 203–10
Paul, Epistles of, 210–24
Pentecost, 199
Peter, Apostle, 162, 170–71, 181, 182,
　199–201, 202, 203
Peter, Epistles of, 227–28
Pharisees, 161, 175, 177, 178, 192, 195
Philemon, Epistle of Paul to, 224
Philip, Apostle, 171, 196
Philippians, Epistle of Paul to, 219–20
Philistines, 59–60, 63, 65, 66, 67, 68,
　69
Pilate, Pontius, 182–83, 189, 192
　wife of, 182
Pisgah, mount, 53
Pit, bottomless, 233
Potiphar, 29–30
Preacher, The. *See* Ecclesiastes, Book
　of
Prodigal Son, 191
Promised Land, 47, 50, 53, 54, 57

Proverbs, Book of, 113–19
Psalms, Book of, 107–13

Rachel, 28–29
Rahab, 54
Rebekah, 26–27
Red Sea, 37, 47
Rehoboam, 75–76, 79
Resurrection of Jesus, 183–84, 186, 197–98, 216
Reuben, 32
Reuel, 33
Revelation, Book of, 230–35
Romans, Epistle of Paul to, 210–14
Ruth, Book of, 61–62

Sabbath, 17, 39, 185
Sadducees, 161
Samaria, 77, 82, 84, 85
Samaritan, 171
  Good, 190
Samson, 59–60
Samuel,
  childhood of, 62–63
  death of, 66
  judgship of, 63–64
  return of, from grave, 66
Samuel, First Book of, 62–67
Samuel, Second Book of, 67–71
Sarah (Sarai), 22–25
Satan, 98–99, 161–62, 184, 234
Saul, 63–64, 65–66
  David's lament for, 67–68
  death of, 67
Saul of Tarsus. *See* Paul, Apostle
Sennacherib, 86
Sermon on the Mount, 162–70
Seth, 20
Shadrach, 141–42
Shalmaneser, 84, 85
Sheba, Queen of, 74–75
Shiloh, daughters of, 60–61
Silas, 206, 207
Simon, Apostle (Simon Zelotes), 171
Simon Peter. *See* Peter, Apostle
Sinai, mount (Horeb), 34, 38, 46, 52
Sisera, 57–58
Sodom, 23, 24, 25
Solomon, 72–75
  birth of, 70

Solomon—*cont.*
  death of, 75
  judgments and wisdom of, 73
  Queen of Sheba and, 74–75
  Temple of, 74
  trespasses of, 75
Song of Solomon, Book of, 123–26
Spirit of the Lord. *See* Holy Ghost
Stephen, 198, 201
Supper, Last. *See* Jesus, Last Supper instituted by

Tabernacle, 41–42, 56, 62, 69. *See also* Ark of the Covenant; Temple
Tamar, 70
Temple, 74, 76, 155, 179, 182, 195, 200, 208
  destruction of, 89, 179
  Jesus' cleansing of, 178
  rebuilding of, 91–92, 153–54
  See also Tabernacle
Ten Commandments, 38–39
Thaddeus, Apostle, 171
Thessalonians, First Epistle of Paul to, 220–21
Thessalonians, Second Epistle of Paul to, 221
Thomas, Apostle, 171, 198
Timothy (Timotheus), 206, 207
Timothy, First Epistle of Paul to, 221–22
Timothy, Second Epistle of Paul to, 222–23
Titus, Epistle of Paul to, 223–24
Twelve Disciples, 171

Uriah, 69

Virgin Mary. *See* Mary (mother of Jesus)

Wise men, 160
Witch of Endor, 66

Zacharias, 187, 188
Zechariah, Book of, 154–55
Zephaniah, Book of, 153
Zerubbabel, 91, 154
Zion, 68, 72, 89, 110, 112, 127, 130. *See also* Jerusalem
Zipporah, 33
Zophar, 100, 103

This book was linotype set in the Times Roman series of type. The face was designed to be used in the news columns of the *London Times*. The *Times* was seeking a type face that would be condensed enough to accommodate a substantial number of words per column without sacrificing readability and still have an attractive, contemporary appearance. This design was an immediate success. It is used in many periodicals throughout the world and is one of the most popular text faces presently in use for book work.

Book design by Design Center, Inc., Indianapolis
Typography by Weimer Typesetting Co., Inc., Indianapolis
Printed by North Central Publishing Co., Saint Paul

DUE